For the best o[...]
decided the[...]

Walking up th[...]
— a[...]

What would follow once they were...

CONVENIENTLY

Wed

Join fabulous, favourite authors
Carole Mortimer, Rebecca Winters
and Melissa James for three
gorgeous, brand-new stories.

100 Reasons to Celebrate

We invite you to join us in celebrating
Mills & Boon's centenary. Gerald Mills and
Charles Boon founded Mills & Boon Limited
in 1908 and opened offices in London's Covent
Garden. Since then, Mills & Boon has become
a hallmark for romantic fiction, recognised
around the world.

We're proud of our 100 years of publishing
excellence, which wouldn't have been achieved
without the loyalty and enthusiasm of our
authors and readers.

Thank you!

Each month throughout the year there will
be something new and exciting to mark the
centenary, so watch for your favourite authors,
captivating new stories, special limited
edition collections…and more!

CONVENIENTLY
Wed

Carole Mortimer
Rebecca Winters
Melissa James

M&B™ and M&B™ with the Rose Device
are trademarks of the publisher.
Harlequin Mills & Boon Limited, Eton House,
18-24 Paradise Road, Richmond, Surrey TW9 1SR

ISBN: 978 0 263 86582 0

009-0208

Harlequin Mills & Boon policy is to use papers that are
natural, renewable and recyclable products and made from
wood grown in sustainable forests. The logging and
manufacturing processes conform to the legal environmental
regulations of the country of origin.

Printed and bound in Spain
by Litografia Rosés S.A., Barcelona

THE MILLIONAIRE'S
CONTRACT BRIDE

Carole Mortimer

Carole Mortimer was born in England, the youngest of three children. She began writing in 1978, and has now written over one hundred and forty books for Mills & Boon. Carole has four sons, Matthew, Joshua, Timothy and Peter, and a bearded collie called Merlyn. She says, 'I'm happily married to Peter senior; we're best friends as well as lovers, which is probably the best recipe for a successful relationship. We live in a lovely part of England.'

Look out for Carole Mortimer's new novel,
The Sicilian's Ruthless Marriage Revenge,
in February 2008, available from
Mills & Boon® Modern™.

Dear Reader,

Three cheers for Mills & Boon's one hundredth birthday!

I hope that you, the reader, feel the same pleasure as I do, as an author, being a part of this celebration.

By sheer coincidence, 2008 also marks my own thirtieth anniversary of writing for Mills & Boon – over one hundred and forty books! It has been fantastic. Being a Mills & Boon author is like being part of a big, happy family – with you, dear reader, at the very heart of it.

Wishing you a truly happy 2008, and congratulations, Mills & Boon, on being one hundred years old!

Carole Mortimer

CHAPTER ONE

'WHAT on earth are you doing here?' Casey gasped. She had arrived home exhausted at almost eleven o'clock after working that evening, only to come to a shocked halt in the doorway to her sitting room and stare at the man sitting there so unconcernedly.

The single source of light in the room came from a small table lamp, casting the man's face in shadow as he sat in the armchair across the room. But even though she had only met him twice—briefly—in her life before, it was still possible for Casey to recognise the dark overlong hair, the wide shoulders and the tall, leanly powerful frame as belonging to Xander Fraser—a man whose brooding good-looks often graced the more prestigious gossip magazines as he attended the premieres of the numerous films released by his production company.

A man she hadn't realised even knew where she lived.

Yes, they both lived in Surrey, but at completely different ends of the housing scale. The Fraser mansion was set in several wooded acres of grounds near the river, while her own home was on an estate and much, much smaller.

If she hadn't been so shocked at finding him here, she might even have found a certain pleasure in having this ruggedly handsome man in her home. After all, he was the first eligible, gorgeous man she had been this close to since her marriage had ended a year ago.

Or perhaps not, she acknowledged with an inward grimace; she was hardly looking her best at the moment. Her hair probably smelt of the food cooked at the restaurant this evening, she was wearing some of her oldest clothes—for the same reason—and wore absolutely no make-up whatsoever to add colour to her naturally pale complexion.

Besides which, it was hardly a good idea for her to be attracted to the ex-husband of the woman who had stolen her own husband!

Xander Fraser shrugged those broad shoulders, shifting slightly so that his face was no longer in shadow, revealing an aquiline nose between high cheekbones, and an arrogant slash of a mouth above a strongly squared chin. He regarded her with hooded blue eyes. 'I was waiting for you to get home, obviously,' he drawled.

'Yes, I realise that,' she answered impatiently; it was why he was here that was important! 'But—where's Hannah?' she asked, her voice sharpening with alarm.

Now that her first shock on seeing Xander was receding, Casey realised the girl she employed to look after her son on the evenings she worked at the restaurant was noticeably absent.

'Is that the name of the babysitter?' Xander Fraser quirked dark brows. 'I told her she might as well take advantage of my being here and go home early.'

'And she just went?' Casey exclaimed. 'But she doesn't even know you! You could have been anybody!'

'Such as?' Those dark brows rose a second time. 'A mass-murderer? Or a kidnapper, perhaps?' He gave a humourless smile.

'Well…actually, yes,' Casey said with a frown, feeling she had every right to be annoyed with Hannah's irresponsible behaviour.

Although Xander Fraser hardly looked the part of either, she acknowledged privately to herself, dressed in those designer label denims and navy blue silk shirt, and possessed of the kind of confidence that only the very rich or very good-looking seemed to acquire.

Xander Fraser scowled. 'Believe me, the complications that go along with the one child I have are more than enough for me to cope with right now!'

His daughter Lauren was six years old—the same age as Casey's son Josh. But there the similarities ended. Lauren Fraser was the daughter of multi-millionaire film producer Xander Fraser, whereas Josh was the son of a single mother juggling two jobs to try and keep a roof over their heads.

She sighed as she put her handbag down on the coffee table, too tired to be able to make much sense out of this man's unexpected presence here, let alone his enigmatic conversation.

It had been a long day for her. She'd got up at seven-thirty, to get her young son ready and at school for nine o'clock, then hurried off to the café she worked in until after the lunchtime rush. Once that was over, she'd collected Josh and spent a couple of hours at home with him, before leaving for her evening job at the restaurant of the local hotel.

Yes, it had been a very long and very tiring day, and she was in no mood to play verbal fencing games with Xander Fraser, of all people. Whether he was sinfully handsome or not!

As he was sitting in the only chair in her sparsely furnished sitting room, Casey remained standing, still very unhappy with Hannah—but that, she promised herself, was something she would take up with the girl tomorrow.

'So, what can I do for you, Mr Fraser?' she challenged tersely.

With her painfully thin frame clothed in a figure-hugging black tee shirt and faded blue denims, and at only a couple of inches over five feet tall, Casey Bridges had all the appearance of a bantam hen aligning itself against a hawk, Xander decided ruefully. Her soft blonde hair was styled wispily about her temples and nape, and her beautiful heart-shaped face was dominated by dark green eyes that did absolutely nothing to dispel that illusion of fragility.

And she looked exhausted… Even as he thought it, she swayed slightly on her feet.

Abruptly, Xander stood up. 'Sit down,' he commanded, 'before you collapse.'

She obviously bridled at the order, but then did as he'd said. Perhaps she realised he was fully capable of picking her up and sitting her in the chair himself, if she refused…

The chair, the coffee table and the lamp were the only furniture in the room. He had noted that with a frown when he'd arrived earlier. There was no television in the room, either, and when he had taken a quick look around the rest of the house he had found that to be no better. Casey Bridges seemed to have taken the 'minimalist' effect to a barren degree.

Or else—as his daughter Lauren had already hinted—there was another explanation altogether for such austerity…

Xander's eyes narrowed as he registered just how fragilely thin the woman before him was. He noted the shadows beneath those dark green eyes, the hollows beneath her cheekbones, and the skin on her hands and wrists that was almost translucent.

'Exactly what's been going on here, Casey?' he asked, his blue gaze uncomfortably penetrating now. 'Where were you this evening?' He had thought she must be out with friends—possibly even a boyfriend, as her husband had left her a year ago—but she hardly had the look of a woman returning from a pleasant evening out.

She gave a firm shake of her head as she seemed to regain some of her composure. 'That really isn't any of your business, Mr Fraser.' She stood up. 'I should go up and check on Josh. I still can't believe— Has he woken up? Is he aware that Hannah has left?' she asked anxiously.

'Josh is fine,' Xander assured her. 'He did wake up once, but when I told him I was Lauren's daddy he wasn't concerned. He and Lauren have become friends—did you know that?'

Yes, she did know that. Ironically, Josh and Lauren had become friends during the eight months when Sam and Chloe had lived together, their visits to their individual parents often coinciding. Casey also knew that Josh had missed seeing the little girl since Chloe and Sam's deaths four months ago.

'Yes, I believe they have—did,' she corrected. 'If you would just like to wait here while I go and check on Josh, we can—continue this conversation when I come back down.' Her gaze didn't quite meet his before she turned and left the room, to run up the stairs to Josh's small bedroom above with a vague feeling of relief.

She had to admit to finding Xander Fraser's powerful presence and fiercely intelligent blue eyes slightly overwhelming in the small confines of the three-bedroomed house that she had lived in first with her parents, then with Sam and Josh, and now just with Josh. The house she was determined to hold on to if humanly possible.

Quite what sort of conversation she and Xander Fraser were going to have she had no idea, but he obviously considered it important enough for him to have gone to the trouble of finding out where she lived.

She very much doubted Xander's ex-wife would have told him. Casey and Xander's previous two meetings had been when they'd happened to call at the same time to collect Josh and Lauren after one of their weekend visits to the house Sam and Chloe had so briefly shared. The dazzlingly beautiful Chloe had had no choice but to introduce the two of them, but her hypnotic blue eyes had been narrowed on them watchfully as she'd done so.

Casey hadn't liked the sophisticated but brittle Chloe Fraser; she knew she wouldn't have liked her even if she hadn't been 'the other woman' in Casey's marriage break-up. The two of them had absolutely nothing in common—except Sam, of course.

Only Chloe Fraser's beauty had been such that her more negative traits obviously hadn't repulsed the golden and handsome Sam, or the darkly brooding and immensely rich Xander Fraser.

But the fact that Chloe and Sam were now both dead—killed four months ago when the private jet they'd been travelling in had crashed—meant that Josh and Lauren's visits to them had obviously stopped, too. And it should have meant that Casey would never have reason to see Xander Fraser again, either.

So why on earth was he downstairs in her sitting room, obviously waiting to talk to her?

CHAPTER TWO

XANDER became aware of Casey's presence behind him as he stood in the kitchen. 'You looked like you could do with a cup,' he explained, as he turned and saw her brows raised at the two steaming mugs of coffee he had just made. 'How was Josh?' he prompted, when he noted the pallor of those hollow cheeks.

The shadows remained in her deep green eyes but she smiled. Deep grooves appeared beside the fullness of her lips, as if humour was something that hadn't come easily to her recently.

And Xander doubted that it had. To Chloe, he knew, the seduction of the man who had come to their home as a landscape gardener had all been a game. A game she had played more times than even Xander was aware of. Or cared about. Although in Sam Bridges' case Chloe had very quickly decided that she wanted to take their relationship to the next level—so the two of them had left their partners and set up home together.

The fact that at the same time she had robbed this

woman of her husband, and six-year-old Josh of his father, wouldn't have been of interest to the spoilt and wilful Chloe. She had seen something she wanted, and taken it without hesitation.

'Fast asleep,' Casey acknowledged ruefully. Then she flushed slightly. 'Er—would you like a biscuit or something to go with that coffee?'

As he had checked all the cupboards in the kitchen while she was upstairs, and found them all bare—just like Old Mother Hubbard's in the nursery rhyme— Xander didn't hold out much hope of there being anything for him to actually have.

'No, thanks—I ate earlier,' he said easily. 'Shall we go through to the sitting room, or would you prefer to stand in here and talk?' Either way, only one of them would be able to sit!

Once again Xander wondered what the hell had been going on in this woman's life these last four months. There was no food in the house, and very little furniture, either, and Casey Bridges looked as if a strong gust of wind would knock her off her feet.

'Here is fine.' Casey took one of the steaming mugs of coffee from him, her hand carefully avoiding coming into contact with his as she did so.

It was ridiculous, she told herself impatiently, to be so aware of this man. So physically aware of him. But there was no denying that her hands were trembling slightly with that awareness.

Perhaps she was just missing having sex?

Surely not! The physical side of her marriage to

Sam hadn't been that good in the first place, and had been completely non-existent for the last six months they'd been together. No, it had to be Xander Fraser himself who had awakened all these sensual longings within her…

Her mouth tightened at the knowledge. 'What did you want to talk to me about—?'

'That can wait,' he cut in abruptly. 'First I would like you to tell me why there's hardly any furniture in the house, and why the fridge is also bare, except for a bottle of milk and a piece of cheese.'

Her eyes widened with incredulous anger. 'You've been looking through my refrigerator?'

'I needed milk for your coffee,' he pointed out with a sardonic smile. His own coffee was black.

'Oh.' Casey felt her cheeks warm at the rebuke. 'But, still, what I do or don't have in my refrigerator is none of your concern—'

'When did you last eat, Casey?' Xander Fraser asked bluntly, ignoring her attempt to put him in his place.

'I don't have to—'

'Yes, you do,' he interrupted again, his tone brooking no more denial or evasions.

She frowned her deep irritation at his autocratic attitude.

'I cooked lamb chops, new potatoes and vegetables for tea before I went out—'

'I'm prepared to accept that *Josh* had lamb chops and vegetables for his evening meal. Unlike you, he looks robustly healthy,' he added pointedly. 'Besides,

I saw the bones from two chops in your pedal bin just now—'

'Mr Fraser, you really do *not* have the right to question me like this!' Casey gasped. 'Let alone go poking around in my pedal bin!' she added indignantly.

No, he probably didn't, Xander acknowledged grimly. And he really couldn't say that he had given this woman, or her son, much consideration during the last year, either. He had been too busy for most of that time trying to deal with the trauma that Chloe's desertion and subsequent death had caused his own daughter to worry about Sam Bridges' family.

But all that had changed since his conversation with Brad Henderson, Chloe's father, four days ago...

Since arriving at Casey's home a couple of hours ago, and seeing the frugal way she lived, Xander was inclined to think the claim Lauren had made once that 'Josh's mummy is so poor she can't buy him any new toys' was probably a true one. Not that it gave Xander any pleasure to know that; it just meant, as he had hoped, that Casey might be the answer to his own dilemma.

In fact, if Casey were willing to be co-operative and agree to what he was about to suggest, she would be vastly improving her own situation at the same time as she helped Xander turn this whole situation around on Brad Henderson.

If Casey were willing to be co-operative...

Looking at her now, he could see just how completely exhausted she was—both physically and emotionally. He didn't think that it was all due to the trauma of the events of the past year alone; from the little Xander had bothered to learn about Sam Bridges, the man hadn't exactly been the perfect husband and provider for his family even before he'd become involved with Chloe.

No wonder his ex-wife had been so drawn to the man. They'd been two of a kind. Spoilt users, the pair of them.

Xander shrugged unapologetically. 'Perhaps if you stop treating me like an idiot and answer my questions honestly I might stop poking my nose into your pedal bin and your business.' Despite the mildness of his tone, he was nevertheless determined to have answers to his questions. 'Where were you this evening, Casey?' He was pretty sure now that she hadn't been out for an evening of frivolity—the woman didn't look as if she even knew the meaning of the word.

Casey looked up at him in a slight daze, still having no idea what had prompted this man's visit, or why he was questioning her so intently. She was only aware that she was simply too tired to argue with him any longer...

'I was at work,' she sighed. 'I work four evenings a week in the restaurant of a local hotel.'

Xander Fraser scowled darkly. 'Wouldn't it have been more convenient, with Josh still so young, for you to have found a job in the day—?'

'I *do* have a job in the day!' she told him impatiently,

feeling at a distinct disadvantage as his body, with its superior height, loomed over hers; Xander Fraser was at least a foot taller than her own five feet two inches. 'I work five days a week cooking at a local café as well as the four evenings at the hotel,' she revealed, still reluctant to discuss her personal business with this man who exuded such wealth and power.

'Why?' he probed.

Her cheeks flushed. 'That is none of your—'

'Business?' Xander finished for her. 'What if I'm *making* it my business?' he added softly, becoming more and more convinced as he talked to Casey that he had found the answer to getting out of the corner Brad was pushing him into.

That what he was about to propose would solve Casey's problems, too...

She gave a disbelieving laugh, at once looking younger, even if the expression in her green eyes was derisive rather than genuinely amused. 'And why would Xander Fraser, multimillionaire film producer, want to do something like that?' she scorned, highlighting the immense gulf between their vastly different circumstances.

Not that she wanted to be mega-rich. Comfortably off would be nice. But the garden centre and the money that her father had left her when he died were long gone—the first bankrupted in a year under Sam's management, the second frittered away as he had struggled to make a success—played at?—landscape gardening.

The only thing Sam had succeeded at was ending their torturous marriage once and for all by meeting Chloe Fraser!

'Well, Mr Fraser?' she said belligerently.

His mouth thinned at her tone of voice. 'I have— a business proposition to put to you,' he finally bit out.

Casey shook her head. 'I'm afraid you've mis-understood my cooking abilities, Mr Fraser. I don't cater for dinner parties—'

'Not that sort of business proposition!' he growled, pacing the small confines of the kitchen, his gaze narrowed to vivid blue slits. 'Are you familiar with Brad Henderson?'

Her eyebrows raised at the mention of the rich, retired owner of a Hollywood film studio. 'Not per-sonally, no.'

'I am,' Xander said.

Casey shrugged. 'You're both in the same business.'

'He's also Chloe's father,' Xander expanded. 'And therefore Lauren's grandfather.'

Casey hadn't known that—although it probably went a long way towards explaining why Chloe had always been so sure of having her own way. A privi-leged, over-indulgent father, followed by marriage to an even richer husband—what choice had the other woman had but to be spoilt and selfish?

All of which was of absolutely no relevance what-soever now that Chloe was dead.

Was it…?

Casey put up a tired hand to brush her hair away

from her brow. 'I really don't see what this has to do with me.'

'I'm getting to that,' Xander assured her impatiently. 'Lauren and Josh are already friends. Things obviously aren't going too well with you if you have to work at two jobs in order to remain even this financially solvent—'

'Now, look, Mr Fraser—'

'Will you just hear me out, Casey?' Xander cut in. 'I have something to say, and your constant interruptions aren't making it any easier!'

She raised blonde brows, indignant colour in her cheeks. 'Maybe if you stopped making this so personal…?'

His mouth twisted humourlessly. 'But it *is* personal, Casey. Very personal,' he added heavily. 'For reasons that I will explain in a moment, I'm here to ask if, in return for my financially providing for you and Josh, you would consider becoming my wife.'

Speechless.

Xander Fraser had rendered her completely speechless with his announcement—his question?

He couldn't possibly be serious!

Could he?

CHAPTER THREE

CASEY felt as if she were fighting her way through cotton-wool—thick, wispy clouds of it that stopped her reaching the surface, stopped her from remembering—

This was all a dream! Xander Fraser was a dream. As his marriage proposal had been a dream—

'Drink this,' rasped an autocratic voice. 'Come on, Casey, open your eyes and drink.'

Unfortunately, that voice was all too familiar. Not a dream, then. Or even a nightmare! Which meant that Xander's marriage proposal had been very real…

'I know you're awake, Casey.' His voice was softer now. 'I'm not going to disappear just because you refuse to open your eyes and look at me,' he taunted gently.

Her lids snapped open and she glared up at her tormentor. She was now sitting slumped in the armchair Xander must have carried her to when she'd fainted, and he was bent over her, holding out a glass of clear brown liquid.

A rueful smile touched those beautifully

sculpted lips as he made no effort to back off. 'Drink some of the sherry, Casey,' he ordered as he held the glass closer to her. 'It should be brandy, I know, but it's all I could find in the way of alcohol,' he added wryly.

It was cooking sherry, Casey recognised with a grimace as she took the glass from him, used to flavour a trifle she had made for Christmas, several months ago. And not a very good cooking sherry, either. But he was right. She needed something to dispel some of the numbed shock she was feeling.

Xander Fraser was the type of man who was always right, she decided, thoroughly disgruntled. She gulped down the sherry, finding it as disgusting as she'd thought it would be, but nonetheless reviving for all that.

Great, Xander muttered inwardly when he saw those green eyes begin to sparkle unnaturally and the flush that suddenly coloured Casey's previously pale cheeks; one glass of bloody awful sherry and the woman was drunk. No doubt the fact that she obviously didn't eat properly hadn't helped.

'That's enough of that,' he said firmly. He took the empty glass away from her and placed it on the coffee table, straightening as he did so to move slightly away from her. His deliberately bland expression showed none of the concern he had felt a few minutes ago, as he'd carried her limp body from the kitchen to place her in the chair in the sitting room.

The woman had been like gossamer in his arms—

so light she'd felt as though she didn't weigh much more than Lauren. As he had looked down at her he'd wondered what difference a few good meals and some TLC would bring to the hollows of her cheeks and the slender curves of her body. How she would look if the worry and stress she was obviously suffering were to be removed and she could actually start to enjoy life again.

Then he had chastised himself for even thinking along those lines. His idea that the two of them marry was a business proposition. Nothing more, nothing less. Far better that he didn't even think of Casey Bridges' undoubted beauty, or the possible allure of her with a fuller, more curvaceous body…

No, thinking about her like that certainly wasn't a good idea. Not if she agreed to marry him.

And he had every intention, now he had actually voiced the idea, of making sure that she did!

Casey looked up at Xander from beneath long golden lashes, easily recognising his leashed strength as he paced the room restlessly. He was a man who wielded power along with supreme self-confidence. A man, she was sure, who never took no for an answer. A man who had just suggested, with the offer of a financial incentive, that she marry him!

She moistened stiff, unyielding lips before speaking. 'I think you had better leave now.'

'I'm afraid I can't do that, Casey. You and I have a lot more to say to each other before I agree to go anywhere.'

'But you can't have seriously just suggested the two of us get *married?*'

'Oh, I'm serious,' he replied grimly. 'Very much so.'

'But you don't even know me—'

'I know all I need to know,' he declared. 'You're hard-working. Independent. A good mother—'

'My teeth are sound, too,' she put in sarcastically.

Xander gave an appreciative grin. 'There—you have a sense of humour as well!'

'It's hysteria, Mr Fraser, not humour,' Casey pointed out, sitting up straighter in the armchair to look at him searchingly. 'Why?' she finally voiced in a guarded tone.

'Add *astute* to your list of attributes!' he teased, not unkindly.

'Well, I certainly know you aren't suggesting I marry you because you've suddenly decided you've fallen madly in love with me!' she retorted.

'No,' he acknowledged seriously. 'Do you want to know why you? Or why I need to get married at all?'

'Both,' Casey snapped.

'Does Josh have any paternal grandparents?' he asked, instead of answering either of those questions.

Casey looked surprised. 'Yes.'

'And have they ever considered trying to take Josh from you?'

'After the way their son behaved? They wouldn't dare!' she assured him, wings of angry colour appearing in those pale cheeks.

'Well, Brad feels no such scruples where his granddaughter is concerned,' Xander said coldly.

'Your father-in-law wants to take Lauren away from you?' Casey gasped. 'But why?'

Xander raised an eyebrow. 'Why does he want Lauren? Or why does he think he has reason to take Lauren from me?'

'Either. Both!' Casey frowned her agitation at his habit of answering her questions with more questions, at the same time wondering how she would have felt if Sam's parents had ever threatened to try and take Josh from her.

As desperate as Xander Fraser obviously did, if his marriage proposal to her was anything to go by!

He sighed. 'Brad is hurting very badly at the moment. His daughter—his only child—died four months ago, and now that his initial shock has receded I believe he sees Lauren as a replacement in his life for Chloe. He informed me on Sunday that he intends applying for custody of Lauren. I tried reasoning with him, and pointed out that he isn't thinking rationally at the moment. He isn't listening,' Xander concluded darkly.

Casey gave him a searching look, knowing by the grimness of his expression that he took his father-in-law's threat seriously. But surely Brad Henderson, no matter how rich and influential, could never succeed in such a threat?

'You didn't answer my other *why*,' she prompted.

Xander Fraser's eyes flashed. 'Why does he think

he might succeed in such a claim?' His lips briefly compressed into a tight line before he continued. 'Whether you believe me or not, I consider myself a good father. But there have been—problems since Chloe and I separated. I'm away on business a lot, obviously. Lauren has been—difficult at school. She has also managed to dispatch the four nannies I've employed in as many months. Brad intends using all of the above as a way of proving he would be a better guardian for Lauren than I am.'

'But those things don't mean anything.' Casey shook her head. 'Josh has been a little—troubled at school, too. But with his father leaving, the strangeness of having another woman in his father's life, and then their sudden deaths—it's only natural that there should be some sort of reaction. I'm sure that's all that's happening with Lauren, too.'

He shrugged. 'You know that. I know that. Brad obviously sees things differently. He's angry, upset, and he's blaming everything and everyone, including me, for Chloe's death. At the moment he simply doesn't see that he helped form Chloe into the selfish person she undoubtedly was. And no doubt he would make Lauren equally selfish if he were to get his hands on her.'

It wasn't too difficult for Casey to imagine the scenario Xander described.

It *was* difficult, however, to understand how proposing marriage to her was going to solve his dilemma!

'So you think marrying a complete stranger is

going to stop him from going ahead with a custody battle?' she said with a frown.

'I think marrying a woman whose young son is already friends with my daughter—she's talked about Josh incessantly the last four months!—and providing Lauren with a stepmother and the stability of a proper family life, is going to stop him from even trying, yes!'

'One big happy family, hmm?' Casey grimaced.

'Can you come up with a better idea?' Xander snapped.

'How about marrying someone you actually love?'

He gave her a pitying glance. 'Don't tell me, after seven years of marriage to a man like Sam Bridges, that you still believe in the love myth? Any more than I do after seven years of marriage to Chloe?'

Her eyes flashed deeply green. 'I think we should leave my marriage out of this.'

'How can we?' Xander asked. 'It's because your marriage was as disastrous as mine that I believed you might be receptive to my proposal—'

'That I might be financially desperate enough to be "receptive" to your proposal you mean, don't you?' Casey bridled angrily, standing up to glare at him. 'I'm sure there must be dozens of women you could find who would marry you without the offer of financial inducement!'

'Someone who would expect more from me than I'm willing to give, you mean?' His mouth twisted cynically. 'I would rather pay up front for the privilege, thank you very much. At least that way we would know exactly where we stood!'

'I don't need your damned charity—'

'No—you're managing just fine on your own, aren't you?" he taunted. 'You're working at two jobs and you still don't have enough money to feed both Josh and yourself. And from the looks of things you've been selling off the furniture a piece at a time, too—'

'Get out, Mr Fraser.' Casey cut him off with quiet determination, her hands clenched into fists at her sides. 'Take your offer and—'

'But you haven't heard what my offer is yet, Casey.'

'I don't need to hear it—'

He ignored her protest. 'As my stepson, Josh would go to the same private schools as Lauren. University later, too. And I would put funds in trust for him to receive when he's twenty-one. Neither he nor you would ever have to worry about money ever again.'

'And in return for all that, what do I give you?' Casey asked, with more than a touch of sarcasm.

'Just your name with mine on a marriage certificate.'

Casey shook her head. 'I understand why you're doing this, Mr Fraser—I really do,' she reiterated as he gave a derisive snort; if anyone tried to take Josh away from her she would do what she had to do to keep him, too. 'But Brad Henderson would never believe in a marriage between the two of us.'

'You're wrong there, Casey,' Xander contradicted her flatly. 'I've had four days to think—to worry

about this—and after my seven hellish years of
marriage to Chloe, I can assure you I've made my
views on marrying again only too plain. Which is
why I think a marriage between the two of us—
Sam's deserted wife and Chloe's deserted husband—
is the only one that Brad would even half believe in.'

'If it was so hellish, why did you stay married to
Chloe for so long?' she snapped, stung by how he'd
described her as *deserted;* he made her sound like
a pair of old shoes Sam had simply laid to one side
and forgotten!

'Why did *you* stay married to Bridges?' he retorted.

But Casey knew the answer to the question even
before they both answered at the same time.

'Because of Lauren!'

'Because of Josh!'

Xander gave a mocking inclination of his head.
'And then, as it turned out, our fears were all for
nothing—because when they did both finally leave
neither of them wanted Lauren or Josh! They only
wanted each other.'

It was true, Casey acknowledged painfully.
Whatever it was that had burnt so fiercely between
Sam and Chloe—love, lust, whatever—everything
else had been surplus to requirements. Including their
two children.

'All I'm asking right now is that you *think* about
marrying me, Casey,' Xander encouraged. 'Think of
what the two of us marrying could mean to you and
Josh, of what I could give you—'

'I said I don't want to hear any of that!' Casey cut in shakily, disturbed by his offer in spite of herself.

Because, the offer of financial security for herself apart, she wanted all those things he had mentioned for Josh, and she hated the fact that she was never going to be able to provide them for him.

And Xander Fraser had to have known that perfectly well when he made his outrageous offer of marriage...

Four days he had said he'd had to think about a solution to his problem, whereas she had only had a matter of minutes to accept that this man really was proposing marriage to her. That the only reason he had chosen her was because he knew she was desperately in need of the financial security he offered.

That he felt confident in making the offer to her because he knew her circumstances were such that he wouldn't need to pretend a love for her he would never feel.

Xander watched the conflicting emotions flickering across Casey's face, realising she was both tempted and repelled by his offer.

He had no idea which emotion was going to win...

CHAPTER FOUR

SHE needed time to think about this, Casey decided. She needed to sit down and think rationally about all that Xander Fraser was offering her.

She no more wanted to marry again than he obviously did—had been just as soured by her unhappy marriage to Sam as he had by his 'hellish' marriage to Chloe.

But that wasn't all that was at stake here, was it? She had Josh's welfare to consider. And, as his stepfather, Xander could give him all the advantages in life that she knew she would never be able to provide for him.

But before making any decision—was she actually *considering* his proposal?—despite his earlier comment, she really needed to know exactly what he would want from her in return.

She looked across at him warily, once again jolted by his sheer physical magnetism. He was an extremely handsome man, his dark good-looks more wild and rugged than the smoothly golden Adonis Sam had been. Yes, Xander was certainly much more vitally physical. That very ruggedness suggested an enjoyment of all the sensual pleasures…

'You said your marriage proposal was a purely business proposition…?' she asked slowly.

He easily returned her gaze, dark brows rising even as a wicked little smile curved his lips. 'Casey, why don't you just come right out and ask whether the marriage would include us sleeping together?'

Colour warmed her cheeks even as she glared at him. 'Well, would it?'

Xander knew he could have continued to play with her. That he would have enjoyed teasing her a little. That he liked the way she blushed when she was embarrassed, resembling a soft, fluffy kitten when it felt itself cornered.

But the situation was too serious for him to prolong this particular conversation. Brad's threats were too painful. He was sure the older man would ultimately lose, but at what cost to Lauren's already delicately balanced emotions?

So instead he shrugged. 'I'll go along with whatever you want.'

'Whatever *I*—?' She broke off incredulously, her eyes wide with shock. 'Are you saying that if I decided I wanted to—wanted to—?'

'To go to bed with me,' Xander inserted helpfully.

She nodded. 'That if I wanted that, you would be willing to—to—?'

'Go to bed with you,' he finished softly. 'Yes, I'd be willing to do that.'

She looked totally stunned now, and Xander realised just how young she was. Perhaps not in years—twenty-seven really wasn't that young—but most definitely in experience, if she didn't know that she could enjoy physical pleasure without being in love with the person she was making love with.

'Why not, Casey?' he added. 'After all, it would be perfectly legal.'

He had a feeling it would be something he would enjoy too. There could be depths to this woman's emotions that she hadn't even discovered fully for herself yet. Yes, he might enjoy administering that TLC he had thought her in need of earlier on...

'It being legal has nothing to do with it!' Casey said indignantly. 'I couldn't just—just go to bed with you because a piece of paper says I can!'

'Why couldn't you?' He came across the room to stand only inches away from her, one of his hands rising to lightly cup the side of her face as his thumb moved caressingly across the fullness of her lower lip. 'You're a very beautiful woman,' he murmured huskily, his gaze roaming over her suddenly pale face. 'Would you find it such a hardship to go to bed with me?' he asked.

Casey found herself mesmerised by those gorgeous firm lips only inches away from her own. What would it be like to feel them moving searchingly against hers? To have him kiss and caress—?

No!

'You would,' Xander said regretfully as she

flinched back from him. 'Casey, thousands of people go to bed together every day for no other reason than that piece of paper.'

'Not me!' she assured him firmly, very aware of the way she still trembled from his light caress, and wondering if she was being truthful—to Xander or herself...

She had been in love with Sam when they'd first married. Or at least she had thought she was. It hadn't been long before she had understood that, at only twenty years old, she had probably been too young to realise she was just dazzled by the fact that someone so good-looking and charming as Sam should have fallen in love with her. But by then it had been too late. They had already been married a year, Josh had been a baby only two months old, and her father had recently died.

But she had continued to be married to Sam for a further six years, hadn't she? And it had only been during the last six months of their marriage that the physical side of things had ended completely.

Yes, but that was different, she told herself firmly now. Sam had been her husband—

Only, if she accepted Xander Fraser's marriage proposal he would be her husband, too!

No, she couldn't go through with this! No matter what the financial inducement to make Josh's life more comfortable and her own life free of the continual financial stress...

'I only said it was an option, Casey.' Xander spoke

evenly as he saw the sudden panic in her easily readable expression.

Her open emotions were certainly a refreshing change after years of Chloe's deceit and machinations!

Chloe had been the most beautiful woman he had ever set eyes on when he met her seven and a half years ago—a beautiful ebony-haired blue-eyed butterfly who had dazzled and beguiled every man she came into contact with. Including him. And Xander had pursued her relentlessly until he caught her.

But after only a few brief months of marriage he had realised that she truly *was* a butterfly—that her emotions, once given, lasted only fleetingly, before she moved on to the next conquest. And the next. And the next.

Only the fact that Chloe had found herself pregnant at the end of their six-week-long honeymoon—at least Xander had been sure that Lauren was his!—had kept the marriage from ending in divorce once he'd discovered Chloe had taken her first lover.

And that was all their marriage had been—a sham, a front for the dozens of men Chloe had enthralled into her bed. Men she would enjoy, but who couldn't demand too much from her when she had the protection of a powerful husband like Xander Fraser.

He should have divorced her years ago, of course, but the possibility of Chloe taking Lauren with her when she left—the daughter he adored—had prevented him from taking such action.

The fact that he was now being threatened in the same way by Chloe's father was totally unacceptable!

'I would be quite happy with a marriage of convenience, Casey; I'm really not that desperate for a physical relationship with an unwilling wife!' he told her, suddenly harsh after recalling such unwelcome memories.

Where had that anger come from so suddenly? Casey wondered.

And who was to say she would be unwilling…?

Her reaction to his touch just now had told her that she wasn't indifferent to him. And she had already acknowledged to herself earlier that she found this man physically attractive—that he exuded a powerful vitality that would make it impossible ever to ignore him—so how much more disturbing was he going to be if he was her husband? If she was living with him on a permanent basis?

She couldn't be *seriously* thinking of accepting his proposal, could she?

But for Josh's sake, she couldn't *not* seriously think about it!

She had been aware for some weeks that she was fighting a losing battle when it came to paying her bills as well as the mortgage Sam had taken out on this house in order to raise extra capital. She knew she might soon have to give up even trying to hold on to her family home, and find somewhere to rent instead. There would be a few thousand pounds to bank once the house was sold, but nowhere near enough to give Josh all the advantages Xander Fraser was offering if he became her son's stepfather.

So how could she *not* accept Xander's marriage proposal?

She moistened lips that had gone dry. 'If I were to accept—I said *if,* Mr Fraser,' she emphasised, when she saw the look of triumph flare in those dark blue eyes.

'I think you had better call me Xander, don't you?' he invited.

She gave him a scathing glance and deliberately didn't respond to his invitation. A childish gesture, perhaps, but she had a feeling that any advantage she might ever have over Xander Fraser was going to be a small one! 'If I accept, exactly when were you thinking of this marriage taking place?'

Xander damped down his feeling of elation that she was even considering his offer—which was pretty strange for a man who, after Chloe's infidelities, had sworn he would never marry again!

But this was a marriage to be made out of necessity rather than choice, he excused himself. It was for his daughter's sake, not his own—exactly the reason he had settled on Casey Bridges—along with her son Josh, who Lauren adored—in the first place!

He shrugged. 'As soon as we can get a licence, I would have thought. The sooner the better, in fact. Why wait, Casey?' he added persuasively as he once again saw that look of panic in her face. 'The sooner it's done, the matter settled, the sooner we can all get on with our lives.'

He had always liked and respected Brad Henderson, and he knew it was the other man's grief at losing Chloe that was making him behave irrationally at the moment; unfortunately, Xander couldn't afford to give the other man time to come to his senses. He was all too aware of the damage that Brad could wreak in Lauren's life as well as his own before that happened.

The sooner he got Casey Bridges to agree to his marriage proposal the better. He found it distinctly unflattering that she viewed marriage to him in so poor a light—most women he knew would have jumped at the offer.

But then, the women who had been in his life the last year were as hard and grasping as Chloe had been. He had chosen them deliberately. At least he knew where he stood with women like that. He would certainly never consider—for *any* reason!— offering marriage to one of them.

Casey wasn't like them—would never be like them—which meant he had to back off a little and give her some time to make her decision. Hopefully, she would realise there were far too many advantages for Josh to allow her scruples to stand in the way.

'Why don't you take overnight to think about it, and I'll call you in the morning?' he suggested lightly.

'Overnight?' Casey echoed with another surge of inward panic. Could she take just a few hours to make a decision that would affect the rest of her life?

And Josh's…

Josh. Her weak spot. A weakness Xander Fraser had already exploited to his advantage…

But apparently not her only weakness, Casey acknowledged thoughtfully as she remembered the way she had trembled, the warmth that had coursed through her body, when Xander Fraser had touched her.

Yes, she had to take into account her unmistakable response to all that leashed magnetism, too. She would be foolish not to do so.

She raised her chin and infused her voice with determination. 'Why don't I take my time to think about it and call you when I reach a decision?'

His mouth tightened, his gaze narrowing speculatively as she deliberately turned his suggestion back on him. 'Why don't you?' he finally growled, taking his wallet from the back pocket of his denims to remove a business card and place it on the coffee table. 'But don't take too long, hmm?' he added.

Or what? Casey wondered with a frown as she watched him turn on his heel and leave.

The front door closed behind him seconds later.

Would she find the offer had been rescinded if she dithered too long in giving him an answer?

Would he decide she wasn't worth the trouble and find someone else—someone more receptive—to make his offer of marriage to…?

CHAPTER FIVE

'MR FRASER—'

'*Xander,* Casey,' he insisted as he easily recognised her voice on the other end of the telephone line.

He should; at almost seven o'clock in the evening, he had been waiting all day for this call!

'I've reached a decision,' she told him without preamble.

Xander wasn't in the least reassured by her businesslike tone. He had an uncomfortable feeling that Casey's scruples might have won out, after all.

'Of a sort,' she added, less certainly.

Xander frowned. His patience was already tried to the limit because he'd had to wait all day for her phone call.

It didn't help that Brad's lawyers had already been in touch with his and suggested that they and their client have a meeting in order to 'try and settle custody of Mr Henderson's granddaughter out of court'!

'Yes?' he prompted, perhaps a shade too tersely.

Casey's mouth felt dry. Her hand was shaking slightly as she held the telephone receiver to her ear, having waited until after she had put Josh to bed before making this call.

She had spent a sleepless night thinking over everything Xander Fraser had said to her, and a distracted day doing exactly the same. And the fact that she knew he wasn't going to like what she had to say certainly wasn't helping her nervousness.

'For God's sake, just say yes or no, Casey!' he bit out as his patience finally snapped.

'I—maybe,' she answered unhelpfully, moistening dry lips. She could feel the tension in Xander's silence on the other end of the line. 'I've thought over everything you said. I can see the benefit to Josh and myself in everything you offered. I just—' She drew in a ragged breath. 'I would need to meet Brad Henderson, to assure myself that his threat is real, before I could possibly give you an answer!' The words came out in a rush as she hurried to get this unpleasantness over with.

It was the only conclusion Casey had come to during the last twenty hours of her thoughts going round and round in circles and always coming back to that one point: maybe Brad Henderson could be made to see how unreasonably he was behaving, that it was grief at his daughter's death that was governing his actions rather than a real belief on his part that Lauren would be better off with him? If the older man could be made to see that then Xander would have no need to think about marrying anyone—least of all Casey.

How was that for shooting herself in the foot?

'Are you serious, Casey?' Xander exclaimed. 'The mood Brad was in the last time we spoke, he would eat you for dinner!'

'Dinner was exactly what I had in mind,' she replied, trying not to feel too concerned. 'In fact, I've already asked for tomorrow evening off work in anticipation of the arrangement. Do you think, if you asked him, he would agree to come? Not here, of course,' she added hastily.

'You're lacking a dining room table, for one thing,' Xander snarled. 'Sorry,' he muttered at her reproving silence, then, 'I can ask him,' he conceded. 'But you had better be prepared for the worst if he agrees,' he warned.

'I think I can cope,' Casey assured him dryly; after dealing with the shock of this man's proposal last night, she was sure she could cope with anything Brad Henderson had to throw at her. 'I think it's the right thing to do—er—Xander.'

'There—that wasn't so hard, now, was it?' he taunted, before adding with a sigh, 'You're pretty insistent on doing what you think is right, aren't you, Casey?'

'I would hate for you to find yourself married to me and then discover you needn't have bothered, after all!' she came back tartly.

He laughed appreciatively, with a husky softness that seemed to move teasingly across Casey's sensitised skin and sent a shiver of awareness down the length of her spine.

'You may not find it so funny if that were to be the case!' she snapped, uncomfortable with the fact that she could be so aware of him just talking to him on the telephone.

This woman was something else, Xander acknowledged wryly. Not only was she hesitating about accepting a marriage proposal from a man who was rich enough to ensure that she never needed to worry about money ever again, but she was also concerned that he should never have cause to regret the marriage!

Incredible.

'I think I would cope, Casey.' He mockingly echoed her earlier assurance to him. 'I'll give Brad a call, and then give you a ring back—okay?' he added briskly, abruptly ending the call. He was not sure what to make of her at all.

It was fine for him to actually *like* the woman he was intending to marry—it would be hell for all of them if he didn't—and it was okay that he found Casey's delicate beauty desirable, too; after all, she might want to change the terms of their marriage some time in the future. But he certainly didn't need to feel anything else for her!

Not even the grudging admiration he now felt after that surprising telephone conversation...

* * *

'He hasn't arrived yet, so you can stop looking so apprehensive,' Xander told her the following evening, after the butler had shown Casey into the sitting room.

How could she help but feel anxious when she wasn't even comfortable in Xander's company, let alone in that of his angry ex-father-in-law—who was arriving at any moment?

'You look—wonderful,' Xander said with slow appreciation.

Casey quirked her brows mischievously. 'I don't always look as if I've been dragged through a kitchen backwards!'

'I didn't mean—You're teasing me,' he realised in surprise.

She nodded. 'I thought we had already agreed that I have a sense of humour?' And she was probably going to need it, too!

But at least she knew she *did* look okay. She had spent a leisurely hour or so in the bathroom before getting ready to come out: blow-drying her hair into silky wisps, keeping her make-up light—a touch of lipstick and blusher, a little mascara emphasising the length of her lashes. The black knee-length sheath of a dress she wore was several years old, but of good quality nonetheless, and the fact that she knew it suited her slender curves gave an added boost to her confidence.

Hannah—suitably chastened after her behaviour the other evening—had readily agreed to babysit while Casey went out for the evening, and had arrived promptly at seven o'clock, assuring Casey that she had no need to hurry back, that she was quite happy to stay for as long as she wanted to be out.

The daughter of a neighbour three doors down, Hannah was probably bursting with curiosity about this unusual evening out for Casey. But it was a curiosity Casey hadn't felt in the least inclined to satisfy. Time enough, if Casey's marriage to Xander Fraser did go ahead after all, for her neighbours' speculation.

Xander had completely misread her emotion when she'd been shown into the sitting room of his beautiful home—she wasn't feeling apprehensive at all, but slightly in awe of the Fraser home. Electric gates had opened slowly at the end of a long driveway after she had given her name over the intercom, and long rolling lawns had edged that driveway as she drove the half-mile or so to the main house. It was a magnificent house of mellow stone, floodlit from the outside, with lights inside gleaming a welcome from crystal chandeliers.

A magnificent house that *she* might become mistress of…

It also didn't help that, having been shown into this gold and cream sitting room, with its genuine Regency furnishings and a fire burning in the huge Adam fireplace, she felt slightly overwhelmed by how wonderful Xander looked in his black evening suit, with a black bow tie knotted meticulously at the throat of his white silk shirt.

He crossed the room in easy strides to stand just

in front of her, his gaze intent as he looked down at her. 'You really do look very beautiful this evening,' he told her huskily.

As a widow with a young son, she was surely too old to blush, Casey told herself, even as she felt the warmth enter her cheeks as Xander repeated his compliment.

'I like the fact that you do this,' Xander murmured, even as his hand moved and his fingers brushed lightly against that blush in her cheeks.

Casey stared up at him, her gaze caught and held by his, her lips slightly parted and her breathing becoming shallow.

The squareness of his jaw looked freshly shaved, his aftershave was alluringly musky, and those sculptured lips curved slightly into a smile as he looked down at her with those dark blue eyes. Eyes that seemed fathomless as Casey suddenly felt herself unable to look away...

'Mr Henderson, sir,' the butler announced haughtily, before what Casey could only describe as a whirlwind swept into the room.

'Xander!' a harsh American voice rasped. 'Who the hell is *this?*' Brad Henderson demanded as he saw Casey standing at Xander's side. 'You didn't tell me we would have company this evening!' he barked at the younger man accusingly.

'That will be all, Hilton.' Xander calmly dismissed the manservant even as he snaked his hand out to firmly clasp Casey's arm before she would have stepped away from him.

Casey was too stunned at the older man's verbal attack to do anything other than remain in Xander's grasp as she continued to stare across the room at the aggressive American. Whatever she had been expecting—an elderly man bowed down by grief at his daughter's death, perhaps?—it certainly wasn't this tall, loose-limbed, energetically vital man in black evening clothes, his still attractive features defying his sixty-something years.

It was obvious, looking at Brad Henderson, where Chloe had got her looks from. His dark hair was showing signs of grey at the temples, but his blue eyes had the same narrowed shrewdness his daughter's had had.

Even on such brief acquaintance Casey knew Xander was right to fear this man's determination to claim his granddaughter!

It was what she had wanted to know, after all— just not quite so forcefully. Or quite so soon…

Well, she couldn't say Xander hadn't tried to warn her!

'Good evening, Mr Henderson,' she greeted him smoothly, stepping forward to hold her hand out politely.

A hand the older man completely ignored as the hardness of his gaze remained fixed on Xander. 'Who *is* she, Xander?' he demanded scathingly. 'Some woman you've brought in for the evening in the hope of distracting my attention from the real reason I'm here? The *only* reason I'm here,' he added harshly.

Casey's breath caught in her throat at the double insult this man had just thrown out so casually. To imply that Xander would stoop to such behaviour was bad enough, but the slight he'd directed at her was incredibly insulting, considering they hadn't even been introduced to each other.

'I can assure you, Mr Henderson, that—'

'I wasn't talking to you, honey. Well, Xander? Are you going to say anything, or just stand there like a dummy all evening?' he challenged.

Xander could clearly feel Casey's tension as he maintained his grasp on her arm. A perfectly understandable tension, considering Brad was excelling himself with his rudeness this evening.

His father-in-law might believe him capable of many things—most of them Brad had already chosen to volubly share with Xander during their telephone conversation on Sunday evening—but being a procurer of women hadn't so far numbered amongst them!

'Casey…?' Xander prompted, and he looked down at her, raising an eyebrow in enquiry, knowing that the next move was up to her—that he couldn't go any further with this conversation without knowing what her intentions were.

She gave him a startled look, her eyes widening as she understood exactly what he was asking of her.

But she had no choice, Xander acknowledged grimly. Whatever method of introduction he were to use, the mood Brad was in he was sure to misunderstand it. Casey had to be the one who decided what happened next.

She gave him a frown, before glancing across at Brad. Her back straightened as that glance seemed to bring her to some sort of decision.

Xander found himself holding his breath as he waited to see what that decision was going to be.

Her chin rose challengingly. 'I'm afraid you've completely misunderstood the situation, Mr Henderson,' she told him with quiet dignity. 'Xander did invite you here this evening so that the two of us could meet, yes. But he intended to introduce me to you as his fiancée, and Lauren's future stepmother, rather than anything else you might have assumed!' There was a slight edge to her voice as she finished this pronouncement.

Xander wasn't sure if he wanted to kiss her more at that moment than he had when she had arrived earlier, looking so stunningly, desirably beautiful!

Her announcement had certainly had the desired effect on Brad. He looked momentarily nonplussed, but he recovered quickly, his blue eyes narrowing speculatively as he shot Xander a derisive glance. 'What is this, Xander? A set-up? You're going to keep a so-called fiancée hanging around for a couple of months in the hope of distracting me from a custody suit?'

Xander's hand tightened on Casey's arm as he sensed her bristling indignation. 'Let me introduce the two of you properly,' he drawled. 'Casey—Brad Henderson. Brad, this is Casey Bridges.'

'I don't give a damn—Bridges, did you say?' The older man's attention sharpened noticeably. 'Are you telling me that she's Sam Bridges' widow?'

'One and the same, Brad,' Xander confirmed softly, now able to feel Casey's slight trembling as the older man turned to give her a closer examination.

'You're marrying *Sam Bridges' widow?*' Brad practically shouted incredulously.

'Am I marrying the woman whose husband your daughter seduced from his marriage? The woman who was left alone and penniless after that bastard walked out on her and her son because he found himself a woman who had more money than sense? Yes, I'm marrying Casey, Brad.' He nodded abruptly, his gaze challenging the other man now, knowing that Brad had disliked Sam Bridges almost as much as Xander had.

Brad's face was florid with anger as he glared at the two of them.

'Damn it to hell, Xander! Sam Bridges' widow?' he repeated, shaking his head in utter disbelief.

'That's correct.' Casey was the one to answer huskily. 'I'm sure Xander—and Lauren, of course— would be pleased if you'd care to attend the wedding next month?'

Brad's response to that was completely predictable. 'You haven't heard the last of this, Xander,' he warned fiercely.

But the threat was bluster, pure bluster, and they all knew it…

CHAPTER SIX

'WHEW,' Casey breathed weakly as she collapsed down into one of the sumptuous armchairs. Brad Henderson had stormed out of the room—and the house—only seconds ago. 'What a truly obnoxious man!'

'Here.' Xander sounded amused as he handed her one of the two glasses of brandy he had just poured. 'He really isn't such a bad guy normally,' he excused with a grimace.

Casey looked up at him, brows raised. 'I'll take your word for it!' she said, before taking a reviving sip of the brandy.

It was obviously an expensive brand—unlike the cooking sherry two evenings ago!—and it slid smoothly down her throat to warm her inside and take away some of the shock of the last ten minutes.

'And can I take your announcement to Brad as yours?' Xander asked as he stood beside her chair looking down at her.

Her announcement that she was his fiancée.

That the wedding was going to be next month.

She avoided Xander's searching gaze. 'I'm sure that normally Brad Henderson is a reasonable man.' She wasn't sure of any such thing, considering his behaviour just now, and the selfish way his daughter had turned out, but she was willing to take Xander's word for it if he claimed otherwise. 'But he certainly isn't fit at this moment in time to have the care and control of an already emotionally traumatised six-year-old girl!'

'You didn't answer my question, Casey…' Xander prompted dryly.

No, she hadn't, had she? Because she felt a little shy with him now that the two of them were once again alone—was very aware that before Brad Henderson had interrupted them she had been on the point of raising her face for Xander's kiss.

The man she had just announced she was engaged to marry!

Xander gave a low chuckle. 'I thought he was going to blow a complete gasket when you invited him to attend the wedding next month!'

Casey winced at this reminder that she had done exactly that. And, considering that tomorrow was the start of the next month, the wedding was destined to take place some time in the next four weeks!

'I did, didn't I?' She chewed on her bottom lip as she looked up at Xander. 'Pure bravado on my part, I'm afraid. I don't think I would be too thrilled if he changed his mind and decided to attend after all!'

Xander smiled as he looked down at her, finding this woman more and more intriguing by the minute.

The two earlier occasions they had met, she had been ruffled at having to collect Josh from the house his father had shared with Chloe, let alone seeing Xander there, too.

Two evenings ago she had been tired and looking less than her best after a hard day working at two jobs.

But tonight—tonight she looked a beautiful and sophisticated woman. Someone he had been proud to present to Brad as his future wife.

If, indeed, that was what she was going to be...

His mouth tightened. 'Casey?' he pressed again.

She couldn't prevaricate any more, Casey knew. It was cruel. She had to give him answer. After all, she'd had no qualms about telling Brad Henderson what her decision was to be!

She sat up straighter in the chair. 'After careful consideration, I—I've decided to accept your proposal—your business proposition,' she amended firmly, determined that Xander should realise that as far as she was concerned this was *only* to be a business arrangement.

Not that Casey imagined he thought of it as anything else—if Chloe Fraser's exotic beauty was anything to go by, she was hardly his type, now, was she?

Which brought her to one of the things that definitely had to be sorted out before any marriage between them took place...

'That's good, Casey.' Xander murmured his satisfaction before she could voice her other concern.

Was it good? she wondered, still filled with doubts

about her decision, but knowing—as, no doubt, did Xander!—that it was the only one she could have made.

She couldn't quite meet his triumphant gaze. 'Obviously we still have to work out the—details of the arrangement—'

'Dinner is served, Mr Fraser.' The tall, imposing butler stood in the doorway, looking completely unconcerned by the fact that there were now only two people left to eat the meal that had been intended for three. Although Casey didn't doubt that Hilton, and the rest of the household servants, were all well aware of the way Brad Henderson had stormed out of the house minutes ago. If not the reason for it!

'Shall we…?' Xander held out his arm to take her through to the dining room.

She didn't really need to stay to dinner now that Brad Henderson had left so suddenly, Casey realised. Although it would probably look even more odd to the staff if she were to leave without eating too!

'Of course,' she answered, and she stood up to place her empty brandy glass down on a side table, her hand trembling slightly as she moved to place her hand in the crook of the arm he held out to her.

'Bring some champagne through, would you, Hilton?' Xander instructed the butler.

Champagne?

To toast their engagement, Casey realised.

Or, rather, she corrected herself firmly, to seal their bargain.

The decision made, the commitment voiced,

Casey could feel her panic starting to rise again at exactly what she had done.

She didn't doubt that Josh would blossom in the ease and comfort to be found in the Fraser household, nor that her young son would be thrilled at finding Lauren was to be his stepsister, and he would benefit from a change of school, too.

Her anxiety was more because she still wasn't sure quite what *her* role was going to be!

Xander's wife, obviously.

No doubt his hostess, too, if he entertained.

But what else?

'Stop worrying so much,' Xander murmured close to her ear as he pulled out a dining room chair for her to sit down. 'It will all work out—you'll see,' he promised.

Would it? Casey wondered, slightly disconcerted by the warmth of his breath against her neck. Would it really?

The fact that the high-ceilinged, ornately decorated dining room was formally set for two—the third placing having been hastily removed, no doubt—didn't exactly instil her with confidence, either. She couldn't help but notice that the snowy white napkins, cut-glass wine goblets and the silver candelabra with candles already alight were a complete contrast to her own cramped kitchen, where most of their last conversation had taken place.

Once again Xander watched the play of emotions that flittered across Casey's telling face. He looked up to give Hilton a frowning glance as the other man returned carrying a silver tray with the requested bottle of champagne and two glass flutes.

'Just leave it on the side there, Hilton,' he said impatiently. 'I'll deal with it myself,' he added less harshly, shooting the butler an apologetic glance as he did so; after all, it wasn't the other man's fault that Xander's bride-to-be was becoming jittery now that she had actually committed herself to the marriage.

'Very well, sir,' the elderly man acknowledged with an inclination of his silvery head, before quietly leaving.

Xander crossed the room to pick up the chilled bottle wrapped in a white linen napkin and loosen the cork; perhaps if Casey got some champagne inside her she might start to relax again.

The sparkling wine poured, he moved across the room to hand her one of the two-thirds-full glasses before raising his own glass. 'To us,' he toasted huskily.

Casey swallowed hard, her fingers tight around the delicate champagne flute. 'To us,' she echoed awkwardly, before taking a grateful gulp of the bubbly wine.

Except it didn't quite work out that way. The chilled wine hit the back of her throat, which was tight with nervousness, and then refused to go down!

She began to cough and choke as the bubbly liquid went up her nose, causing her eyes to water, too, holding the glass away from her so that she shouldn't spill the rest of the champagne down herself or over the ornate Aubusson carpet.

She couldn't even see properly when Xander took the glass from her unresisting fingers, patting her lightly on the back as he stood in front of her to use one of the snowy white napkins to wipe away the tears that were now streaming down her face.

This was just too embarrassing, too awful, on top of everything else! What on earth was Xander going to think of her? That she was too gauche even to drink champagne properly without—

Casey became suddenly still as, the choking stopped, her cheeks wiped, she found herself standing only inches away from Xander, looking up into the handsome ruggedness of his face.

Her breath felt strangled in the tightness of her throat and she was completely captured by the sensual heat of Xander's gaze, her heart starting to beat so loudly that she was sure he must be able to hear it, too. She felt so sensitised, so aware, that it seemed as if she could feel the blood rushing through her veins.

She must look a fright, an absolute mess—her eyes teary, her nose red, her cheeks flushed—

None of which seemed to bother Xander in the slightest as he slowly lowered his head and his mouth claimed hers.

Casey melted against him as his arms moved about her waist to pull her into the hardness of his body, and the soft flick of his tongue against her lips encouraged them to part so he could deepen the kiss.

Her own arms moved up, her hands gripping his shoulders to feel the ripple of muscles there, the promise of power as he tensed beneath her touch—a leashed power that she sensed could be so easily released, overwhelming her...

One of his hands caressed the length of her spine as his mouth continued to plunder hers, fingers light against her before his hand cupped the curve of her bottom and drew her even closer against him.

She could feel his body, that leanly muscled force, hard with desire, pulsing against her thighs, filling her with the warmth of her own rising need—a need that was rapidly spiralling out of control—

'Mr James is on the telephone from New York, Mr Fraser,' a voice interrupted them regretfully.

Casey drew back guiltily and turned to look at the butler, standing so stiffly in the open doorway. She couldn't miss seeing the amusement in Xander's gaze before she pulled abruptly away from him to move over to the window and stare out sightlessly into the darkening evening.

What was she *doing?*

Minutes ago she had realised that any relationship between herself and Xander had to be clearly defined—that they would both need to know exactly what each would expect from the other during their marriage—and that it wouldn't include any sort of physical relationship between the two of them.

What had happened between them just now only increased the urgency for that conversation!

'I'll take the call in my study, thanks, Hilton,' Xander said. 'That will be all,' he added, dismissing his servant and waiting for the other man to leave before turning back to Casey. 'We—'

'Please go and take your call, Xander,' she told him shakily, without turning.

Xander stared in frustration at the rigidity of the slender back Casey kept so firmly turned towards him.

Maybe kissing her hadn't been the most sensible thing in the world. But, no matter what she might be thinking now, it hadn't been the worst thing that could have happened, either. The two of them were getting married, for goodness' sake, and if their response to each other just now was anything to go by then it didn't have to be a celibate marriage. For either of them.

'Casey—'

'Would you please go and take your call, Xander?' Her voice was brittle with the tension obvious in her expression as she turned to face him. 'And then I think it would be a good idea for us to discuss the— details of our marriage, when you come back,' she told him coolly.

Details of their marriage?

She had mentioned something about those details earlier, too, hadn't she…?

And, if that determined look in her face was any indication, Xander didn't think he was going to particularly like them!

CHAPTER SEVEN

CASEY had her emotions, and herself, firmly under control by the time Xander returned to the dining room ten minutes later.

It had just been a kiss, she tried to persuade herself. A kiss that shouldn't have happened, and must never be repeated, but nevertheless still just a kiss. And once she and Xander had discussed the terms of their marriage she need never worry— fear?—that it would happen again!

Xander seemed to have put the incident behind him too, as he moved once again to hold a chair for her to sit down at the dining table. 'I think we should start to eat some of this delicious meal my cook has prepared for us, don't you?' he suggested, before taking his own seat opposite hers at the twelve-foot-long table.

It would certainly be easier with Xander seated so far away for her to gather her chaotic thoughts together. To start the discussion that had been interrupted twice already.

But she took a sip of the white wine the butler poured to go with their smoked salmon and waited for the man to leave before attempting to do so. 'I think it might be better if there were some sort of formal contract drawn up between us before we marry,' she told Xander, her long lashes fanning over her cheeks as she looked down at her food, rather than down the table at him.

'A formal contract…?' Xander repeated guardedly.

'Yes.' She chanced a glance at him, and as quickly looked away again as she met the hard glitter of his gaze. 'I think that would be best,' she added nervously. 'So that we both know where we stand and what—what to expect of each other.'

A silence heavy with tension stretched out between them. She really wasn't going to be able to eat any of this lovely food at all if Xander continued to look at her so fiercely, his mouth unsmiling, his jaw clenched.

'A prenuptial agreement, you mean?' he finally bit out.

'Something like that, yes.' Casey nodded, relieved that he was the one who had actually given it that label. For her to have done so would have sounded— well, rather materialistic, perhaps.

But it wasn't just her future she was talking about, was it? She had Josh to consider, too. In fact, if it weren't for her young son she would never have considered Xander's businesslike offer of marriage in the first place.

Besides, she had no idea why he was so obviously displeased by this conversation when the marriage of convenience had been his idea. After all, there had to be guidelines, didn't there? For both of them. Otherwise the whole thing would just be a mess.

And so it began, Xander acknowledged with weary cynicism as he leant his elbow on the table and took a swallow of his wine. He somehow hadn't seen Casey Bridges as mercenary, but he really should have known better. He hadn't met a woman yet who wasn't.

'And what exactly do you have in mind for the contents of this prenuptial agreement?' he asked, almost pinning her to her chair with the force of his piercing gaze.

She made a fluttering movement with her hands. 'I don't know— Well, I would obviously like something in writing concerning the security of Josh's future,' she amended quickly, as Xander raised dark, mocking brows at her prevarication.

He showed his teeth in a humourless smile. 'And of course your own?'

Casey really wished he would stop looking at her like that. Almost as if she were a specimen he had placed under a microscope!

She shook her head. 'I'm more interested in securing Josh's future than my own.'

'Oh, come, Casey—let's not be coy about this,' he drawled, ignoring the food in front of him but continuing to drink his wine. 'Once your house is sold, and you move here, I will obviously pay all household bills, school fees, and so on, but I appreciate you will need access to money of your own for other—expenses,' he rasped. 'In return you will be expected to give up both the jobs you have been working at in order to become a full-time mother to Lauren and Josh.'

Well…yes. She had already worked that out. It wouldn't be too much of a hardship when being a full-time mother was exactly what she had always been—until Sam's desertion a year ago had forced her to juggle motherhood with two jobs in order to support them both. She accepted that it might not be every woman's ideal to be a full-time mother, but she had always enjoyed the role, and had no doubt she would enjoy being stepmother to Lauren, too.

Although she wasn't so sure about selling her family home…

What if Xander changed his mind and this arrangement only lasted a few months? Brad Henderson might calm down more quickly than Xander expected, and so remove the threat of a court battle over Lauren, in which case he wouldn't need a wife any more.

Whereas she would still need a home for Josh and herself…

These were exactly the sort of details that needed to be worked out before they were married, so she had no idea why Xander should continue to look at her in that sceptical way.

'Is that all?' he snapped.

'Er—no. There's also the matter of the—the

intimacy, or lack of it, in our relationship,' she added uncomfortably. 'Of course I accept that you're only in your thirties,' she rushed on, before she lost all her courage under Xander's steely gaze, 'that you will want—er—have needs… But as long as your—relationships are kept discreet, I see no reason why they should interfere with our arrangement in the slightest,' she concluded awkwardly.

Xander continued to look at her for several long seconds without speaking, his hooded blue gaze unreadable. 'You don't think,' he finally said softly, 'that after our earlier—exploration of the possibility, perhaps it might be easier—less complicated—if we were to have that sort of relationship ourselves, in order to satisfy those *needs?*'

No, she didn't!

She didn't care about his previous claim that there were thousands of couples who had a sexual relationship but didn't love each other. She had already had that with Sam, and she had no intention of repeating the experience with Xander Fraser!

'No, I don't,' she told him firmly.

Xander's fingers clenched so tightly around his wine glass that he was in danger of breaking it. Damn it, that earlier kiss might have been a little—unwise on his part, and the timing absolutely lousy, but couldn't this woman see that there was a sexual attraction between the two of them that they would be foolish to ignore?

That it could be dangerous to ignore!

Did she seriously expect them to live together in close proximity, as husband and wife, and not explore the possibilities of the desire they obviously felt for each other?

He could see that she did. That green gaze was clear and determined as she looked down the table at him so intently.

'We will, of course, have separate bedrooms,' she added briskly.

That would be no hardship—he and Chloe had occupied separate bedrooms for years, by his choice!

He raised a mocking eyebrow. 'And what of your own—needs? Do you intend to satisfy them *discreetly* too?' His voice hardened. He was not at all happy with the thought.

The blush that he found so intriguing once again brightened her cheeks. 'Certainly not!' she denied indignantly.

Xander frowned, but something inside him eased a little, and he loosened his death-grip on the wine glass before he shattered it. 'Then what do you intend doing about them?'

She shook her head, the candlelight bringing out the gold highlights in her hair. 'I don't intend doing anything about them!' she assured him tartly. 'The— physical side of marriage is not something that interests me in the slightest.'

She really thought she meant that, Xander realised as he took in the set of her mouth and the determined tilt of her chin.

For a woman who had been married for seven years, who had a six-year-old son, Casey was surprisingly naïve if she didn't realise exactly how sexually responsive she was—of how she had melted against him minutes ago, her mouth as hungry as his own.

Xander's gaze narrowed as he wondered again about her marriage to Sam Bridges.

He had despised the other man almost as much as he had despised Chloe—had thought them two of a kind, considering only their own interests of importance. But had that selfishness also permeated Bridges' physical relationship with his own wife?

What business was it of his? Xander instantly rebuked himself; Casey was very firmly setting down the terms of their marriage, making it perfectly clear that the financial security he offered was all that interested her. That he would have to look elsewhere if he wanted to satisfy his physical 'needs'!

'Fine.' He gave a sharp inclination of his head. 'Is there anything else you want written into the contract besides what we've already discussed?'

Casey looked at him uncertainly, knowing she had displeased him in some way, but completely at a loss to understand how. She was being reasonable, wasn't she? More than reasonable, she would have thought.

'No, there's nothing else,' she confirmed.

'Then I'll go ahead and make the necessary arrangements.'

The arrangements for their wedding.

The arrangements for her and Josh to move into this house.

The arrangements for her to be Xander Fraser's wife. In name only…!

CHAPTER EIGHT

FOR Xander, the three weeks leading up to their wedding day were some of the most puzzling—and frustrating—he had ever known.

Used to making decisions, to controlling his multimillion-pound production company both here and in America, he found dealing with the complexity of the woman who had agreed to become his wife—in name only!—more challenging than anything or anyone else he had ever encountered.

In response to that telephone call from David James he'd initially had to go to New York for five days. While there he had received a telephone call from Brad Henderson, and the older man had made it clear that he didn't believe any marriage between Xander and the widow of Sam Bridges would ever take place.

Which had been enough of a spur—if Xander had needed one!—to set the marriage plans in motion.

Which was when his troubles with Casey had really begun!

Telling the two children of their plans had gone smoothly enough—although Xander had been a little thrown when Josh, with his mother's candour, had innocently asked if he was going to be his new daddy.

Casey had been the one to smooth over that awkwardness by stating that she thought it better if Josh called him Xander for the moment, and Lauren called her Casey.

But following that Casey had flatly refused to comply with his suggestion that she immediately give up her two jobs at the café and the hotel restaurant, claiming that she still had to live and pay the bills until after they were married.

When he had asked why she hadn't put her house on the market yet, he'd been given the same answer.

His question as to whether or not she had any guests she wished to invite to the wedding had also been met with a negative. Well, he didn't, either.

And she had absolutely refused to even consider his suggestion that she make any changes—either to Fraser House, or the running of it—she deemed fit for the comfort of herself and Josh. She had assured him there would be plenty of time for that later, *if* she deemed it necessary.

This had given him some insight into the reasoning behind Casey not doing any of the things he had asked of her—she wasn't sure that he was going through with the wedding, either!

As a way of showing her he was completely serious about the marriage, he'd had his lawyer draw up the contract Casey had asked for—only to have her request that it be sent on to her own lawyer for perusal.

The bundle of fury that arrived at the house that evening, only two days before the wedding, wasn't what he had been expecting!

He was working on some papers in his study when Hilton announced Casey's arrival. The fact that she was here at all was surprising enough, but the angry glitter in her eyes and the flush to her cheeks were even more so as she stormed into his study seconds later and threw the contract down on his desk in front of him.

'I can't sign this!' She scowled.

Xander frowned darkly. 'Why can't you?'

'Because I can't!' she snapped. 'Because it's wrong! Because it's—it's damned insulting!' she finished furiously, her hands bunched into fists at her sides as she confronted him across the wide width of the leather-topped desk.

She really was beautiful when she was angry, Xander thought abstractedly, even as he wondered exactly which part of the contract she found insulting.

Her face was less strained than it had been a couple of weeks ago—those dark circles beneath her eyes having disappeared, and the hollows of her cheeks having filled out a little.

But as for what was wrong with the contract, he had no idea. He had given her what she'd asked for, hadn't he? Financial security for herself and Josh. So what the hell was the problem?

Casey stood her ground when Xander stood up to

move round and rest his hips against the front of the desk. But the movement brought him dangerously close to her in the process, making her totally aware of him—of his warmth, of the air of sensuality that he held in control but which was never far beneath the surface whenever the two of them met.

Not that she showed by the flickering of an eyelid that she was in the least disconcerted by his close proximity. Xander Fraser was a man used to having his own way. She had quickly learnt that this last few weeks. But, as a woman who had become used to running her own life, and Josh's, this last year, she wasn't about to cede any of her independence without a fight.

'Tell me what's wrong and I'll have my lawyer change it,' he promised.

If he had returned her anger, or even if he had spoken to her in that coldly distant tone he sometimes adopted, Casey knew she would have found it easier to maintain her own fury on reading the contract he'd had drawn up.

As it was, she felt a little like a deflated balloon at his reasonable response. 'I— It's just— *That* paragraph is complete nonsense!' She moved to jab a finger at the offending paragraph in the contract.

She was now even closer to Xander, her arm brushing against his before she moved back abruptly to look at him from beneath lowered lashes.

There was a dark shadow to the squareness of his jaw where he was in need of a shave, and his overlong hair was slightly dishevelled where he'd been running his fingers through it as he'd worked at his desk. Dark hair, that shone with ebony lights... The sort of hair that made Casey long to reach out and touch it, to run her own fingers through its silky length as Xander's mouth once again plundered hers—

Casey gave an inward groan. She'd had a lot of fantasies like this these last couple of weeks— moments when she had found herself thinking of Xander, of the way he had kissed her, caressed her...

Imagining what would have happened if Hilton hadn't interrupted them that evening...

After all her talk of a marriage of convenience between them, her insistence that she wouldn't object to him having other relationships as long as he was discreet, Casey now knew that she found the very idea of Xander being intimately involved with another woman completely abhorrent.

Which was pretty ridiculous when she had absolutely refused to even contemplate the two of *them* having an intimate relationship.

But there was a good reason for that.

A very good reason.

She didn't want Xander to know—for him to discover, just how inept she was at lovemaking. 'Frigid' was one of the words that Sam had used, along with 'unresponsive' and 'cold'.

Sam had not been amused by her inexperience on their wedding night—had been slightly put out that he'd had to be the one to initiate her into lovemaking—and the whole thing had been painful and awkward for Casey. The fact that she had found herself pregnant only three months later had been something of a relief because Sam had claimed to find the whole idea of making love to a pregnant woman repugnant.

Their lovemaking had resumed after Josh's birth, of course, but it had never been something that Casey had enjoyed—more something to be endured.

But she had been attracted to Sam before their marriage—had thought herself in love with him— and look how disastrously that had turned out!

No—no matter how attractive she found Xander, she did not want to repeat the experience with him, to see the same impatience in his face when he found out what a disappointment she was in bed.

Luckily he wasn't looking at her, but at the contract he had picked up, a slight frown between those deep blue eyes as he finally looked up to shake his head. 'I can't see what the problem is—'

'There!' Casey moved forward to point to the appropriate paragraph, drawing in a sharp breath as once again she found herself standing so close to him she could smell the musky tang of his cologne, could see the dark hair that grew lightly on his bared arms beneath the black tee shirt he wore, see the quiet strength of his hands, his fingers long, the nails kept short.

Hands that last night she had actually dreamt of— touching her, caressing her—

'I still don't see it,' Xander protested. 'All it says is "the amount of one million pounds is to be paid into the bank account of Casey Bridges, then to be Casey Fraser, on the day of the marriage"—'

'All it says?' Casey repeated incredulously, stepping back slightly. 'A *million pounds,* Xander?'

Xander found himself very aware of the woman standing so close to him. In fact, he acknowledged with self-derision, he had often found himself thinking of Casey lately, when he should have been concentrating on other things.

Apart from Lauren, who was something else entirely, work had always come first with him these last seven years—had been the constant that kept his life with Chloe bearable.

But this past few weeks he had found himself musing about Casey even in the middle of business deals. Found himself wondering about the soft curves of her body, of how it would feel to have her nakedness against him, under him, on top of him. Imagining parting the litheness of her thighs, touching her there, feeling her flower and blossom…

He wanted to touch her, to kiss her, taste her, to watch her face as he slowly, oh, so slowly entered her, and the heat of her engulfed him—

He was doing it again!

Except that this time Casey was standing right here beside him, looking up at him with those huge green eyes, her cheeks flushed, her lips slightly parted, as if waiting for his kiss.

He couldn't fight this any longer, Xander decided achingly, and he reached out to grasp the tops of her arms and pull her hard against him, shutting off her angry words as his mouth captured hers.

He slowly lay back on the desk behind him and took Casey with him, her thighs lying between his parted ones, the softness of her breasts crushed against his chest, as his mouth claimed hers with the fierceness of three weeks' longing.

CHAPTER NINE

CASEY had no idea how she came to be lying on top of Xander on his desktop as his mouth plundered hers—none of the fantasies she'd had about him had ever been *this* immediate—she only knew that she felt empowered, above him like this, as she raised her head slightly to nibble and suck his bottom lip, to taste him as he was tasting her.

Xander groaned low in his throat, his hands moving restlessly along the length of her spine as he encouraged her to deepen the kiss. A move Casey denied him as she took her time running the warmth of her tongue against his parted lips.

But it was her turn to groan with pleasure as she felt Xander push her tee shirt up over her back, his hands, those big warm hands, against the bareness of her flesh, spreading fire wherever they touched.

Casey's hands tangled in the dark thickness of his hair as she kissed him hungrily, her lips apart as he returned that hunger, his tongue plunging into her hotly as she squirmed her hips against his hardened thighs.

Xander broke the kiss to push her tee shirt completely out of his way before his hands moved about her slender waist and he easily lifted her slightly above him, so that his tongue circled and licked the hardened nub of her bared breast.

Casey arched her back as her breasts tingled and swelled to the caress, gasping breathlessly as Xander drew the tightened nipple into the heat of his mouth, sucking and licking, that tingle spreading to her thighs as she moved rhythmically against him.

He was so hard against her, his hardness rubbing against the heated centre of her even as his mouth continued its attention on her breast.

She was on fire, her eyes closed, her breathing ragged, the heat between her thighs becoming unbearable as Xander's hand cupped and captured her other breast, his thumb moving caressingly against the hard tip in the same rhythm as he sucked its twin.

'Xander, I can't—!'

'Yes, you can,' he assured her gruffly as he released her to roll over, so that she was the one now lying on the desktop, his gaze held hers as his hand moved to unsnap the button on her denims, before reaching beneath to unerringly seek the centre of her need.

As soon as he touched her there Casey arched against him, wanting more, wanting something—

Xander's mouth claimed hers even as he found her centre, his thumb moving softly against the swollen nub even as his fingers touched her moisture, circling but not yet entering.

Casey breathed shallowly, her eyes closed as she gave herself up to the pleasure she could feel deep inside her—a pleasure that spread and warmed, burned as Xander increased the rhythm of his caress, as his fingers finally entered her to move in the same rhythm.

She couldn't take any more—felt as if she were about to explode with pleasure—needed, needed—

She gasped, her eyes wide, as Xander satisfied that need with the firm caress of his thumb. Casey exploded around him in spasms of unrelenting pleasure as she stared up at him in the sheer wonder of her release, the whole of her body throbbing with the ecstasy he'd made her feel.

Xander watched her unashamedly as she found her release, his caresses continuing until he was sure she was completely spent, until he had given her every last moment of pleasure.

Then he bent his head to once again claim her lips with his, his caresses soothing now, gentling, as he smoothed her tee shirt back over her breasts before entangling his hands in the silkiness of her hair, his lips moving to kiss the tiny shell of her ear before trailing down the column of her throat to the tiny pulse throbbing at its base.

Casey moved restlessly beside him. 'But you didn't—' She drew in a shaky breath. 'You haven't—'

He raised his head to look down into her stricken face. Her cheeks were flushed, her eyes darkened by dilated pupils, and she couldn't quite meet his gaze. 'I don't need to,' he assured her gruffly.

And he didn't. What had happened just now, seeing and feeling Casey's pleasure, had been the most erotic experience he had ever had in his life. The throbbing of his own body was sweet evidence of that.

Casey's skin was like velvet, her breasts so small and perfect, so responsive to his hands, lips and tongue. *All* of her was so responsive that he felt that to take his own pleasure would ruin something that was already perfect.

'I don't need to,' he repeated huskily, smiling down at her as his hand moved to lightly caress one pink cheek.

Casey stared up at him wordlessly. Why didn't he need to? Sam had always—

Now wasn't the time to think about Sam, or their marriage!

Xander had just—

No, *she* had just climaxed—for the first time in her life.

Ever.

And it had been the most wonderful experience she had ever known. She had never dreamt—never realised—

What must Xander think of her?

She had come here to tell him that one of the details in the contract he'd had drawn up outlining the terms of their marriage was unacceptable to her, and had ended up having an orgasm on his desktop!

Not only that, but Xander had obviously found

her lack of control so shocking that it had killed his own desire!

She turned her head away. 'Would you let me up, please?' She spoke quietly.

'Casey—'

'Just let me up, Xander!' Her voice rose forcefully as she turned to glare at him.

Sighing, he complied, standing up to look away as she moved to adjust the fastening of her denims.

Casey swayed dizzily as she stood up, her legs feeling weak from the onslaught that had just racked her body, still aware of that tingling sensation between her thighs.

She closed her eyes briefly, wondering how she was ever going to be in Xander's company again without remembering—remembering how she had—

'I have to get to work,' she told him abruptly.

Xander turned slowly to look at her, frowning as he saw the closed expression on her face—her eyes unreadable, her mouth set hard with determination. 'Don't you think we need to sit down and talk more than you need to go to work?' he finally suggested.

'Talk about what?' she challenged.

Yes—talk about what? Xander wondered as he continued to look at her.

The last half an hour might have been the most incredibly erotic experience of his life, but it obviously hadn't meant the same to Casey...

He drew in a deep breath before moving quickly

away from her. He was afraid of what he might do if he didn't!

'So I'm supposed to ignore what just happened, huh?' he growled.

She blinked, swallowing hard before answering. 'I think that might be for the best, don't you?'

It wasn't a question, and Xander didn't bother granting it an answer. If she could forget what had just happened then he would obviously be wasting his time talking about it.

'Just put in whatever you want that paragraph to say.' He held out a pen and the contract without looking at her, his clenched hands returning to his sides as he resisted the impulse to reach out and kiss her senseless as she made the necessary adjustment.

Despite the sexual attraction that existed between them, Casey obviously regretted having given in to that attraction. She was making it perfectly clear that she didn't want a repeat of it, either, that it had meant nothing to her.

All this marriage meant to Casey—all it would *ever* mean to her—was financial security. And the sooner he got used to that idea the better.

'Fine.' He nodded as she placed the adjusted contract back down on the desk. 'As Josh and Lauren won't be at the wedding on Friday, I think it would be a good idea, after you and Josh have moved in here tomorrow afternoon, for the two children to stay up and have dinner with us. I know it's a school day the following morning,' he continued as she would have spoken, 'but they need to feel a part of this.'

Oh, God. She and Josh moved in here tomorrow afternoon…!

How could she go through with this after what had just happened?

But how could she not? She had already handed in her notice at her two jobs—had already finished at the café earlier today. This was the last evening she would be working at the hotel. Her own and Josh's things were packed back at the house, ready to move in here tomorrow.

In less than forty-eight hours she was due to become wife to Xander.

A man she had just discovered could so easily take her to the heights of pleasure.

A man she had come to like these last three weeks.

A man she had come to…love?

She gave him a startled look. *Did* she love Xander? Had she fallen in love with the man who was only marrying her to provide a mother for his daughter, to stop his father-in-law from attempting a custody suit for that daughter?

Could she really have been so stupid?

'What is it now?' Xander asked wearily as he watched the play of emotions cross Casey's face. 'After what just happened, you want it actually written into the contract that we maintain separate bedrooms? Fine.' He nodded. 'You want it in writing that there won't be a repeat of just now? Again, fine,' he snarled. 'Now, if you wouldn't mind, Casey, I have some work to do, too.' He moved pointedly to sit back behind his desk, too tired, too bone-weary now, to engage in any more verbal battles with this woman this evening.

Casey's face had first flushed, and then paled at his outburst. 'That won't be necessary,' she told him coldly. 'Just the adjustment I've made will be quite sufficient.'

'Then don't let me keep you. I would *so* hate for you to be late to work,' he added. And he knew he sounded so like Lauren when she was in a fit of childish pique that he was surprised Casey didn't tell him to grow up.

She didn't—simply giving him one last pained look before turning on her heel and making a dignified exit, her head held high.

What an idiot he'd been, Xander instantly berated himself.

Had he really thought, when Casey had come here to complain that a million-pound settlement on her wasn't enough, that the two of them making love would make any difference to her completely financial motivation for marrying him?

He was a fool.

Not only that, but he had been so beguiled, so enchanted with Casey's loss of control, that he hadn't even wanted to find his own release in the warmth of her body—had found her pleasure more than enough to satisfy him.

He was worse than a fool.

Chloe had used her body to manipulate and control him too. Until he had become wise to her machinations and refused even to share her bed any more.

He couldn't believe he had fallen for that trick a second time!

How much more than a million did Casey want? How much did she think that sexual encounter was worth?

Xander's eyes glittered angrily as he picked up the contract. But his anger quickly turned to a puzzled frown when he looked down at the adjustment Casey had made.

That whole paragraph concerning the settlement of money directly on Casey on the day of their marriage had been completely erased, with firm, black strokes of his pen!

Casey didn't personally want *any* settlement of money from him.

He didn't feel angry or puzzled any more—he felt stunned!

CHAPTER TEN

'IT's going to be great living here, isn't it, Mummy?'
Josh said excitedly as the two of them returned to his
new bedroom, after sharing a swim with Lauren in
the indoor pool at the back of Fraser House.

Oh, yes—great, Casey echoed wearily in her head,
outwardly giving her blond-haired young son an encouraging smile as she went through to the adjoining bathroom to run the shower for him.

The two of them had moved in that afternoon, as
planned. Xander had been conspicuously absent
when they did so—for which Casey had been very
grateful, still not sure how she was going to face him
again after yesterday evening.

The worst part about it, as far as Casey was concerned, was that she only had to close her eyes to
relive the way Xander had kissed and caressed her,
her body tingling anew as she remembered how it
had felt when she had completely lost control.

Wonderful.

Like nothing else she had ever known in her life.

Something she craved—longed to have happen again!

But she knew that she couldn't let it.

There was absolutely no point in continuing to explore a sexual relationship with Xander. Especially when his comments afterwards, concerning the inclusion of clauses in their contract about separate bedrooms and there being no repeat of what had happened between them, had to mean that their time together couldn't have meant the same to him as it had to her. It was obviously no hardship on his part to forego an intimate relationship with her.

How could it be? Xander was gorgeous, extremely sexy, and there had to have been dozens of woman in his life—both before and since his marriage to Chloe. Unlike Casey, who had previously only ever known Sam as a lover. And even that one time with Xander had shown her just how awful Sam's love-making had been in comparison!

Once Sam had realised on their wedding night that she was still a virgin, he had never particularly cared about initiating her into pleasure.

He'd seemed to think she should know what to do—that her inexperience was nothing but a liability he had no time for, and it was her own fault she never reached a climax in their lovemaking.

And she had accepted what he told her—had been sure that he was right, that there must be something wrong with her because she didn't enjoy sex with her own husband.

She had enjoyed it with Xander last night.

Because she had instinctively known what to do with Xander!

He had allowed her to kiss and caress him, pulling her on top of him as he'd invited her to take the initiative.

And he had felt so good. So—

'Is everything okay?'

She spun round guiltily as Xander suddenly spoke behind her, spraying him with water because she still held the showerhead in her hand.

'Thanks!' he murmured ruefully as he looked down at the water soaking into his pristine white shirt.

'Oh, Lord!' Casey gasped her dismay as she realised what she had done, quickly turning off the water to drop the shower head into the bath.

She picked up a towel and moved across the room to wipe ineffectually at his shirt-front, her movements slowing and then finally stopping when she found her gaze caught and held by the way the shirt clung to him, the material almost see-through now, the dark hair on his chest clearly visible.

She looked up at him from beneath lowered lashes, and then quickly looked away again as she found him looking down at her with enigmatic blue eyes.

'I'm really sorry about that,' she mumbled awkwardly.

'Forget it,' he dismissed.

Forget the way the shirt was clinging to him, outlining his muscled arms, the powerful expanse of his chest, making him look more sexy than if he actually hadn't been wearing a shirt at all? Impossible!

'Perhaps you had better go and change—'

'I said forget it, Casey. I'm more interested in whether or not you have everything you need,' he said gently.

She swallowed hard, knowing that he wouldn't want to hear what she needed at that moment!

Because she needed *him.* His arms about her. His mouth on hers. His hands caressing her.

She moistened lips that had gone suddenly dry. 'Josh and I are fine. Thank you,' she added.

'I've already spoken to Josh and established that he's more than happy. Lauren, too,' Xander said. 'I was asking about *you,* Casey.'

What did he want her to say? That she was fine, too? That all of this was fine with her? That she was already as comfortable with her drastic change in lifestyle as Josh obviously was? That she wasn't bothered by the fact that Xander's idea of separate bedrooms was actually to have adjoining ones?

What she really wanted to say was that she had made a mistake in even *thinking* that she could go through with a marriage of convenience now that she had realised how she felt about him.

That in the three short weeks she had known him she had fallen in love with him…

Oh, yes—she could just see herself telling Xander all of that!

'Everything is fine.' She nodded, still not able to meet his gaze.

How could she, when yesterday evening she had behaved like a complete wanton in his arms and for every hour since then had wanted a repeat of what they'd done?

Xander's gaze rested thoughtfully on her bent head as he saw her total unease in his company—not that it was surprising after what had happened last night.

Casey had made it perfectly clear to him—several times!—that she wasn't interested in a physical relationship with him.

Something he'd had no trouble in totally ignoring once he had her in his arms.

In fact, a part of him had been surprised to discover she had moved in as planned when he'd got home this evening. He had half expected that she might have decided she couldn't go through with marrying him, after all.

What the hell had he been thinking of when he'd taken her on his desktop like that?

The problem was he hadn't been thinking at all—had been driven to kiss and caress every silken inch of her, to feel her nakedness against him, to taste her.

Not what she would have been expecting when she'd only come to discuss some changes to the contract he'd had drawn up!

Changes he had spent most of the day trying to make sense of—when he hadn't been thinking of how Casey tasted and felt, that was!

This woman—a woman he had three weeks ago cold-bloodedly decided to marry—made him feel anything but cold-blooded. Even standing next to her now, his wet shirt clinging to him uncomfortably, he knew that he wanted her. Wanted her wild and wanton beneath him as he entered her, as he felt himself engulfed by her, possessed by her, as they both reached a shuddering climax this time.

It had all seemed so simple when he'd first come up with this plan—so uncomplicated: marriage to a woman he didn't love, who made no pretence of loving him, and both of them knowing exactly what was expected, wanted from the marriage.

After last night it didn't seem that uncomplicated at all.

There was no way—absolutely no way—he was going to be able to share this house with her, occupy the adjoining bedroom to hers, without wanting to make love to her again.

In fact, as things stood, he wasn't sure that *he* could go through with this marriage of convenience at all!

'I need to talk to you, Casey,' he rasped. 'Alone,' he added, as Josh could be heard singing happily in the adjoining bedroom.

She gave him a startled look. 'I—we're due to have dinner with the children,' she reminded him.

He nodded curtly, well aware that he was the one to have suggested the arrangement. He just hadn't realised at the time how desperately he would need to be alone with Casey.

'Once they're both in bed will do,' he said.

'I—of course,' Casey agreed slowly, shooting him an uncertain glance as she did so.

Xander's eyes, as he returned her gaze, were dark and unreadable—although the harsh expression on his face certainly wasn't encouraging.

What did he need to speak to her about so urgently? she wondered, with a sickening jolt in her stomach.

Had he spoken to Brad Henderson today and worked out some sort of compromise with him?

Had Xander decided not to go ahead with their marriage, after all?

CHAPTER ELEVEN

SITTING through dinner, with Xander now looking incredibly sexy in black trousers and a black silk shirt that showed off the broad width of his shoulders and the flatness of his stomach, trying to pretend, for Josh and Lauren's sake, that they really were going to be one big, happy family, was absolutely excruciating for Casey.

Especially when, as the minutes slowly passed, and the brooding Xander seemed to have trouble addressing even the most casual of remarks to her, it became more and more obvious he wished her anywhere but here in his home.

If he had changed his mind—if he had decided not to go ahead with the marriage—then he should have sought her out earlier today and told her so. Before she'd had a chance to actually move herself and Josh in here, Casey thought. It was going to be much harder for all of them if she and Josh simply had to move out again.

When Lauren requested that Casey be the one to

put her to bed as well as Josh, Casey felt even more of a fraud, and her cheeks were flushed with anger when she returned to the sitting room minutes later, to find Xander standing beside the fireplace enjoying a glass of brandy.

'Like one?' He held up the bulbous glass.

'Am I going to need one?' she returned sharply.

'That depends on your perspective on things!'

Casey's mouth set unhappily. 'In that case, I'll have some,' she said, before moving to stand on the other side of the fireplace to stare down sightlessly at the crackling flames as she waited for Xander to return with the brandy.

She was wearing a green off-the-shoulder dress this evening, Xander noted admiringly, glancing across at her as he poured her brandy and refreshed his own glass. The soft material clung to the pert thrust of her breasts and the slender lines of her waist and thighs.

In fact, Xander had been looking at her admiringly all evening. Casey was beautiful—more subtly, quietly so than Chloe had ever been, but it was a beauty that came from within. He didn't doubt that in fifty years or so Casey would still be radiantly lovely.

Fifty years or so…

Where would *he* be in fifty years?

Still here at Fraser House, he suspected, with Lauren and Josh having left long ago to make their own way in the world. Casey would be gone too, once there were no children to bind them together. So it would be just Xander, rattling around in a house that would no longer have a family in it to make it a home.

The thought of growing old alone had never bothered him. His marriage to Chloe had been over for years before she'd actually left, and he had long been used to being alone.

Alone was good. Alone was undemanding. Alone was the freedom to do what he wanted, when he wanted. Alone was uncomplicated.

Alone sucked!

He crossed the room to hand Casey her glass of brandy, a frown creasing his brow as he noted the way she deliberately avoided her hand coming into contact with his.

She could no longer even bear for him to touch her casually!

He took a swallow of his own brandy before speaking. 'Casey—'

'I'm sorry to interrupt, Mr Fraser—'

'Not now, Hilton!' Xander growled, and he turned to glare at the manservant standing in the doorway.

Damn it, he had never realised what an intrusion household staff could be until Casey came into his life! Every time he tried to talk to her, it seemed for one reason or another Hilton came in and interrupted.

Except yesterday evening, in Xander's study…

It was probably just as well that the butler hadn't walked in on that particular scene!

The elderly man had the grace to look apologetic.

'I really am sorry for the interruption, Mr Fraser, but Mr Henderson has called—'

'Tell him I'll ring him back later,' Xander instructed, not at all interested in yet another confrontation with his ex-father-in-law.

'You misunderstand me, Mr Fraser,' Hilton persisted. 'When I said he had called, I meant that he's here—at the house.'

'Here?' Xander repeated, with a scowl. 'Now?'

'He's waiting in the hallway, sir.'

Xander looked at Casey, noting that her eyes were wide with an apprehension she couldn't hide. 'If you would rather go upstairs while I talk to Brad…?'

He was offering her a way out, Casey realised. A chance to escape any further insults from his ex-father-in-law.

She straightened her shoulders, her chin rising. 'No, I don't think so, thank you,' she refused quietly, surprised when Xander reached out and gave her hand a reassuring squeeze.

'Good girl,' he murmured approvingly, before turning back to the waiting butler. 'Show Mr Henderson in, Hilton.'

Casey was aware of Xander's hand still holding hers when Brad Henderson was shown into the room. The older man's gaze narrowed immediately as he took in that outward show of intimacy.

Which was probably why Xander had done it, Casey thought.

Obviously the two men hadn't come to any compromise after all—so what had Xander needed to talk to her about so urgently earlier on?

'Brad,' Xander greeted him curtly, once the three of them were alone.

'Xander,' the older man acknowledged with a nod. 'Mrs Bridges,' he added, surprisingly.

'Casey will do,' Xander was the one to suggest.

Brad Henderson gave a brief smile. 'I—I believe the two of you are to be married tomorrow?' he began awkwardly.

'Yes, we are,' Xander replied firmly.

Yes, they *were?* Casey thought, relieved.

Xander hadn't changed his mind about the marriage, after all?

Or was he just saying the wedding was going ahead for the other man's benefit…?

'Yes. Well.' Brad Henderson looked decidedly un-comfortable. 'I—' He broke off, breathing heavily.

'Can I get you a drink, Brad?' Xander offered gently. 'You look as if you could do with one.'

The older man quirked a rueful brow. 'That obvious, is it?'

'Yes,' Xander drawled, releasing Casey's hand to move across the room to the drinks cabinet. 'Bourbon on the rocks?'

'Thanks,' the other man accepted, glancing at Casey once Xander had handed him his drink. 'I believe I owe you an apology, Mrs—Casey,' he amended stiffly.

'You do,' Xander agreed, before Casey could think

of an appropriate reply. 'You were extremely rude to her three weeks ago,' he pointed out as he moved back to stand at Casey's side.

One thing was becoming very clear to Casey—Brad Henderson had had some sort of change of heart. Perhaps it meant the wedding didn't even need to take place.

It was what she had feared from the beginning, of course. The reason she had insisted on meeting Brad Henderson three weeks ago—to ascertain that his threat was genuine.

Although the reasons for her misgivings now were no longer the same as they had been then!

She had fallen in love with Xander over the last three weeks.

She *wanted* to marry him.

She wanted to wake up beside Xander every day for the rest of her life. Wanted to have more children with him. Wanted the two of them to watch all their children grow up together. Wanted to grow old with him…!

Brad tried to smile. 'I'm afraid I wasn't quite myself when we last met, Mrs—Casey,' he offered.

She inclined her head graciously. 'It was perfectly understandable, following your recent loss.'

'Perhaps,' he accepted.

'It wasn't understandable at all after what Casey had already been through,' Xander refuted. 'You were bloody insulting, Brad,' he added grimly. 'To both Casey and myself.'

The other man had put him in an unacceptable

position because of his threats concerning Lauren, and Xander, for one, didn't intend letting him get away with it that easily.

Brad ran a hand through the thickness of his hair and he looked shame-faced. 'I was, wasn't I?' he acknowledged with a grimace. 'I really do apologise, Casey,' he turned to tell her gruffly. 'I—if you and Xander have managed to find some happiness together out of this mess, then I sincerely wish you well.' Brad raised his glass and took a huge swallow of his bourbon. 'I may have been an over-indulgent father, Xander, but I wasn't blind. I always knew that you and Chloe weren't particularly happy together—'

'We weren't happy together at all,' Xander said bluntly, welcoming Brad's apology.

'No. Well.' Brad gave a shuddering sigh. 'I knew that, of course. But she was my daughter, Xander,' he appealed. 'And despite everything I loved her.'

'Of course you did.' Casey was the one to answer him soothingly.

'But that's no excuse, is it, Xander?' Brad looked across at him regretfully. 'I put you in a terrible position three weeks ago, with my threats concerning Lauren.' He gave a self-disgusted shake of his head. 'If it's any consolation, I've come here this evening to eat humble pie.'

Xander watched as Casey moved gracefully across the room to Brad's side, to place her hand lightly on his arm. 'Why don't you sit down for a while, and perhaps the three of us can talk quietly together?' she invited.

She really was the most incredible woman, Xander acknowledged with growing wonder. Most women in the same position, having previously been insulted and ridiculed, would have told Brad just what they thought of him. Chloe certainly would have done. But Casey, being Casey, was being gentle and understanding.

He could only hope for that same gentleness from her when the two of them talked together, once Brad had left.

Brad was just as amazed. 'I can't believe someone like you was ever married to that complete—' He broke off, realising he was about to be rude again. 'Insulting the man isn't going to bring Chloe back,' he acknowledged shakily.

Xander felt for him, he really did, and his own anger faded. He knew what it must be costing the other man to come here this evening and abase himself like this.

Brad continued. 'I want you both to know that I'd no idea Bridges was even married until I called to see Chloe one weekend and Bridges' son Josh was actually staying there with them. Chloe didn't tell me that the two of them setting up home together had broken up two families, not just one. And even once I knew about Josh, Chloe assured me that the marriage had been over long before she'd entered Bridges' life. But that wasn't true either, was it?' He sighed.

Casey felt so sorry for this man. She knew that he must have faced some harsh realities about his daughter in the three weeks since he had met her, and

Xander had told him the truth about the break-up of her marriage.

'No, it wasn't.' Xander was the one to answer the other man harshly. 'I told you three weeks ago what really happened.'

'Yes.' Brad Henderson nodded. 'But even then I couldn't believe it—couldn't accept that Chloe had done such a thing. It was only after I spoke to you on the telephone in New York, when you insisted you were telling me the truth, that I sat down and realised how wrong I've been. You've never lied to me in the way that Chloe did, Xander. I want you to know I'm not going ahead with any custody battle over Lauren. I—she's better off with you. And Casey,' he added, with a brief smile in her direction. 'I had better go now.' He stood up abruptly to drain the last of his bourbon, before placing the empty glass on the coffee table. 'I hope that some time in the future you will be able to forgive me for the trouble I've caused, and that—that you will let me see my granddaughter from time to time.' He gave Xander a hopeful look.

Casey looked at Xander, too, willing him not to remain angry with the older man.

At the same time she recognised that Brad Henderson backing down on the custody battle now meant that Xander *definitely* didn't need to marry her!

CHAPTER TWELVE

'WELL...that was pretty traumatic, wasn't it?' she said over-brightly, once Xander had returned from walking Brad out to the door.

Xander looked at her from between narrowed lids, pleased that Brad had backed off from a custody battle over Lauren, and more than happy to forgive the man and assure him that of course he could see his granddaughter—any time he wanted to.

It was the fact that there was now no reason for Casey to marry him that was causing him to frown.

Causing him to frown? He wanted to hit something!

'Another brandy?' he offered.

'I think I've already had enough, thanks,' Casey declined. 'Well, what do we do now?' she asked, in that bright voice that grated Xander's already frayed nerves.

'What do you want to do?' he asked cautiously.

'I don't think that's up to me, do you?'

'Who else is it up to, then?' Xander challenged.

Casey smiled wryly. 'I suppose we should cancel the wedding. Move my own and Josh's things back to the house. You see—it was just as well that I didn't put it on the market.'

She could look a little less happy about this, Xander fumed, wanting to wipe that smile right off her face.

Her heart was definitely breaking, Casey decided, as Xander took his time in answering her. Probably trying to find the words that would cause the least awkwardness, she acknowledged leadenly.

There was nothing he could say that wasn't going to hurt her!

He no longer had any need to marry her. She wasn't going to have more children with him that they could watch grow up together. She most certainly wasn't going to grow old with him!

'It's a little late for Josh and I to move out this evening, so if it's okay with you I think we'll leave it until the morning,' she suggested, trying desperately to keep her voice steady.

'No, that most certainly isn't okay with me!' Xander snarled.

'You want me to wake Josh up and take him away from here *tonight?*' Casey gasped, and she stared across at him incredulously.

Surely he couldn't be that cruel? It was going to be difficult enough explaining to Josh why there was no longer going to be a wedding, or a stepsister and stepfather, without waking him up to tell him that in what was the middle of the night to him!

'No, of *course* I don't want that,' Xander almost roared.

She gave a dazed shake of her head. 'I don't understand…'

Xander's mouth tightened. 'We had—have a deal, Casey. We get married, and I provide for Josh's future, remember?'

Well, of course she remembered. But with Brad Henderson's visit, his apology, surely the reason for their marriage had now been removed…

'Don't worry, Xander, I'm not going to hold you to any of that.' She shrugged. 'After all, neither of us have signed the contract, so there was never actually anything in writing, was there? Besides, the fact that the marriage isn't going to take place makes that contract null and void anyway.'

Xander's expression was stormy. His hands clenched at his sides in an effort to control his rising temper.

Casey was being so damned calm about all of this. So understanding. So unconcerned!

He drew in a ragged breath. 'You don't think we should consider going ahead with the marriage, anyway?' he finally managed to bite out through gritted teeth.

Her eyes widened. 'Why on earth would we do that?'

Because the thought of her just walking out of his life tomorrow was totally unacceptable! Because he wanted to marry her!

But not on the terms they had agreed. Oh, no, he wanted more than that. Much more than that…

'It seemed like a good idea yesterday, so why not today?' he queried.

'But you heard Brad Henderson. He isn't going ahead with the custody battle—'

'Forget the custody battle!' Xander growled. 'Forget Brad Henderson! I'm talking about you and me. I'm—I'm attracted to you. And after yesterday evening I don't think you can deny your own response to me, either. Isn't that mutual attraction enough to be going on with?'

Casey stared at him, slightly stunned. Of course mutual attraction wasn't enough to base a marriage on. She already knew from being married to Sam how fleeting, how insubstantial that was—and surely Xander had learnt that lesson only too well himself from his years with Chloe. Long, bitter years, when there was neither love nor respect on either side.

As for mentioning that embarrassing time in his study last night…!

She couldn't quite meet the intensity of his gaze with her own as she answered him. 'Xander, if you haven't realised it yet, my marriage to Sam—the physical side of our relationship—was less than—satisfactory—'

'In what way?' Xander probed remorselessly.

'In every way,' she snapped back. 'He was my first and only lover before—before yesterday. And by the time my marriage ended I couldn't even bear to be in the same room with him, let alone have him touch me in that way. He was mocking and sarcastic about our—our sex-life. And I never—I never— It just never worked between the two of us,' she choked.

'What do you mean, mocking and sarcastic?' Xander asked more gently.

'Can't you guess?' Casey whispered. 'Sam never lost an opportunity to tell me how frigid, cold and un-responsive I was. How it was my own fault that I could never reach—that I never—' She looked up at Xander through tear-drenched eyes. 'Do I have to actually spell it out for you?' she cried.

No, she didn't have to spell anything out to Xander. Not Sam Bridges' deliberate cruelty to the young and inexperienced girl who had become his wife. Not the other man's years of emotional batter-ing that had made it impossible for Casey to ever be able to relax enough with him to find release for her own pleasure.

A pleasure that Xander knew she'd had no problem reaching in *his* arms.

While he'd had her lying on a desktop!

He still cringed at the thought of how that must have seemed to Casey. Even more so now that he knew he had been the first man to ever give her physical pleasure.

'In the circumstances, I think it's totally wrong for the two of us to marry now that there's no reason for us to do so.' Casey's voice cracked emotionally, her eyes awash with unshed tears.

Tears that he had caused by his insensitivity. Tears

that he wanted to kiss from her eyes. That he wanted to banish from her life for ever!

'Casey—'

'Don't, Xander!' she choked, as he would have reached out and grasped her arms. 'I don't want you to touch me again!' She turned away from him blindly. 'I will move my own and Josh's things out of here tomorrow, once I've taken him to school, and after that you need never see either of us ever again,' she added brokenly. 'Until then I think it would be better if we just stayed away from each other!'

'Casey, *please*—'

'No!' she told him forcefully, as he would have reached for her a second time. 'The last thing I need is your pity!'

Pity? Xander was too filled with a burning rage at Sam Bridges' complete callousness towards Casey, the lies he had told her in order to cover up his own inadequacies as a man, to be able to feel such a feeble emotion as *pity*. And he certainly didn't feel that emotion towards Casey...

Casey blinked her tears away as she looked up at Xander, able to see the same disgust and anger on his face she had so often seen on Sam's. 'See what a lucky escape you've had, Xander?' she whispered. 'I'm sure you no more want a frigid wife than Sam did.'

He shook his head in denial. 'You aren't frigid, Casey—'

'No?' she said scathingly. 'Then I must just be cold and unresponsive!' She squeezed her eyes shut.

'I have to go, Xander. I have to get out of here! I have to get away from you!' She turned quickly on her heel and fled the room.

CHAPTER THIRTEEN

SHE barely had time to close the bedroom door behind her before it was forced open again. She turned sharply to face Xander as he followed her into the room and closed the door firmly behind him to lean back against it.

'I told you—'

'I know what you told me,' he cut in softly. 'I heard every word that you said. Now I want you to listen to me for a few minutes, okay?'

She eyed him warily, but could see only warmth in that blue gaze now. His jaw was no longer clenched, and an encouraging smile was now curving those sculptured lips.

Her hands were fisted at her sides even as she swallowed hard before speaking. 'I don't see what else there is to say…'

'Don't you?' he breathed. 'Dear Lord, Casey, there is so much. So much! The first thing you need to know is that you are not any of the things Bridges told you that you were.'

'But—'

'*None* of them, Casey,' he insisted. 'You were a young girl of twenty when the two of you married, and Bridges was already in his late twenties; he was the one who should have been responsible for tenderly and lovingly introducing you to physical pleasure—'

'I really don't want to talk about this!' Casey groaned in embarrassment as she turned away. 'You didn't even want me enough last night to finish what you started!'

'Casey.' Xander spoke urgently from just behind her. 'Turn around and look at me. Please!'

She drew in a ragged breath, tensing her shoulders before turning to face him, keeping her gaze fixed firmly in the centre of his chest.

'Touch me,' he encouraged softly.

She raised startled eyes to look up at him, frowning with confusion, not knowing what he wanted of her.

Xander reached up and began to unbutton the black silk shirt he wore—slowly, taking his time over each button as he watched the play of emotions across Casey's oh-so-telling face. He saw the way her breath caught in her throat as the muscles of his chest and the flatness of his stomach were slowly revealed, the way the fiery colour caught and held in her cheeks as he pulled the shirt from his trousers and opened it.

'Touch me,' he repeated huskily.

She hesitated for only a moment, and then her hands moved up tentatively, lightly caressing as she touched the dark hair that grew on his chest, those caressing fingers leaving a trail of fire wherever she touched.

Xander held back none of his response to her slightest touch—his laboured breathing, his muscles clenching at her lightest caress. He practically stopped breathing altogether as her touch became bolder, moving silkily up the length of his chest, seeking, knowing, exploring each dip and curve of his flesh, until she finally pushed the shirt off his shoulders and down his arms, leaving him naked from the waist up. She came closer, not quite touching him as her hands moved along the taut width of his shoulders.

He wanted to be completely naked—wanted Casey's hands, her lips, to know all of him before she took him inside her and he let the warmth of her completely engulf him.

'Can you feel how I want you?' he groaned. 'Feel how *much* I want you!' He spoke more fiercely as he took one of her hands and placed it against him—against the throbbing heat of him.

Casey's eyes widened as she felt the outline of Xander's need. He was so big and hard, and as her hand ran the length of him she felt him surge at her lightest touch.

Xander *did* want her!

Now!

Urgently!

'Let me show you how far from frigid, cold and unresponsive you are,' Xander pleaded as his hands moved down to clasp hers within the warmth of his. 'Trust me, Casey,' he urged as she looked up at him uncertainly. 'Trust me not to hurt you. I promise I'll never do anything to hurt you. If I do anything—anything at all that you don't like—you have only to tell me and I'll stop, okay?'

'But—'

'We can talk later. We have all the time in the world to talk. Now I want to show you, to let you see, that you are the most sexy, arousing, erotically beautiful woman I have ever known.'

'But Chloe was so beautiful—'

'Chloe was an immoral alleycat!' Xander said harshly. 'I have absolutely no doubts that she and your husband were well matched, that they found together whatever it was they were looking for. But you, Casey…' His voice deepened to a husky growl. 'To me you're perfection. You are everything a woman should be. Beautiful. Warm. Kind. A loving, unselfish mother. With a body that is so incredibly, sexily, magnificently arousing that I only have to look at you to want to make love to you.' He drew in a ragged breath. 'I didn't stop last night because I didn't want you. I stopped because lovemaking should never be about taking, Casey, but about giving. And last night giving you pleasure was all that I needed or wanted.'

'And now?' Casey breathed softly.

'Now I would like us to make love to each other,' he told her, and he shed the rest of his clothes to stand before her completely naked. 'Slowly. Tenderly. Fiercely. I want us to love each other in every way there is between a man and a woman.'

'You really do want me?' she voiced shyly.

'Oh, Casey, how can you doubt it?' He took her hands in his and once more drew them to his body, his gaze holding hers as he slowly moved those hands across his chest, down the flatness of his stomach, and lower, placing them against him, around him, gasping as he allowed the fierce heat to flow through him. 'I think you may be a little overdressed for the occasion, though,' he murmured softly, and his arms moved about her and he slid the zip of her dress down her spine, before allowing the garment to fall to the carpeted floor.

Casey stood before him wearing only silky French panties and hold-up stockings, the style of her dress not having allowed for a bra. Her breasts were full and pouting—and begging for his kiss!

Casey's breath drew sharply in—and then stopped as she felt Xander's lips and tongue against her breasts, her back arching instinctively as she offered herself.

The bed was soft and welcoming as Xander laid her back upon it. His kisses and caresses were unrelenting in their intensity, and he shuddered his own pleasure as Casey caressed him in return, keeping nothing of his responses back as he allowed her the freedom to touch and kiss wherever she chose.

'Oh, God, Casey!' he moaned as her lips and tongue drove him mad. 'No more!' he finally gasped hotly, sitting up to lie her gently down beside him. 'Your turn now,' he promised, even as his mouth moved moistly, hotly, down the length of her body.

Casey lay before him unashamedly naked as he stripped the last of her clothes from her body. His lips and tongue tasted every inch of her, suckling and laving her breasts until she lay weak and gasping beneath him, and her cry was one of appeal as he moved lower and unerringly found the core of her, tasting her, savouring her, as he brought her to the very brink of release.

She looked up at him through half-closed lids as he moved up and above her, his weight on his arms as he settled between her thighs. Then he surged into the raw heat of her with slow, stroking thrusts.

She cried out hoarsely, her hands against the tautness of his spine as he moved harder and faster and her body convulsed around him. There was a look of pure rapture on Xander's face as he reached his own release.

'I could lie with you like this for ever,' Xander murmured some time later, his lips against her creamy throat, his arms tightly about her, their bodies still joined.

'So could I,' Casey acknowledged huskily, her hands lightly caressing his silky hair as it rested on his shoulders in tangled disarray.

Xander looked at her with intent blue eyes. 'I love you, Casey.'

Casey closed hers briefly, hardly able to believe he had said those words to her, before opening them and saying, 'Do you really, Xander?'

'More than life itself,' he vowed. 'Forget the past. Most of all, forget the cold-blooded way I asked you to marry me three weeks ago.' He groaned. 'As you've just seen, there is nothing in the least cold about the way you make me feel!'

Casey laughed softly, knowing a freedom with Xander that she had never experienced before. 'Or the way you make me feel,' she echoed huskily. 'I do love you—so very much, Xander.' She moved so that she could look down at him, careful not to dislodge him, loving the feel of him inside her, knowing him to be a part of her that was as necessary as breathing.

'Will you marry me, Casey?' Xander asked. 'For no other reason than because I love you. Because you love me. Will you, Casey?'

'I thought—before Brad arrived I believed you were going to tell me that you couldn't marry me, after all!' She breathed shakily, hardly able to believe that such happiness was really within her grasp.

'I was,' Xander confirmed. 'But only that I couldn't marry you under the conditions we had agreed,' he added quickly, as she frowned. 'I couldn't have been married to you and not wanted to be with you like this!' he told her fiercely. 'I would have been lying to you as well as myself if I had allowed us to sign that contract disclaiming any physical relationship between us. I want you too much, need you too much, to ever be able to agree to that!' he assured her gruffly. 'And I want, always, to give you the same honesty you've always given me,' he murmured, even as his hands moved to caress the softness of her hair. 'Marry me, Casey, and make me the happiest man that ever lived.'

'Oh, yes,' she said. 'Yes, I'll marry you, Xander!'

For a time there was only silence in the bedroom as they kissed each other with fierce hunger.

'When did you know that you loved me?' Casey finally asked wonderingly.

'I'm not completely sure of the exact moment I fell in love with you. But I knew for certain that it was love I felt for you when I looked at the contract last night after you left and saw that you refused to accept any money for yourself. You see, my darling, I had assumed you weren't happy with the contract because a million pounds wasn't enough—'

'Xander Fraser, I don't *want* your money—'

'I know that, my love.' He smiled. 'I know that only too well. But it seemed, after the way you left me last night, that you didn't want me, either.'

'How can you say that, after what happened?' Casey gasped incredulously.

'You seemed—unhappy that you had allowed it to happen.' He grimaced.

'I was stunned,' she corrected huskily. 'I really did believe that I was one of those women who simply don't enjoy the physical side of a relationship.'

'And now?' Xander teased.

'Now I would like us to make love again,' she admitted softly, even as she felt him stir inside her. 'In fact, I would like for us to stay in bed for a week, with absolutely no distractions but each other!'

'I think that might be arranged,' Xander muttered as he moved to kiss her. 'I'm sure the children won't mind if we ask Brad to stay with them while we disappear for a few days on our honeymoon.'

'We're really going to get married tomorrow, as planned?' Casey looked up at him with wondering eyes.

'I think perhaps we had better, don't you,' he said indulgently. 'I love you so much, Casey, and I'm not going to be able to keep my hands off you for some time to come.' His hand moved caressingly down the flatness of her waist to the silky curls beneath.

Love.

To have Xander love her.

To love Xander in return.

Love was what made all the difference...

CHAPTER FOURTEEN

'Xander...?'

'Hmm?' he murmured sleepily against her throat, having fallen into a satiated sleep after their lovemaking.

Casey took a few moments for contented reflection before answering him.

Even after a year of marriage they still couldn't get enough of each other—of being together, of loving each other.

Xander often deferred business trips if Casey couldn't accompany him—something that wasn't always possible when they had two small children to think of. And Casey's late stage of pregnancy meant she hadn't been able to fly anywhere at all these last two months.

This last year of being Xander's wife, of uniting their two families—Brad had become grandfather to both Josh and Lauren—of making a child of their own, had been the happiest time Casey had ever known in her life.

And it was about to get better…

'I think we need to go to the clinic, Xander,' she told him softly.

'Hmm?' he murmured sleepily again. 'What?' he gasped, sitting up as her words penetrated his drowsy brain, with a panicked look on his face. 'Are you sure? Isn't it too early? The baby isn't expected for another couple of weeks!' he muttered worriedly, even as he got out of bed and began to pull on his clothes.

Casey gave a happy smile as she watched him put on his trousers without putting on his boxer shorts, and having to start all over again. 'I think the baby has decided otherwise,' she told him as she moved to the side of the bed.

'Fine.' He nodded distractedly, his hair a dark tangle as he ran an agitated hand through it. 'First I have to call Brad and get him to come and sit with Lauren and Josh. Then I have to—'

'Slow down, Xander.' Casey laughed. 'It isn't going to happen for hours yet,' she assured him. 'I just don't think it's going to wait until morning,' she added, as another contraction gripped her.

Xander paled and quickly crossed the bedroom to her side. 'You're going to be all right, aren't you, Casey?' he asked, gripping both her hands in his as he stared down at her intently. 'I couldn't bear it if anything happened to you—'

'Nothing is going to happen to me except that in a few hours' time we're going to have another son or daughter,' she said warmly.

Xander sat down on the bed beside her. 'I love you, Casey!' he told her fiercely. 'I love you, want you, and need you so very, very much!'

She leant forward and kissed him lingeringly on the lips. 'I love, want and need you in exactly the same way.' She straightened. 'Now, let's go and give birth to our son or daughter!' she added, with an exultant laugh.

Their daughter, Anna Louise, was born three hours later, with her father's glossy black hair and eyes of blue already tinged with her mother's green.

'I want half a dozen more,' Casey warned Xander as she watched the gentle way he cradled their daughter in his arms.

'Only half a dozen?' he teased, and he looked at her lovingly, an emotional catch in his voice.

Life was good—so very, very good, Casey acknowledged, even as her eyes began to close sleepily.

With Xander to love, and be loved by, she knew that it would always be that way…

ADOPTED BABY, CONVENIENT WIFE

Rebecca Winters

Rebecca Winters, whose family of four children has now swelled to include three beautiful grandchildren, lives in Salt Lake City, Utah, in the land of the Rocky Mountains. With canyons and high alpine meadows full of wild flowers, she never runs out of places to explore. They, plus her favourite vacation spots in Europe, often end up as backgrounds for her novels because writing is her passion, along with her family and church.

Rebecca loves to hear from her readers. If you wish to e-mail her, please visit her website at www.rebeccawinters-author.com

**Look out for Rebecca Winters' new novel,
The Italian Tycoon and the Nanny,
in March 2008, available from
Mills & Boon® Romance.**

Dear Reader,

It boggles my mind that, as long ago as 1908, Gerald Mills and Charles Boon formed a publishing company that not only has stood the test of time, but a hundred years later is still the unquestioned leader of romance sales worldwide!

What boggles my mind further is that I've been fortunate and blessed enough to become one of their authors. To celebrate their one hundreth birthday I've written *Adopted Baby, Convenient Wife*, a marriage-of-convenience novella that epitomises what I believe to be the essence of virtual, romantic romance.

Is there anything greater than a lovable woman, a noble man and a precious baby, all coming together under unusual circumstances to give us the hope and promise of a happier tomorrow? I don't think so.

Long live Mills & Boon. Long live the romantic souls of the publishers, editors, authors and especially you wonderful READERS, wherever you are.

Rebecca Winters

This book is dedicated to you, Bonnie K Winn, a real Texas Bluebonnet who's one of America's top-selling romance authors. I'm lucky enough to call you my dear friend and mentor. Would you believe this story takes place on the Bonnibelle Ranch? Enjoy!

CHAPTER ONE

THE wizened old cowboy filling his pickup truck at the service station in Elko tipped his hat back. "The Bonnibelle, you say?" His head turned toward the mountains. "Everyone knows it's right over there in the valley, beneath those snowcapped peaks."

Catherine had heard of it, of course, but coming from the other side of Nevada she could be forgiven for not knowing exactly where to find it.

"Biggest cattle ranch around," he expounded. "Thirty-five thousand acres. Can't miss it. After you leave town, take the 227 and follow it all the way."

Straight as the crow flies? she wanted to respond, but quashed the impulse because the older man thought he was being helpful. To his mind, he'd given her all the directions she needed.

O ye of little faith, she chided herself before thanking him. Then she got back in the car.

Having made her visit to the ladies' room, plus purchasing a cold bottle of water along with the gas, she was ready to go. But who knew how many more miles she had to travel before she reached her destination?

There wasn't any point in consulting the map she'd bought before leaving Reno. It was of no further use to her now except to tell her she was headed toward the Ruby Mountains.

In the heat waves rising from the highway, Bonnie's precious little image swam before her eyes.

If your daddy's there, my darling baby girl, I'll find him. If he's not, then I'm going to make you mine no matter what I have to do.

After losing track of time beneath a sweltering July afternoon sun blazing down on miles of rangeland, she finally spied an arch of deer antlers to her right, signifying the entrance to the Bonnibelle. A name like that must have come from the heart of some homesick Scotsman who'd settled here many years earlier and staked his claim.

It took another fifteen minutes before the dirt road climbed higher past alpine paintbrush and lupine to a crystal blue lake where an immense three-storied log ranch house hugged the shoreline. The spectacular backdrop of mountains against such splendor caused Catherine to suck in her breath.

Your daddy picked a piece of heaven when he decided to work here, sweetheart.

Beyond the main house there were clusters of immaculate outbuildings and a huge barn erected amid clumps of dark pines. Some of the structures looked as if they dated back to the second half of the 1800s.

Catherine surmised that it not only took a small army of hands to keep this place in mint condition, but a cattle king with exceptional gifts and an iron hand to make certain its inner workings ran with all the precision of a fine Swiss watch.

An odd assortment of luxury cars mixed with pickup trucks and horse trailers stood parked along the border of grass planted in front of the main house. Considering the ranch was such a big business concern, she didn't question their presence or the number of vehicles with the state's official seal decorating the car doors.

Perhaps she might have done if she hadn't been so intent on her desperate mission. With time running out, she needed to act fast. Otherwise she could lose Bonnie.

At the mere thought, stabbing pain brought fresh tears to her eyes.

The idea of someone else raising Bonnie was unthinkable to Catherine. Once she'd confirmed Bonnie's father turned out to be the no-account drifter she'd labeled him—once she heard him say he wanted nothing to do with his own flesh and blood—she was ready to go to court and claim the baby for her very own.

After finding a parking spot behind a blue Mercedes sedan, she levered herself out from the front seat of her vehicle and stepped out into the dry heat. At six thousand feet it was certainly cooler than in Elko.

Since she'd left her condo seven hours ago, the sun's position had altered. Catherine's willowy body, dressed in a crushproof two-piece suit, cast a shadow against the bank of cars. She headed for the main entrance of the ranch house, grateful she'd worn medium-sized heels to navigate. They made a soft crunching sound on the gravel driveway.

A deep porch ran the full length of the beautiful old structure. Upon climbing the steps, she saw the sign that told visitors to ring the bell.

Not long after she'd pressed the button a maid answered the door. Catherine caught the cool breeze of the air-conditioning and welcomed it. As she breathed in, she detected the strong scent of fresh flowers.

Beyond the young woman she noticed several massive sprays of roses and lilies placed at either side of the bottom of the grand staircase. The interior of the spacious foyer had more the look of an English manor than its rustic western exterior conveyed.

While Catherine was wondering if she'd interrupted a wedding or some such thing, the maid said, "Everyone's gathered in the great room. If you'd like to follow me."

"Oh, but I'm not—"

Catherine stopped talking because the maid had already disappeared through two paneled doors on the right, leaving Catherine in a dilemma. Whatever social event she'd walked in on, she hadn't been invited.

Making a decision to err on the side of caution, she hurried outside again. She would wait in her car until she saw someone leave the ranch house. At that point she would approach them to find out what was going on. Depending on the answer, she might have to double back to Elko for the night and return in the morning.

Her reasons for coming here were private and personal. After suffering a troubled childhood and teenage years, Catherine had been given a second chance at life. Now, years later, she was in a position to fight for someone who couldn't.

The problem was, any information she gave to the wrong person could jeopardize everything. She refused to let that happen, not when she'd made promises to Terrie she intended to keep.

"Mr. Farraday?"

"Excuse me, Hal," Cole said to the Lieutenant Governor and his aide before turning to face Janine, the newest member of the household staff. The tone in her voice held a certain nuance that prompted him to walk her over to one of the windows where they could be apart from the thirty or so people left in the room. "What is it, Janine?"

"A woman I've never seen before came to the door just now. I assumed she must be a friend of the family, so I asked her to come in and follow me."

Making that kind of assumption was Janine's first mistake, but Cole let her continue uninterrupted.

"When I turned around, she was gone! I don't know if she's somewhere in the house, or if she left. I alerted Mack, but thought you should know."

Cole schooled his dark features not to reveal his

thoughts. "You did the right thing to come to me. Give me a description."

"She was a tallish blonde wearing a yellow outfit."

"How old?"

Janine shrugged her shoulders. "Maybe twenty-five, twenty-six."

Or maybe thirty-five, thirty-six, all disguised by a series of surgical makeovers? One of Buck's bimbos from the past? Some exotic dancer his thirty-year-old brother had gotten involved with at an XXX-rated bar in Elko before he'd cleaned up his act?

Buck had the kind of looks women couldn't resist. He came from money and was always ready for a good time. For the last few years it had taken everything Cole and his brother John could do to keep Buck's nocturnal activities under wraps. In secret, Cole had even asked his uncle Richard, who lived in Reno, to take Buck under his wing for the latter part of last summer in the hope of straightening him out.

He smothered a groan of protest, because this woman had dared to trespass even though she knew Buck had married Lucy two months ago. That was all his shattered sister-in-law needed right now.

He knew how she felt. Ten years ago Cole had lost his wife, Jenny, and his dream of a family of his own had died with her. Maybe the Farraday clan was cursed after all.

While his flint-like gaze swerved to a white-faced Lucy, who was surrounded by her family and

Cole's married sister Penny, a feeling of rage swept through him.

After watching his youngest brother's body being lowered into the ground earlier in the day, he'd been so full of pain he hadn't thought there could be room for any other emotion.

"Thanks, Janine."

The guests were congregated in groups, among them his attorney Jim Darger and his wife. On one side of the room John and Cole's brother-in-law Rich had their heads bent together in serious conversation. On the other, he observed Brenda, a woman he'd been seeing lately, talking with a group of friends. His nieces and nephews had long since disappeared, making him wish he could have joined them.

Under the circumstances no one would notice if he headed for the nearest exit and slipped from the room. The less anyone in the family knew about this the better.

If the intruder in question was enjoying a tour of the place, like some stalking voyeur, his ranch manager Mack would quickly catch up with her.

Acting on a hunch, he let himself out of the house through the study doors and started walking toward the vehicles parked out front. In case she made a dash for one of them, he'd be waiting for her.

To his shock, a woman answering Janine's description got out of a white compact car and called to him in a slightly husky voice. "Excuse me?"

His jaw tightened.

She wasn't at all what he'd anticipated. For one thing she couldn't be in her thirties. For another, her suit was a pale lemon color, subtle and sophisticated. Her healthy, natural ash blond hair didn't look anything close to the cheap image that had filled his mind.

With or without clothes on her slender yet rounded body, there was an elegance to her bones. Those long legs enabled her brilliant blue eyes to meet his without difficulty, and he was a tall man.

Her upswept hair caught in a loose knot revealed classic facial features that needed no enhancement flushed from the heat. He saw intelligence in her glance. More disconcerting to him was the passionate flare of her mouth, as if she could read his mind and enjoyed confounding him. But of course she didn't have the power to do that.

He made the mistake of drawing too close to her. The combination of her own feminine scent and the fragrance either from her hair or perfume, or both, assailed him. Cole hadn't thought anything could drown out the cloying scent of lilies coming from the funeral sprays.

"What can I do for you?" he asked, congratulating himself for sounding willing to help her without revealing the full state of his churning emotions thrown by her presence. But the fact that he had an inordinate curiosity about her proved to be the cause of a deeper irritation at his own undisciplined thoughts on this black day.

"I came to talk to the person who does the hiring

on the ranch, but I'm afraid I arrived at an inopportune time. Did someone just get married?"

At the thought of his recently reformed brother gone from this world, leaving Lucy and the whole family in despair, a fresh shaft of pain, sharp and swift, pierced his gut. He rocked back on his handtooled cowboy boots. "There was a funeral today."

She bit her lower lip, drawing his attention to that succulent part of her mouth despite his darkest thoughts. What in hell was the matter with him? There'd been women since Jenny died, but none of them had stirred him the way this stranger did. It made no sense.

"Then I'm glad I didn't intrude. Thank you for talking to me." Summarily dismissing him, an experience he couldn't remember ever happening before, she climbed back in her car. In a few seconds she'd be gone.

The sensible part of him wished he could allow her to drive away, but he wasn't finished with her. She'd claimed she wanted to talk to the person in charge of personnel. He did the hiring himself. No one worked at the Bonnibelle—either in the house or on the spread—unless he okayed it.

Whatever the qualifications she might bring for a position she wanted, she'd be the last person he'd consider. Not even then…

She didn't come off flirtatious, which was a surprise. Yet her unconscious sensuality would play havoc with the harmony he'd worked like the devil to maintain among the stockmen since their parents' death in a light airplane crash three years back. Buck had fallen apart after that. It had taken Lucy's sure, steady love for him to start putting himself back together.

Exhaling heavily, Cole took the few steps necessary to place his body next to the door she'd just closed. He braced his hands against the open window and lowered his head.

She turned a surprised gaze to him, giving him the full benefit of her dark fringed eyes, an unusual combination on a blond. A man could think he was falling through a cloudless western sky just looking into them.

"I'm in a position to know there are no job openings, Ms....?"

"Catherine Arnold," she supplied evenly. "Then I should consider myself fortunate I already have a job I love," came the evasive comment.

"I meant no offense."

"None was taken."

Her guileless response disarmed him. She had a lot of ready answers without asking the right questions. There was a reason she'd come to the ranch, but she didn't intend to tell him any more than she had to. That was too bad, because he was determined to learn the truth one way or the other.

"The maid thought you had followed her into the house. When she couldn't find you, she called Security."

Though her expression didn't change, he watched in fascination the way her slim fingers tightened around the steering wheel. She wore no rings, only a gold wristwatch. A clear polish covered her manicured nails. He could see the half-moons of her cuticles clearly.

Everything about her appealed to his senses. That was another thing that hadn't happened to him in years.

A trace of a smile formed on her lips. "And here I was hoping someone would come outside to enlighten me, Mr....?"

"Farraday, but I answer to Cole."

"Thanks for your help, Cole," she said, without as much as a flicker of those long lashes.

Cole wasn't a vain man, but it was a fact that their family's name figured prominently in the settling of this part of Nevada. If she recognized it and was playing dumb, she was a superb actress, particularly since Buck's death had been highly publicized in the media.

Angry at himself for letting her get to him, his chiseled features formed a grimace. "Why do you want to speak to the man who does the hiring?"

"That's my business, surely. No offense," she added in a pleasant tone.

"None taken," came his superficially calm response. "Only I'll have to ask you to step out of the car and accompany me to the owner's office." He'd give her one final chance to own up.

"Why?"

Cole sucked in his breath. Evidently she'd decided not to take it, which could mean she really didn't know who he was. Then again...

"Let's just say it's my job. From here on out you'll have to answer to him." He opened the door, relishing the moment when he exposed her little game, whatever it was.

Her lissom body stiffened. "This is ridiculous. I haven't done anything wrong."

He elevated his dark brows. "Look at it from his point of view. He buried his youngest brother today and came back to the ranch house to be with his closest friends and family. In the process of trying to give comfort to his bereaved sister-in-law, a perfect stranger walks in from out of nowhere with an agenda she refuses to reveal."

While he'd been talking, he didn't think she could fake the growing concern on her face, most likely for the trouble she could be in.

She stirred restlessly. "Doesn't the fact that I called out to you for information prove I have no evil intentions?" The straightforward hint of pleading in her voice almost convinced him.

"On the contrary," he rejoindered coolly, "your behavior is more suspect than ever. Shall we go quietly, or do I take you inside in a manner guaranteed to embarrass you in front anyone who might see you?"

Her face filled with color. "You wouldn't—" she whispered.

Not today, no… He'd find another method. But she didn't know that.

"Try me, Ms. Arnold." He checked his watch. "I'll give you thirty seconds to make up your mind."

CHAPTER TWO

CATHERINE didn't dare call his bluff, not with those cold pewter eyes bearing down on her features, pinning her to the seat.

Standing easily at six-three or four, this powerful-looking security guard, wearing an expensive looking formal suit of midnight-blue in deference to the funeral proceedings, had the hard-muscled physique of a male at home in the out-of-doors.

He was probably in his mid-thirties. She had to admit, albeit begrudgingly, that with his black hair and burnished skin he resembled a rugged facsimile of Adonis. To her ear the name Cole sounded too western for a man who exuded an almost international sophistication.

Having worked the front desk on the night shift at one of Reno's top hotels while she'd finished college, she'd met attractive, wealthy men from all over the world. But if she had to pick just one who was the most memorable, he still wouldn't measure up to the force standing next to her.

That was what this man was—a dynamic, living, breathing force. He radiated a potent male energy that set him apart from those less endowed. She had to concede she'd more than met her match here. If she could appeal to his honor—

Catherine sensed something that told her he was a highly principled male with a superior intellect who probably demanded more discipline from himself than those around him.

How she knew that she couldn't explain, but she recognized that the owner of the ranch had known what he was doing when he'd hired Cole Farraday. She was left with little choice but to reveal what he'd immediately perceived was her secret motive for coming here.

"All right," she exclaimed with a resigned sigh, feeling more vulnerable than ever with the door still open so he could view every inch of her body, which he'd been doing. But in case someone came outside to get in their car, she didn't want to attract attention by standing next to hers in the presence of the security guard.

At least sitting here in the driver's seat, people would think they were simply chatting. Heavens— there was no acceptable way out of this except to get it over with as quickly as possible.

"The truth is, I'm searching for someone."

He kept a hand on top of the open door, perpetuating the fiction that they were acquaintances brought together by the death of a friend. She noted inconsequentially he wore no rings, but that didn't mean he wasn't married. Not that it mattered. She was here for Bonnie's sake, and ultimately for her own.

"That's a start. Man or woman?"

Without looking at him she said, "I've been given reason to believe he might be working on this ranch, or maybe he used to work here."

"Your lover?" he insinuated. "A disgruntled fiancé, perhaps?"

"Neither one," she said, refusing to rise to the bait. But on second thought—considering the circumstances—he'd posed some logical questions. She decided it was his blunt way of speaking that led her to believe he was goading her. After all, the man was only doing his job.

She heard his intake of breath, harsh and distinct. He was growing impatient. "Why do you want to find him?"

The operative question.

Catherine could be blunt too. "To let this man know the teenager he got pregnant gave birth to his baby."

"Ah. That's a very sad story," he answered, with an element of sincerity she didn't doubt, "but, cruel as this will sound, he probably doesn't want to be found."

"You're right," she agreed in a less than steady voice now. "They never do. The story gets even sadder. The mother, Terrie, died from complications, leaving the baby without a mother or father."

In the periphery she could see the rise and fall of

his broad chest. After a tension-filled pause, "This teenager wouldn't be your sister by any chance?"

After her emotional gaffe, he'd made another logical assumption, one that happened to strike too close to home. He couldn't know that despite the difference in their ages, she and Terrie had bonded much like two siblings because of similar life experiences growing up.

Summoning her resolve to hold on to some vestige of control, she said, "No. She's no relation."

"A friend, then?"

She grasped on that. "Yes—" It was the truth, after all, but she was already growing too emotional and he sensed it.

"I noticed from the rim of your license plate you bought this car in Reno. Is that where you live?"

The man's radar didn't miss anything. Whether she chose to tell him or not, he'd be able to find out the pertinent details about her with one simple phone call to the authorities. Considering the nature of his job on such a renowned ranch, the man probably had an inside track. Since he would have friends in high places, she'd save him the trouble.

"Yes."

"Did the teenager in question give birth there too?"

"Yes."

He shifted his weight, an ominous sign which could mean any number of unpleasant things. "Does this cowboy have a name?"

She craned her head in order to look at his brooding features.

REBECCA WINTERS 145

"I think he probably made it up so Terrie would never know who he really was for fear she'd try to trace him."

"Out with it, Ms. Arnold." He'd come to the end of his tolerance for what had turned out to be a fencing match. In truth she was tired of dancing around the subject too.

"If I tell you, and you recognize it, you have to promise me you won't reveal it to anyone else—" she cried, then moaned inwardly, wishing she hadn't sounded like she was begging.

"Why do I get the feeling you're trying to protect *him?*" came the silky question.

Her jaw clenched. "I have no love for this man, believe me. But even he has rights I have to honor."

He studied her as if she were a paradox. "In that case, why bother to look him up at all?"

"Because I promised Terrie I would. All she wanted was for him to know he had a daughter. What he does with that information is up to him." Catherine had no doubts he'd do nothing with it. That was what she was counting on. "It's no one else's business."

"What about you?" he questioned.

"I don't understand," she dissembled, vying for time, though she didn't know why because no one was going to come and rescue her from this precarious dilemma.

"Let's not play games." His lips broke into a forbidding curl. "In my gut I know there's a lot more at stake here than your being the simple bearer of this kind of news."

Catherine couldn't afford to lose her cool now. Not in front of this all-seeing, all-knowing watchdog who was sounding much more like a chief prosecutor. She needed to stay calm and collected, like the professional she purported to be.

Filling her lungs with air, she said, "I'm here because of Bonnie."

Though his expression didn't change, a silver flash coming from those suspicious gray eyes indicated she'd hit some kind of nerve. "Bonnie…" he repeated quietly. For want of a more precise word, he sounded haunted.

"Yes. That's the name Terrie gave her baby."

After an almost eerie interim of silence his deep voice spoke again, this time in a gravelly tone. "And the father's name?"

"I-it's one of those nicknames that could belong to any number of men or their horses, especially those living in this part of the country."

"I'm still waiting." He was about to take the action he'd threatened. A small shiver ran down her spine. She was going to have to trust him.

"Terrie said he called himself…Buck."

The second the name left her lips a daunting stillness pervaded the atmosphere. While she could feel the adrenaline driving the speed of her heart, her interrogator carefully shut the door, as if he'd come to some monumental decision.

But when he finally spoke through the open

window, the last thing she'd expected to hear was, "Start your car, Ms. Arnold. You're going back to Elko. I'll be right behind you. When we reach the first exit, follow me into town."

So he *did* know Buck and had decided to take her to him.

Catherine experienced a moment of triumph to realize she'd be able to fulfill one of Terrie's dying wishes. For herself she'd been waiting months to confront the amoral male who'd taken advantage of Terrie's youth and naïveté, then discarded her so cruelly, never worrying if there'd be consequences.

"I'll see you there, then," she responded quietly.

With a mixed sense of anxiety and anticipation over what she would learn, Catherine turned on the motor, willing to cooperate with this enigmatic man who held the keys to Buck's whereabouts.

Once she'd made contact, and had satisfied herself he couldn't care less how many children he might have spawned in his selfish need for gratification, she'd be able to carry out Terrie's other wish.

A wish that had become Catherine's *raison d'être*.

Evening had come to the Rubies, prompting Cole to turn on his headlights. The woman at the wheel in front of his power wagon drove at a fast clip, forcing him to concentrate while he made a couple of phone calls, the last one being to his brother.

"John? Hold down the fort, will you? I'm on my way to Elko to take care of some important business."

"I saw you leave a little while ago. Anything I can do to help?"

Cole's thirty-two-year-old married brother was a rock he could always lean on in an emergency. They'd shared pretty much everything in life, but not this time. Not until Cole knew if their little brother had truly fathered a child.

"I'll tell you about it later."

He could hear the question John didn't ask. That was what made him the good man he was.

"When will you be back?"

"I'm not sure."

"Fair enough. Brenda's waiting for you. She's going to be disappointed when I tell her business called you away."

Business, hell—

Cole rubbed his jaw. Brenda was attractive, and he enjoyed her company, but that was all. Unfortunately she wanted more. This was as good a time as any to end it with her. She would have to understand he needed his space to mourn Buck. If she didn't, then he couldn't do anything about it. Catherine Arnold's bombshell had blown him from the path where he'd been letting his life drift. But no longer.

"I'll call her later." He rang off, his thoughts already concentrated on the female who'd managed to get beneath his skin long before he'd learned her visit had anything to do with Buck.

When she took the first turnoff, he sped ahead of her and drove on to the Midas Inn, located in the center of town. Pulling around the side to a private entrance, he jumped down from the cab to help her from the car she'd parked alongside his truck.

Her long, elegant legs distracted him as she got out of the car. "Is this where we're meeting Buck?"

"No." With that one word he'd extinguished the hope in those fabulous blue eyes. "We need to talk. The Midas is one of the ranch owner's investments," he explained, aware of her questioning glance as he pulled her overnight bag from the backseat. "I phoned ahead to arrange a room for you. If you made a reservation somewhere else, let me know and I'll cancel it."

"It's at the Ruby Inn."

"In your own name?"

"Yes," she answered tentatively. "Why do you ask?"

"You come off sounding like you might be an attorney. If so, you could have made your reservation in the name of the firm you work for."

"I'm a social worker at a facility for young single mothers, but I'm not here in an official capacity. My reason for coming is strictly personal, if it's any comfort."

It wasn't.

Buck had shown poor judgment in a lot of cases— but getting involved with an underage girl while he'd been working on their uncle's stud farm outside Reno last summer?

"Maybe that explains why you exhibit the instincts of a clever PI."

"Not that clever, apparently, but I'm not going to

complain if it means you can lead me to Bonnie's biological father."

He ushered her inside the building as far as the door of the manager's office. "Follow this hallway to the front desk and give the night clerk your name. He'll take care of you. After you've freshened up, meet me in here."

"Thank you." She managed to get the words out before taking the bag from him. "I won't be long."

"In that case I'll ask the restaurant to bring us a sandwich."

Cole doubted he'd able to eat, but he preferred she didn't suspect he felt like he'd been trampled in a wild mustang stampede no one had seen coming seconds before it happened.

CHAPTER THREE

TEN minutes later Catherine knocked on the manager's door.

"Come in."

Recognizing Cole's deep voice, she walked inside the office. The sight of him standing behind the desk, in a beautiful white dress shirt with the sleeves pushed up his tanned arms to the elbows, rocked her to the foundations.

Minus his tie and suit jacket—the outer trappings of civilized society—his virility was even more in evidence.

By comparison she knew she looked washed out. Other than pulling her hair back in a ponytail, she still wore the suit she'd arrived in. Until she saw the club sandwiches and sliced melon placed on the desk in front of him, she hadn't realized how hungry she was.

"Sit down, Catherine."

The use of her first name indicated progress. Despite their precarious beginning, she liked the sound of it on his lips. She liked the play of muscle across his shoulders and arms. Too much.

Murmuring her assent, she pulled up a chair. Now that the fencing was over, they could get down to business.

He pushed one of the plates toward her, no doubt recognizing the signs of someone who was starving. She reached for a sandwich half and began devouring it. Cole, on the other hand, drank cola from the can while he watched her through shuttered eyes.

Anticipating her needs, he handed her a cola, which she gratefully accepted. She drank most of it before putting the can back on the desk.

"Thank you. I needed that," she exclaimed, glancing at the food he hadn't touched. "Aren't you going to eat?"

"Later. For now I want to hear the details about Terrie and her relationship with Buck." His probing gray eyes were like an assault on her senses. "When they first met—where—how long it lasted—how and when you came into the picture—"

On the drive back to Elko she'd determined to tell him everything she knew in the hope her candor would be rewarded.

"A year ago this month Terrie ran away from her foster home in California. She had the help of another runaway. They stole money and a car. En route they ditched it and stole a van. Once they arrived in Reno, they changed the plates and lived out of it while they washed dishes for a local café called the One-Eyed Jack. On their breaks, they were given free meals."

His brows furrowed. "Resourceful girls."

"The street-smart ones are. They'd been there a month when this 'hunky cowboy'—Terrie's words—showed up and took an immediate interest in her. In fairness to him, she could make herself up to look closer to twenty. He could be excused for not knowing she was only seventeen. After she got off work he would take her dancing, spend money on her. He told her she was beautiful, which she was," Catherine added in an unsteady voice. A brunette with hazel eyes...

Bonnie had been born with a head of dark hair and a rosebud mouth. The sweetest, dearest little baby on earth.

Clearing her throat, Catherine continued. "Soon Terrie was sleeping with him. She didn't have the experience to realize it couldn't last, let alone turn into anything permanent like a wedding ring on her finger. By September he was gone from her life without a trace, leaving her pregnant and ill with morning sickness. The café manager had to let her go, but she gave Terrie the name of a home run by private donations called Girls' Haven."

"You're the case worker there?" He sat back in the chair with his strong arms folded.

"Yes. I've been working there for three years. Stories like Terrie's are all too common. Her friend dropped her off in the van, then drove away. Terrie never saw her or Buck again."

"Did this Buck actually tell her he worked on the Bonnibelle?"

"He didn't tell her anything concrete about his life except that he was a cowboy. The night before he disappeared, someone came in the café looking for him while he was waiting for her to go off shift. She overheard this person tell Buck he'd better call the Bonnibelle on the double. Terrie went through her pregnancy assuming the other man had been referring to a woman Buck hadn't told her about, and that's why he'd abandoned her. It wasn't until she was dying from an infection following the delivery that she broke down and told me about the incident. That's when I told her Bonnibelle was the name of a famous ranch somewhere in Nevada."

Their eyes held for a brief moment, sending an errant thrill through her body that had nothing to do with business.

"At that point Terrie said she wanted the name Bonnie put on the birth certificate. She begged me to find Buck so he'd know he had a daughter."

Maybe it was the dim light of the office, but lines of what could be interpreted as exasperation mixed with sorrow gave Cole's hard-boned face an almost haggard appearance. She had to remember he'd attended a funeral earlier in the day. The mention of Terrie's death must have triggered emotions still close to the surface.

Catherine could relate. She was still in pain and shock that the teen she'd grown so close to in the last year was gone, and wouldn't be able to raise her little girl. Life could be cruelly unfair to some people—

"What's the name of the hospital where she delivered?"

"Reno Regional." Her voice caught.

"When was the birth?"

"June twentieth."

"Five weeks old already?" He echoed her concern. She nodded.

"The only reason she hasn't been adopted yet is because she was born five weeks premature. For a while she was on a ventilator and had to be fed through an IV. They had to recreate conditions in the womb. She also had a bad case of jaundice and had to be placed under lights."

Catherine had spent every possible minute with Bonnie after work and on weekends, touching her through the holes of the hospital incubator until she could hold her and feed her the special formula. She couldn't love her more if she'd given birth from her own body.

"Where's the baby now?"

"In a temporary foster home awaiting adoption." That familiar jabbing pain tore at her heart. "A newborn baby is in such high demand, Bonnie will probably find a permanent home with an adoptive family within the next week. That's why it's necessary I speak to Buck right away."

"Provided he's the father," his voice grated.

"A DNA test will put the matter to rest one way

or the other," she reminded him, though of course he didn't need to be told that. "The hospital already has the results on Bonnie. It's a routine procedure for prospective adoptees."

Cole rubbed the back of his bronzed neck. She had the further impression he was near exhaustion, unknowingly soliciting her sympathy. Whoever had died must have been a close friend.

A strange sound escaped his throat before he sat forward in the swivel chair. "I'll arrange for Buck's DNA to be sent for comparison."

"Can you ask them to put a rush on it?" She knew he had the clout to light fires.

"I'm as anxious to clear this up as you are," he ground out. "What was Terrie's last name?"

"She went by Cloward with a C. That's on her records both at Girls' Haven and the hospital. But I'm sure she made it up, since she told the café manager it was Markham. No doubt Terrie told Buck something altogether different. They both had their secrets," she lamented, surprising a troubling bleakness coming from his eyes.

"In case he pretends not to recognize her description, I have a photograph you can give him. It was taken before she was showing. In this one she's not wearing makeup or clothes that tend to make her look older."

She pulled it from her purse and handed it to Cole, who studied Catherine intently several seconds before looking at it.

"You're right," he eventually murmured. "She's

attractive in the way a girl is who's standing on the brink of womanhood."

Despite Terrie's history, Catherine could tell Cole could see what Catherine had seen in her…a young, troubled teen in need of help. A girl much like Catherine had been once upon a time. The knowledge caused her to warm to him unexpectedly.

"Buck's charm managed to turn her into one." Catherine tried to keep the bitterness out of her voice, but failed. "She said he was her first experience, and that it was wonderful. *He* was wonderful. Tender. Again, those were Terrie's words. I—I have to admit I was glad for that at least," she stammered.

"You believed her?"

"Yes." She drew in a quick breath. "Terrie had no reason to lie about him. Not after admitting to breaking several laws. But it doesn't really matter. The fact is, she loved him and died of a broken heart long before the infection became impossible to stop."

Reaching in her purse, she pulled out more photos. "These show Bonnie in the premie ICU, hooked up to all those tubes."

He reached for them.

"Newborn pictures never do a baby justice, especially when they have as hard a time as Bonnie. You can see her swollen eye and how yellow she is there, poor darling."

Silence filled the office while Cole took his time studying them.

"Here's one I took of her two days ago. If this is

any indication, she's going to be a real beauty like her mother."

While he examined it she said, "Am I allowed to ask a question now?"

Slowly he lifted his dark head. "Go ahead." His voice grated.

"What's his marital status?"

His face closed up. "He was married two months ago."

"That news would have killed Terrie," she whispered. "Assuming he *is* Bonnie's father, I can't imagine him wanting to claim her now. But on the outside chance that there's a part of him wanting to do the right thing, then I—"

Before she could finish the rest of her sentence, Cole was on his feet, stunning her with the speed that had propelled his powerful body out of the chair.

"I have something to do before any more time passes." He reached for his suit jacket, where he pocketed the photos. "I'll call you in Reno tomorrow," he said, grabbing for his tie. "Give me your cellphone number."

She wrote it on her business card and handed it to him.

He came around the desk and accompanied her to the door, moving with that careless male grace that distinguished him from other men. Like a wall of heat, she felt the sweep of those silvery flecked eyes.

"Your bill's been taken care of. Have a good sleep and a safe trip home, Catherine."

* * *

"Bonnie had her mid-morning bottle but she still fussed before going to sleep. She gets all excited when you come, and misses you when you're not here. It's amazing!"

Uh-oh.

"What's her schedule like?"

"She's eating every three hours."

I know. I was there from the beginning.

Catherine had just driven in from Elko. Normally she would have gone to her condo and showered before starting her work day. But she hadn't seen Bonnie for twenty-four hours. Driving to the ranch and back had made it feel like she'd been gone a week. Babies changed every day. She envied Carol Wilson for being able to take care of her on a round-the-clock basis.

Unable to restrain herself, she kissed the baby's cheeks several times before raising up. "She looks contented now. I'll be by again tomorrow, Carol."

The best part of Catherine's job was to visit the foster parents and check on the babies. But her pleasure had become pain because Bonnie didn't belong to her.

Assuming Buck was the father, and he wanted his daughter, then they had the God-given right to be with each other and Catherine would have to find a way to live with it.

But if he gave up all parental rights to her…

"She's a sweetie pie," Carol said, walking Catherine

to the front door. "Makes me baby-hungry again, but Phil says three children are enough." She winked. "Between you and me, this one's going to be hard to give up. I swear I couldn't do your job or I'd want to take every baby home with me."

Catherine murmured something appropriate and hurried out to her car. The last thing she wanted was for Carol to witness her emotional turmoil. Already she was wondering how she would make it through the day while she waited for Cole Farraday's phone call.

She had an idea the man could move mountains. When he called, he would have news for her, and he'd deliver it in that deep, cultured voice. Anticipating even talking to him again made her feel breathless.

CHAPTER FOUR

As IT turned out, she didn't hear from him until she got home from work at six-thirty that evening. She'd just stepped out of the shower and changed into a T-shirt and jeans when her cellphone rang. The caller ID indicated out of area, which might or might not be the call she'd been waiting for all day.

She clicked on, aware her pulse was racing. "This is Catherine Arnold."

After a pause, "You do realize that in answering the way you do, you give any crazy out there more information than you might want him to know."

Her hand tightened around the phone while a fire and ice sensation spread through her body. It was a little like eating crème de menthe on top of vanilla ice cream.

In truth no man had ever shown her this kind of concern before. She was so used to fending for herself. Cole Farraday's unexpected comment reminded her he was that exceptional kind of male who would protect his own to the death.

What would it feel like to be loved and taken care of by a man like that for the rest of your life? Catherine couldn't comprehend it any more than she could imagine what it would be like to have a mother and father, or siblings.

"You're right, but since a lot of troubled teens phone me when they're most vulnerable or desperate, I want them to know they don't have to go through a third party to find me."

"Point taken, Catherine. No offense," he murmured.

She sank down on the edge of her bed, attacked by a sudden weakness. "None taken."

"Are you still at work?"

"No. I—I'm home." Her voice faltered.

"Alone?"

Did he ask that question because he wanted to keep their conversation private, or was she hoping something of a more personal nature was behind it?

"Yes," she said quietly. "Do you have news for me yet?"

"I do, but I need to see you in person."

So the Buck he knew *was* Bonnie's father! Otherwise he would have told her there was no DNA match and she could check at the hospital for the results herself.

Did it mean Buck wanted to see his daughter?

Torn by conflicting emotions, she jumped to her feet. "When can you be in Reno?"

"I flew in this morning."

Her heart leaped. He'd been here all day? Now she

wouldn't have to wait until tomorrow. "Where are you?"

"I'm just leaving the hospital. For the sake of everyone concerned I'd prefer to meet you in private."

Catherine felt the same way. After pressing her lips together she said, "Come to my condo. I'm in a fourplex southeast of the hospital." She gave him the address and instructions to get there. "It's a little complicated."

"I'll find you."

She had no doubt of it.

With a fluttery feeling in her chest, she clicked off before racing back to the bathroom to fix her freshly washed hair and change into a cotton shirt.

Cole's first thought when he walked into her cozy living room was that she was even more beautiful than he remembered from the night before. The dusky rose of her top, pulled down over white pants covering womanly hips, blended with the blush of her complexion.

Like a gossamer curtain, she'd allowed her hair to fall loose from a side part. It swished against her shoulders with each step she took.

Following the long line of her shapely legs to sandaled feet, he could find no flaw in the way she was put together, let alone her color scheme.

"Won't you sit down?" She indicated the couch opposite the chair she'd claimed, ensuring some distance between them. Cole had the distinct feeling the awareness between them was growing stronger for her too.

Though she presented a poised, professional attitude, he sensed a barely suppressed anxiety coming from her, apart from her eagerness to get straight to the point.

She couldn't afford to get this involved with every case, otherwise she'd burn out from the intensity. If she'd spent a lot of time in the premie nursery with the baby, it would explain why she'd become so emotionally attached.

It was a situation beyond the norm—an occasional hazard in her line of work, he surmised. She'd said her visit to the ranch was unofficial.

Who would have imagined his brother being at the core of Terrie Cloward's heartbreak and ultimate demise?

"Buck's the father, isn't he?" The question brought him back to the source of his bone-deep sorrow with a jolt.

"Yes. His paternity's not in question."

She sat forward. "Did he fly here with you?"

Cole detected a distinct throb in her voice. Her behavior was all the more intriguing in spite of his pain. "No. His DNA results were faxed from the hospital in Elko."

She stood up, evidently too restless to stay seated. "Does that mean he didn't want anything to do with Bonnie, even when he discovered he had a daughter?" she cried.

Something earthshaking was going on inside her to lose control like that. Join the club. Dear God.

How in the hell would Buck have responded upon learning he was a father? Poor Lucy… Still in the honeymoon stage, who could say how she would have handled the shock? With news of that nature even the strongest marriage would be tested to the ultimate degree.

The questions bombarded him, bringing him to his feet. "Since I can't speak for him," he began solemnly, "I can't honestly answer you."

Catherine faced him with an incredulous look. "What do you mean, can't? Surely when you told him he needed to go to the hospital to have the DNA test done, he knew exactly why?"

He massaged the tight cords at the back of his neck. There was something he needed to do before this went any further.

"I'd like to see the baby, then I'll answer all your questions."

She searched his eyes in bewilderment before shaking her head. "My hands are legally tied. Only the father can have access, or, in the unlikely case of his death, his next of kin."

Cole inhaled sharply. "You're looking at him."

A myriad of emotions chased over her face until comprehension dawned. Then she gasped softly. "The funeral—"

He gave an almost imperceptible nod of his head. "My youngest brother, Patrick Farraday. Killed in a riding accident out on the range last week. Our father called him Buck at an early age and it stuck."

She clung to the back of the chair. "But you said it was the *owner* of the Bonnibelle who—"

He wasn't destined to hear more, because a moan had escaped her throat, preventing the rest from coming out. She'd finally put the pieces together.

"Until his recent reformation, my little brother didn't always do the right thing—as you've already discovered. But for all his faults and virtues, he was my brother and I loved him."

Her eyes grew suspiciously bright. "Naturally you wanted to protect him. You did a superb job of it, Mr. Farraday."

"So did you," he riposted. "Another person in your official capacity might have taken it into her head to expose some of the family secrets last evening, damaging Buck's fragile widow."

She searched his eyes. "They'd only been married two months?"

"That's right. After working on a relative's stud farm outside Reno part of last summer, I told him he was needed at home. To my surprise he actually showed up without an argument. When he arrived he declared his partying days were over. Evidently something had happened to make him realize he'd been going in the wrong direction."

His eyes caught hers. "Now we know what it was. In one of his sober moments, he must have realized his mistake in getting involved with someone as young as Terrie. At least I'd like to think so. A couple of months later he announced his engagement to Lucy, the girl who'd been crazy about him for years."

Catherine rubbed her arms. "How old was Buck?"

"Thirty last birthday."

"It's too tragic," she whispered.

He nodded. "A double tragedy considering Terrie died so recently. I'd like to see Bonnie tonight."

His request seemed to startle her. "It's too late to make arrangements with her foster family. But, more to the point, it's my professional opinion it wouldn't be a good idea."

Cole shifted his weight. "Good idea be damned. She's a Farraday. She has a birthright she shares with uncles, aunts and cousins."

Catherine studied him through veiled eyes. "Nevertheless, you're grieving the loss of your brother. You don't need this to compound it, not when she's going to be adopted. It would be better not to put yourself in a position where you could form an attachment."

His teeth ground together. "Simply knowing I have a niece, I already feel attached to her. You gave me pictures of her I'm not likely to forget, remember?" he challenged.

She stiffened. "At the time I didn't realize you were her uncle."

He stifled an oath. "Without proof from the DNA, neither did I."

"Look, Mr. Farraday—" She spread her hands in

a conciliatory gesture. "Let's not make this any harder than it is. Terrie asked me to find Buck. I've honored her wishes, and my heart goes out to you and your family. But the reality is, Bonnie's a ward of the court. A judge will decide her new home."

He had to tamp down his temper. "It will never take the place of that spot of earth her ancestors settled and gave their life's blood for."

"But would it be her home if Terrie hadn't died?" She held her ground with surprising tenacity. "Do you honestly believe your married brother would have wanted visitation rights?"

From the first Cole had been asking himself that question. "The reformed Buck would have," he theorized. "But since both parents are gone the point is moot. It's a new playing field."

"You're right. And that playing field has to serve Bonnie's best interests. Do you have any idea how many people incapable of having children are dying for a baby like her to love and raise?" Her voice trembled. "Some have been preparing years for the privilege."

From the raw emotion she exuded, he could almost believe she was talking about herself. If she'd been at Girls' Haven three years, she undoubtedly grew close to the teens who found themselves in trouble. It wasn't that different from him getting to know the stockmen who worked for him. At times their problems became his.

Terrie's death had to have been hard on her, not to

mention Bonnie's hospital stay. Much as he hated this situation, Cole admired her wisdom and dedication to the job. On top of everything else, she'd shown discretion, a noble attribute when all was said and done.

Changing tactics, he said, "I only want to see her. Will you arrange it for me?" He could call his attorney to do it for him, but, for several reasons he hadn't examined too closely yet, Cole preferred to deal with her alone.

She let out a sigh that sounded troubled, if not anguished. "How long will you be in Reno?"

"For as long as it takes."

A battle seemed to be going on inside her. After a tension-filled silence her gaze fell away and she gave a brief nod. "Come by at nine in the morning and she'll be here."

Without further word she walked to the door, indicating it was time for him to leave. No woman of his acquaintance had ever done that to him before. Contrarily, he didn't want to go. There was a lot more he wanted to know about her.

She didn't wear a wedding ring. As far as he could tell she wasn't living with another man. He saw no signs of a male occupying her home, but that didn't mean there wasn't one in the picture. A woman who looked and moved like her would attract them in droves.

Hell—he'd been drawn to her from the moment her husky voice had called out to him yesterday. Being with her tonight, those feelings had only intensified.

He moved toward her. "I'll get out of here so whoever you're expecting won't jump to a hasty conclusion."

"Thank you, Mr. Farraday." Ignoring his gambit, she opened the door. But satisfying color swept into her cheeks, intensifying the electric blue of those fabulous eyes, giving him the answer he sought. For the moment anyway.

"I'll be here on the dot of nine," he assured her before walking toward his rental car.

No sooner had he driven away than he pulled out his phone to check his messages. He'd turned off the ringer so he wouldn't be disturbed while he talked to Catherine.

Two were from Brenda, the others from John and Penny. If he'd seen one from Mack, then he would have known something was wrong at the ranch.

Under the circumstances he didn't feel like talking to anyone. From the second he'd taken a look at Bonnie's pictures an idea had been percolating in his brain. After talking to Catherine this evening, it had taken on critical mass.

CHAPTER FIVE

CATHERINE brought the baby into the living room. "When I picked her up this morning, she'd just finished her bottle. I'm afraid she's about to fall asleep again."

Their eyes met for a moment. Cole's were alive with anticipation. "No problem."

As if he were used to taking care of an infant, he plucked Bonnie from her arms and carried her across the expanse to the sofa.

Such a tiny bundle nestled securely against the broad shoulder of a powerfully built man like Cole caught at Catherine's heart. She heard low, happy laughter rumble out of him as he laid Bonnie on the cushion and began examining her.

Catherine had been guilty of doing the very same thing before he had arrived. Now she was guilty of examining *his* body, dressed in a navy polo shirt and pleated trousers.

Terrie had fallen in love with a "hunky" cowboy named Buck.

Now that Catherine had met his big brother—the dynamic owner and head of the Bonnibelle Ranch—she understood the power of the Farraday charm. It was lethal.

Bonnie must think so too. While she focused on the man speaking to her in that deep, rich voice, giving her all his attention, her whole tiny body seemed to wriggle with new life.

Without conscious thought Catherine drew closer, marveling at certain similarities between the two of them. Though she saw a look of Terrie in Bonnie's mouth and nose, her hair color and widow's peak, the shape of her eyes was genuine Farraday. Was it any wonder she was such a beautiful child?

Cole seemed captivated by her, as if he'd forgotten Catherine was in the room. Pleasure in the baby caused the lines of his face to disappear for a moment, making him look younger and so handsome it hurt.

It was only natural he was thinking of his brother and the little girl he and Terrie had produced. Yet every minute spent with her would make it that much harder for Cole to let her go.

No one understood that better than Catherine herself.

Time was passing. She had to bring this love-fest between uncle and niece to an end.

"Cole?" she called softly to him. "I've bent the rules by bringing Bonnie here. She has an appointment with the pediatrician in a half-hour. Now that you've had the opportunity to see her, I'm afraid we have to leave."

That brought his dark head around. "Is there something still wrong with her?" he demanded quietly.

After the way he'd been playing with the baby, testing the strength of her fingers and kissing her sweet neck, it shouldn't have surprised her he'd reacted to Catherine's words like any typical anxious parent.

"Not at all, otherwise the hospital wouldn't have released her. It's standard procedure that while the babies are in foster care routine checkups are done with more frequency than usual because they can be adopted at any time." She flashed him an apologetic smile. "I don't want to be late."

Actually the doctor would fit the babies' visits in without an appointment, but Cole didn't need to know that.

Perhaps it was an unconscious gesture on his part, but in the next breath he'd laid Bonnie against his shoulder, exhibiting an undeniably possessive hold on her that was at once stunning and touching.

The thing Catherine had hoped wouldn't happen had already come to pass. His next words confirmed it.

"No stranger is going to adopt her. I won't allow it."

Cole Farraday was used to his word being law, but in this case the situation wasn't so black and white. Catherine took a fortifying breath. "Then you'll need to tell that to the judge. I'll warn you now that, even with money and power on your side, he'll want what's best for Bonnie."

"She's going to come home to her rightful family," he declared in a forceful tone.

"Are you married, Cole?"

His jaw hardened. "I'm a widower, but in this day and age having a wife isn't a prerequisite, surely?"

It appeared he'd known a lot of sorrow in his life, but then so had Catherine. She couldn't let sentiment dissuade her from her course.

"Perhaps not always, but there are other considerations."

"What consideration could possibly be more important than the fact that Bonnie is already loved by her own surviving flesh and blood?"

Panicked, Catherine could feel the baby slipping away from her, figuratively as well as physically.

"Terrie left written wishes before she died," Catherine answered him. "They hold weight with the court."

She caught the glint of fire coming from his eyes. "You fulfilled them by driving to the ranch to find Buck." His expression mirrored a faint respect for what she'd done, but that was all.

Her heart kicked against her ribs. "There was another wish."

She could almost feel his arms close tighter around Bonnie. "Am I going to have to pry that out of you too?"

His black brows took on a threatening slant, but she was fighting for her life and refused to be intimidated.

"In the event I couldn't find Buck, Terrie designated someone specific to raise Bonnie."

The sudden indrawn breath she heard sounded like ripping silk.

"Someone waiting in the wings, you mean, yet you wouldn't tell me even if the law didn't forbid you," he reflected bitterly, in what she guessed was a rare show of temper.

In the stillness that followed, he rubbed the back of the baby's head with a tenderness that melted Catherine's insides.

She sensed his frustration. Under other circumstances she'd be on his side all the way. "I'm sorry. As it is I shouldn't have let you come here to see Bonnie."

But he wasn't listening, and she heard his next words delivered with barely veiled hostility. "That explains why you were in such an all-fired hurry to get the DNA match done."

"Cole, I—"

"Obviously it's someone in Terrie's confidence." He continued with his train of thought, staring at her as if he'd suddenly been given second sight. "A woman with a vested interest in her wellbeing and that of her child."

He took a step toward her. "It's *you,* isn't it?"

Catherine started to shake.

"I *knew* there was something different about you, something that didn't quite add up. A social worker's job doesn't include driving across Nevada to find a man who might have impregnated one of the teens at Girls' Haven."

His gunsmoke eyes impaled her. "Now it's

making sense. You had to be certain Buck wouldn't claim his rights before you put in your petition to adopt Bonnie yourself."

Catherine could see there was no point in denying it, not when his steel trap mind had figured it out.

He kissed the top of the baby's head. "Terrie may have wanted you to raise her daughter, but, considering your position as the social worker for Girls' Haven, I can guarantee that a judge will see your petition for adoption as a conflict of interest."

"I'm sure he will," she admitted to him. "But the circumstances were extraordinary. I spent five weeks at the hospital with Bonnie, and now she needs me. I'm counting on the judge to weigh the facts that I love this baby with all my heart, and I have Terrie's blessing. Don't make me out to be some kind of monster. Terrie wanted to give Buck the chance to claim Bonnie. So did I," she defended. "Every child deserves its parents if it's humanly possible. The truth is, I was orphaned as a baby, never knowing who mine were. Like Terrie I lived in various foster homes and ended up at Girls' Haven, pregnant at the same age."

His lips thinned, undoubtedly in revulsion.

"Terrie's and my stories are very similar, except that I planned to keep my baby. But it wasn't meant to be because I miscarried at four months. I never got the chance to hold my little girl or love her."

Don't break down now, Catherine.

"But thanks to Girls' Haven I was given a second chance at life and I took it. That was eleven years ago.

A lot has happened since then. After university I came to work for them, hoping to give back what they gave me. Getting to know Terrie and her situation was like experiencing *déjà vu*. Over the last months we grew very close," she explained, endeavoring to get through to him. "She always planned to give up her baby for adoption. When she realized she was dying, she begged me to be Bonnie's mother." Her voice shook. "I told her that if I couldn't find Buck, or if he didn't want Bonnie, I—I'd do everything in my power to adopt her."

Catherine had a struggle to hold the tears back. "It wasn't hard to make that promise. She's the most precious, adorable baby on earth."

Though his hand spanned Bonnie's little back lovingly, his eyes still glittered dangerously. "A wise judge will suspect you used your considerable influence to coerce Terrie into putting her wishes in writing."

"A good judge will take the extenuating facts into consideration and rule what's best for Bonnie," she countered, swallowing hard. "In all probability we'll both lose out, and he'll award the adoption to a couple so Bonnie will grow up with a mother *and* father. It's something neither you nor I can provide."

The tension between them sizzled.

"That's unacceptable."

"You think I don't feel the same way?" came her anguished cry.

Catherine understood his anger since she felt defeated by the same ineffectual emotion. This was a situation she would never have envisioned. Not in a lifetime.

"Will you please give Bonnie to me? I have to get her ready to go to the doctor."

She expected another argument, but shockingly he said something quite different in a low aside. "Let me help. Where's her carryall?"

It was in her bedroom, but she didn't want him of all people going in there. "I'll get it."

When she hurried back with it, he lowered Bonnie into it as if he'd done this sort of thing many times before. He'd mentioned having nephews and nieces, so it wasn't surprising he seemed a natural.

As she tucked a receiving blanket around Bonnie, who was being a perfect angel, her arm brushed against Cole's. He didn't act as if he'd noticed, but she felt sudden warmth spiral through her body.

"Come on, sweetheart," she said a bit unsteadily. "It's time to go get checked out."

"I'll carry her out to the car for you."

Catherine didn't say anything because she knew she couldn't stop him. His proprietorial interest in Bonnie was nothing short of astounding.

He must have seen her vehicle out in the carport because he knew exactly where to go.

Amy, the good-looking redheaded Realtor who lived in the next condo, was just walking toward her car. She almost tripped over a crack in the cement while she stared at Cole. As an afterthought she said hello to Catherine, who could read the other woman's mind.

Unfortunately Catherine knew her aggressive neighbor would be over later to find out who the mystery man was, because there was no question about it, Cole Farraday was an incredibly gorgeous man. However, this was one time Catherine didn't intend to satisfy Amy's curiosity.

After she unlocked her car, Cole fastened Bonnie's carryall into the base of the back seat. Through the rearview mirror Catherine watched him kiss the baby's nose and cheeks. His display of affection wasn't feigned. This was his brother's baby and he was crazy about her.

But so was Catherine!

He approached her window, which she had to put down. "What time do you eat lunch?"

His deep voice disturbed her as much as his nearness. She might have known Cole wasn't going to let this go. "Most of the time I don't," she said, playing for time so she could think.

"Then I'll come by Girls' Haven later and we'll talk."

"No!" she cried in panic. "That would be the worst thing you could do." She clung to the steering wheel.

His presence would create a major upheaval, starting with Sylvia, the director, who would ask questions Catherine would be forced to answer. It could get her into serious trouble and he knew it!

A satisfied gleam had entered those silvery eyes. "We have unfinished business, Catherine. You name the place."

"There *is* no place that would be safe for us to be seen together," she confessed.

"My thoughts precisely."

He had the upper hand. If she didn't know better, she would think he was actually enjoying this.

"Meet me here at two. I can spare a half-hour. No more."

Needing to get away from him, she started the car and began to back out. He stood there with his hands on his hips in a totally male stance. After driving away, she could still feel his penetrating eyes following her.

Cole's motive for wanting to see her again was transparent. With family blood on his side, he believed she didn't have a chance of adopting Bonnie. But rather than fight her he intended to use that potent Farraday charm to gain her cooperation in helping him win custody of the baby. He wasn't the head of the Bonnibelle for nothing.

But Catherine didn't plan to make Terrie's mistake and be drawn in by male persuasion at the hands of a master. Watching Cole interact with the baby had given her an idea, one that grew as the day wore on. Under the circumstances it made the most sense.

A few hours later she tried it out on him. For an answer Cole's mocking tone resounded in her living room. "You'll grant *me* liberal visitation rights?"

She'd been five minutes late returning to the condo from her work, and was still out of breath. They faced each other like adversaries.

"Yes. I've been thinking about it since I took the

baby back to her foster family. You and I could petition the judge in the same pre-trial hearing. Don't you see it might strengthen both our cases if we show that we're willing to work together for Bonnie's ultimate welfare?"

Cole's mouth compressed. "Who's going to raise her during the day while you're at work?" At least he'd cooled down enough to have a conversation.

She was ready for that question. "Terrie and I talked about it. There's a wonderful daycare facility right across the street from Girls' Haven. I'll be close to her and can oversee everything on a constant basis."

He made a dismissive gesture. "My housekeeper could provide the same care, but I doubt the judge will be impressed with either scenario."

"So what are you saying?" she blurted, trying to tamp down her alarm.

His gaze wandered over her features with a lazy sensuality he probably wasn't aware of. "That your original assumption was correct. The ideal for Bonnie would be to have a stay-at-home mother whose husband provides the necessary income."

His pessimism over her idea of a joint petition acted like a giant hand crushing her heart. If Cole, with all his resources and a last name like his, didn't think they could sway the judge, what chance did she really have to fight for Bonnie on her own?

Tears glazed her eyes before she could turn away. She buried her face in her hands, trying not to make a sound. In searching for Buck, the dream world she'd been living in for the last five weeks had shattered. "No stranger will ever love her as much as I do."

"That makes two of us," he whispered behind her. "I see my brother in her, and it kills me."

The pathos in his voice reached down to the core of her being. Catherine had no more desire to fight him.

She sniffed before wiping her eyes with the back of her hands. "I-if you plan to fight for her, I'll help any way I can. The judge needs to hear how much Terrie loved your brother, and how much you loved him. Just promise me that if you win you'll let me see her once in a while?" her voice throbbed.

"Oh, I plan to win," he finally said in a low, husky tone. "I have an ace up my sleeve guaranteed to produce results."

The hairs prickled on the back of her neck. Catherine turned to him, staring at him through blurry eyes. "What is it?"

"I've decided to get married."

She received the news like a physical blow, but by some miracle she remained standing.

"Th-that ought to do it," she stammered helplessly. "With or without my help."

"I'll need that too, but we'll talk about it this evening over dinner. I'll be by at six."

"I'm afraid I can't tonight. A new case is coming in. I probably won't be leaving the office until nine or nine-thirty." For once she was grateful she had to work late. The bombshell he'd just dropped had disturbed her in ways she didn't dare examine.

"You can ask someone else to cover for you."

"It would have to be an emergency."

"What if I told you it is?"

He sounded deadly serious.

"I don't understand."

"How could you when you don't know all the facts?"

Cole seemed to be talking in riddles.

"Have you arranged to meet with your attorney? Is that why you need me there? So I can give him the relevant details?"

"We'll do that too. But first I've made an appointment with a justice of the peace."

She blinked. "Surely you don't need me to witness your marriage—"

A strange smile broke out on his arresting features. "No. I need you to marry me tonight."

She let out a caustic laugh. "Oh, please—"

"My word exactly," he came back in a frighteningly sober tone. "Following that we'll fill out adoption papers on Bonnie that my attorney will present to the judge. You were the one who warned me time was of the essence."

The world tilted for a moment.

Catherine lost cognizance of time and place, because she knew Cole never said anything he didn't mean, or wasn't prepared to carry out.

"It's the only solution," he added, taking advantage of her silence. "We're both free and we both want to be a parent to Bonnie. As Buck's brother and

Terrie's choice of woman to raise her daughter, we can offer something no one else can. There's one caveat, however," he added, sounding mysterious.

She was still too deep in shock to respond, and he knew it.

"When I take you and Bonnie home to the ranch, I'll be introducing you as the woman I fell in love with a year ago. We found out we were expecting a baby, but you refused to marry me because you were afraid I was still too in love with the memory of my deceased wife."

"Are you?" she fired hotly.

"I'll always love Jenny, but she belongs to my past. Unfortunately there are people who for reasons of their own insist on believing otherwise."

"Meaning your ex-girlfriends?"

An amused gleam entered his eyes. "After our daughter was born you realized I really did love you. Hoping it wasn't too late for us, you came to the ranch on the day of Buck's funeral and asked me to marry you. Naturally I was overjoyed and insisted we get married immediately."

Catherine shook her head, finally managing to find her voice. "In the first place, two strangers don't meet one day and get married the next—and even if by the remotest possibility we did, I couldn't live around your family with a lie like that—"

His features hardened. "Then we'll tell the truth in front of everyone, which will include Lucy. She'll learn that Buck got involved with a teenager and the baby is his. That we had to get married in order to adopt her. Lucy will put two and two together, figuring out Bonnie was conceived just weeks before Buck returned to the ranch and asked her to marry him."

"No—" Catherine cried. "That would be too awful, too cruel to her. It could destroy her faith in love. She'd grieve forever."

"Then which is it?" he inserted suavely. "You can't have it both ways if you want to be a mother to Bonnie."

Catherine wanted it more than anything in the world. She'd promised Terrie. But to get married to a man she'd only met two days ago…

What did she really know about him except that he was the owner of the famous Bonnibelle Ranch?

He wants Bonnie as much as you do, her heart reminded her. *He wants you to help him raise his brother's baby. That's what you know about him, deep down in your soul.*

Her body trembled. Was that enough reason to do something so drastic it would change her whole life and his?

"Do you know the odds against a marriage like that working?" she cried.

"Probably as good as the odds of any marriage making it," he countered, with a cynicism she vaguely shared.

"Where would we live?"

"In my house."

"You mean the ranch house?"

"No. My brother and sister and their families live

there. Buck lived there with Lucy, but I suspect that one of these days she'll move back to Elko to be near her family. My house is on the other side of the lake."

"Is it where you lived with your wife?"

"No. Like everyone else, Jenny and I began our married life in the ranch house."

Though she hated asking the next question, she had to know. "How did she die?"

"A drunk teenager ploughed into her car one night as she was driving back to the ranch. She died instantly."

Catherine's face crumpled in pain. "I'm so sorry."

She felt his eyes studying her. "After she was gone, I built a place of my own to get away from the memories. My sister Penny jokingly calls it the bachelor pad, but with your help we can make it family-friendly. I dare you to come and live in it with Bonnie and me." He flashed her a rare white smile that turned her heart over.

Shaken by his proposal, she drew in an unsteady breath, attempting to keep her wits. "Supposing I were to say yes to this ludicrous idea of yours, and we get married only to learn that the judge turns down our petition?"

He gave an elegant shrug of those masculine shoulders. "Then we get an annulment. I'll have my attorney put it in writing. But if we win Bonnie, our marriage is forever."

Forever.

She reeled in place.

He paused at the door. "I'll be by at six for your answer. If you're not here, then I'll know she isn't your *raison d'être* after all."

CHAPTER SIX

AT FIVE to six Cole pulled up in front of Catherine's condo. He'd come early because, frankly, there was nowhere else he wanted to be.

Throughout his life he'd relied on gut instinct to get him through some rough moments. By asking him if he would let her visit Bonnie sometimes, she'd admitted defeat. It was the pain he'd heard in Catherine's voice that had made up his mind for him.

Now it was a waiting game to see if she had the courage to do this outrageous thing and marry him.

"Coletrane—" he could hear his father "—whether you like it or not, you're a natural-born leader. I'm depending on you to hold this family together after I'm gone someday. Buck bears watching, and Penny and John will always look to you, whether in good times or bad."

Cole ground his teeth.

Watching Buck self-destruct despite many unsuccessful interventions on Cole's part had turned him inside out. But he could do something for his brother now. He *wanted* to do it.

Already he thought of the baby as *his* little Bonnibelle. She was a fighter to have gotten through those first difficult five weeks. Nothing in life seemed more important than being a father to her. With Catherine helping him, they could be the family Cole ached for and Bonnie deserved.

He checked his watch. Five after six.

His chest grew tight. If he was wrong about Catherine and she couldn't bring herself to marry him, not even for the baby's sake, then he'd call out every favor to influence the judge to let him adopt Bonnie alone.

It might entail an all-out battle with the court. That was okay. He was ready for the fight, even if it meant pretending *he'd* been Terrie's lover. A white lie God would understand. His and Buck's DNA would be a close enough match.

But he much preferred the thought of being Catherine's husband.

Since the idea had come to him, it was all he'd been able to think about. She was a beautiful woman. Her haunting image had played havoc with his sleep. He couldn't forget how careful she'd been to protect Buck, or how brave she'd been to stand up to Cole no matter what he threw at her.

They would have something going for them most newlyweds didn't have—a ready-made child they both loved. In that regard he and Catherine shared an unassailable bond. It was what had brought them together. Who knew what the future might hold for them?

In two days she'd become so important to him he felt a stunning sense of loss at the thought of never seeing her again. Nothing close to this had happened to him before, except for the way he'd felt about Jenny when they'd first been introduced.

He knew for a fact that, having met Catherine, he would pursue her under any circumstances. But with the minutes ticking away, and no sign of her, he had to conclude she couldn't bring herself to say yes to him, not even with Bonnie as the prize.

Cole unconsciously pounded the flat of his hand against the steering wheel. He could swear she was aware of the instant chemistry between them. Hell, he *knew* she could feel it. The tension between them was palpable.

But he had to remember Catherine had been deprived of her family from birth. She'd obviously struggled through her teens. Clearly she'd been let down by the man who'd impregnated her.

After the miscarriage she would have been devastated, yet she'd gone on to make a total success of her life. She couldn't have achieved her goals without using her native intelligence to make unimpulsive decisions.

By proposing marriage, he'd asked something of her that meant she not only had to let go of old fears, she had to trust him and herself enough to face the unknown. Hopefully the possibility of raising Bonnie was reason enough for her to make that leap of faith.

Going on the hunch that she needed more time to make up her mind, he started the car and drove three blocks to a convenience mart he'd passed on the way.

Alighting from the seat, he went inside for a cup of coffee. Once back behind the wheel, he decided it was time to make the phone call he'd been putting off. Whether she was at work or home, he could reach her on her cell.

She picked up on the second ring and said hello.

"Brenda? It's Cole."

"At last— I know how much you're hurting. I guess I was beginning to wonder if I'd hear from you before the weekend."

This was the last time.

"Buck's death has set me back, no doubt about it. But I'm dealing with another issue right now." He paused. "I'm afraid it's going to prevent me from seeing you again."

"You don't need to lie to me," she said in a brittle tone. "I know I don't measure up to Jenny. No woman does."

Her comment didn't faze him. Like a glorious rainbow over the Rubies following the most violent of storms, Catherine's unexpected appearance had changed the entire landscape of his life.

But Brenda didn't need to know that. He expelled a controlled sigh. "I'm sorry."

"So am I. It's been ten years. You should have gotten over her by now, Cole."

The sound of the click came as a relief.

He finished his coffee, then backed away from the curb and headed for Catherine's once more.

Bringing another colleague up to speed on the case coming into Girls' Haven had taken longer than Catherine had realized. It was six-twenty before she turned the corner of her street so fast her rear wheels squealed.

She strained to discover if Cole's rental car was parked out in front. When she couldn't see it, her heart pounded sickeningly. He'd said six o'clock and it appeared he'd meant it!

Suddenly any misgivings she might still have been entertaining about the wisdom of marrying him vanished. She wanted Bonnie, and so help her she wanted Cole too, but it looked like she was too late!

He would have come for an answer. Not finding her here, he'd gone. For all she knew he was halfway to the airport and she'd never see him again—

Like a drowning victim her life flashed before her, giving her glimpses of the three of them living in that glorious piece of heaven. But the thrill of it only lasted a moment, because it was a dream she hadn't reached for in time.

Too many old demons about trust issues had clouded her thinking. She'd taken too long to make up her mind. Now all could be lost.

Shattered by the realization, she doubled over the steering wheel in pain. She might not have known

Cole for more than a few days, but she knew enough to understand he was a man of action.

Once he made up his mind about something, he didn't deviate from it. Those who couldn't meet that high standard were left in the dust. One way or another he would claim his brother's child, only Catherine wouldn't be a part of it, and it was her fault.

Maybe it wasn't too late to catch up to him, wherever he was—

Unfortunately he'd never given her his cell number. If she wanted to get in touch with him she would have to phone the ranch and leave a message.

But she didn't dare do that. Cole had done everything to ensure this matter remained ultra-private. Too much was at risk for her to make a call that might alert his family and raise unwanted questions.

Barring another visit to the ranch, which would be a disaster, she didn't know how to contact him without letting anyone else know.

Unable to stem the tears gushing down her hot cheeks, she opened the car door with every intention of making it inside her condo before someone saw her. But as she swung her legs out into the heat, she found her way blocked by a powerful male body.

"Cole—" she cried, on a little sob of joy he couldn't have helped but hear.

He stared down at her, studying her moist face with an intensity she could feel travel the whole length of her body.

"How am I supposed to interpret those tears?" he asked in a thick-toned voice.

The time for truth had come. She would never get another chance.

"I was late b-because I had a lot of thinking to do."

Like the sun penetrating a dark cloud, his eyes filled with light. "But the point is, you came."

She moistened her lips nervously. "I had to. I love Bonnie too much to let her go without a fight. If I become your wife, we'll have the optimum chance to win custody."

Beneath the expensive brown silk sport shirt he was wearing, his chest rose and fell visibly, a sign of vulnerability she wouldn't have guessed at considering he kept such a tight control on his emotions.

"We'll be taking solemn vows in a little while. There'll be no going back," he declared with a refined savagery, reminding her he was a cattle king with an iron hand and those exceptional gifts. The idea that he was about to become her husband sent another shiver through her body.

"No."

"If the judge grants our petition, our marriage is for real." His eyes trapped hers. "You do understand that?"

She knew what he was asking. Her breath got trapped in her lungs. "Yes."

He straightened away from the door. "Good. Let's get you inside so you can pack."

"Pack?"

"After the ceremony we'll be staying at the Atlantis Reno to enjoy our honeymoon. Only you and I will know what goes on behind closed doors at the hotel. Hopefully Bonnie will be ours in a matter of days."

She froze. "I thought the whole point was to do all this in secret. If we check in there, you're bound to be recognized."

One corner of his mouth curved, almost knocking the breath out of her. "It could happen. More to the point, you and I have to make this look as romantic as possible. That's why I booked a luxury suite in the Concierge Tower there. It will help carry off the myth that we've been secret lovers over the past twelve months. Our family and friends will expect that we celebrated our marriage in the open like any besotted newlyweds."

Her legs almost buckled. "Since you live so far away from Reno, is anyone going to believe we ever had a relationship?"

"I've been flying here on personal business to see my uncle three to four times a month for years," he confided. "Finally the family will understand why I was willing to console myself away from the ranch as often as I did. My brother John and his wife Rosemary will be delighted with our news."

Not so the women who would like to be Cole's exclusive love interest, Catherine surmised.

"Bonnie's going to come as a huge surprise."

His eyes softened. "She's going to breathe new life

into the Farraday clan at a very critical period. So will you," he added silkily. "As for my sister Penny and her husband Rich, they'll be overjoyed I've found love again after all this time. She'll tell you she's been worried I'd end up wifeless and childless."

"Is she one of those sisters who never leaves you alone?"

A chuckle escaped, giving her the answer. Its deep male timbre excited her.

"You're lucky."

He stared down at her through narrowed eyes. "Right now I know I am." When he said things like that her insides melted.

"Maybe it's bad luck to get too far ahead of ourselves."

"I don't believe in bad luck, just bad timing."

Her thoughts reeled. If there was one man who could impress a judge and make things happen with lightning speed, it was Cole.

No sooner had he helped her from the car than Amy drove in the next parking stall. She didn't waste any time walking over to them with a flirtatious smile centered on Cole. There wasn't a woman alive who wouldn't be attracted to him.

"We meet again." Her eyes swerved to Catherine's "Aren't you going to introduce me?"

"I'm her fiancé," Cole declared, effectively negating any reason for Catherine to speak. "We're about to be married, so forgive us if we have to rush off…"

Her heart thudded at the possessiveness in his tone.

After he'd ushered her inside the condo, Catherine turned to him. "She didn't like me before. I'm afraid that encounter just made things worse."

"Since you won't be living here from now on, it's no longer your concern. You'll need to give notice at your work."

He moved too fast for her.

"I asked for a week's emergency leave for personal reasons, and got it, but until we know whether Bonnie is ours, I'll wait to call the chairman of the board who actually hired me."

"The adoption's going to happen," he stated, as if it were a *fait accompli*. His innate confidence was a sheer revelation to her. "Now, what can I do to help? Since we can drop by here any time during the week, just bring what you need for the next few days."

She paused in the doorway to the hall. "Are we getting married in one of those wedding chapels?"

"No." A simple word, but she sensed his distaste at the mere idea. He regarded her steadily. "The ceremony will take place at the judge's home, with only his wife and my attorney present."

Thank you for that, Cole.

"I'm glad," she confessed in relief.

"Once we know Bonnie's ours, we'll repeat our vows at church in Elko."

She bowed her head. "I'd like that." Suddenly his presence in her small living room was too overpowering for her to function with any coherence. "I-if you'd like to sit down and read a magazine, I won't be long," she called over her shoulder before disappearing into the bedroom.

Catherine had been making a mental list: a dress to be married in, a business suit to wear in front of his attorney, a couple of tops and pants, a nightgown and robe.

The choices staring at her from her closet were hardly awe-inspiring. The more she examined her wardrobe, the more anxious she became.

On impulse she rushed back to the living room, where she surprised Cole in the middle of the room talking on his cellphone. His glance darted to hers. "What's wrong?"

"I don't have anything appropriate to get married in."

"Then we'll buy you something in one of the boutiques at the hotel and change in our suite before we drive to the judge's residence."

"I was hoping you'd say we had enough time. I'll hurry."

Though this was more of a business merger between rational adults than the romantic elopement of two young lovers, she didn't want to embarrass Cole. He was a well-known figure. Becoming his wife would bring her into the spotlight.

There hadn't been time for them to talk about their public life together as man and wife, but she knew enough about him to realize he expected her to be a woman he could introduce with pride.

She couldn't bear the idea of his friends and

family thinking he'd made a serious mistake in his choice of bride. Perish the thought they'd feel sorry for him. For tonight she determined to go all-out to look beautiful for him.

Earlier Cole had asked her if she understood this was to be a "real" marriage and she'd said yes. On the outside chance it would have to be annulled, she hadn't allowed her thoughts to drift that far.

That was then. This was now.

She was really getting married in a little while, and found to her shock that she wanted it to last—even if they couldn't adopt Bonnie.

CHAPTER SEVEN

THE suite on the twenty-third floor of the hotel had adjoining rooms leading off a private lounge, both of which overlooked the Sierra Nevadas. Cole had just emerged from his room wearing a new stone-gray suit with a deeper hued shirt and silver monogrammed tie.

On the eve of his first marriage, he hadn't known the meaning of the word nervous.

This was different. He wanted Catherine to trust him. Otherwise the plan he'd devised would never come to fruition.

Up to now he was used to making unilateral decisions without looking back when certain situations demanded it. But he realized he couldn't do that with her. She'd come too far, fought too hard for her independence to imagine she'd follow blindly where he led.

He'd made a big mistake telling her she'd have to give her boss notice. She'd tossed it right back in his face.

When she'd found the fantastic soft cream crêpe

dress and shoes she'd liked, and had reached for her credit card, they'd clashed because he'd told her he'd pay for them. Up had come her softly rounded chin in a mutinous gesture she probably hadn't been aware of. But he'd noticed it, like he noticed everything about her, and backed down.

Small things could grow into big ones. He would have to learn to choose his battles more carefully. They were going to be parents, with their own ideas of how things should work. Theirs needed to be a partnership of equals. If she felt he didn't respect her opinions, she'd keep her emotional distance. He refused to let that happen.

They weren't even married yet, and already he knew he wanted her in all the old ways he'd thought had disappeared when he'd buried Jenny. He couldn't wait to explore what was coming.

Whatever else you do, Farraday, just don't blow it.

He heard a sound and turned in its direction. Catherine had left her room and was walking toward him. Her eyes looked like two dazzling sapphires.

"What do you think?" She smiled. "Too much? Too little?"

He cleared his throat. "You look like a bride. But I think you don't need me to tell you your taste is impeccable."

"Thank you, Cole. You make a very striking groom. I'm going to be the envy of every female when we leave this room."

There was nothing coy or artificial about

Catherine. She didn't have theatrics in her. If he took this moment to reveal the depth of his intimate thoughts where she was concerned, she'd run a thousand miles.

He'd seen her wear her silvery blond hair several ways. Tonight she'd caught it back in a loose chignon. A few strands tipped by the sun had escaped and framed her oval face, bringing out the mold of her high cheekbones.

The simple elegance of the knee-length dress with its draped neck and long flowing sleeves brought out the singing curves of her sylph-like figure.

He'd given her a corsage of creamy roses whose petals blended with her flawless complexion. She'd already fastened it to her shoulder without his help. Another signal to let him know she needed her space.

After reaching for the digital camera he'd purchased that afternoon, he crossed the room to the glass elevator of their suite.

"It's time, Catherine."

As she moved toward him on those long elegant legs, he snapped half a dozen pictures. He planned to have one framed for his den at the house. The rest would go in an album Bonnie would come to treasure.

"Your turn," she said, taking the camera from him. "I wish I'd had this while you were playing with Bonnie." She took several shots of him.

His lips twitched. "We'll have a lifetime to immortalize ourselves."

A worried expression crossed over her face as she handed the camera back to him. "I hope so."

"Believe it." He grasped her hand to draw her in the elevator, aware of a latent fire building inside him.

"After the ceremony we'll bring my attorney back here to do the paperwork. That way he can file it with the court first thing in the morning and get a date for a hearing with the judge right away."

"Congratulations, Mr. and Mrs. Farraday. May your life together be one of joy and happiness."

The judge who had married them spoke with an eloquence that had added the right amount of reverence and dignity to their wedding ceremony. Both he and his wife were very gracious and conveyed a sincere cordiality.

Catherine muttered her thank-you, but after the thorough kiss Cole had just given her, her palms ached and her legs had grown weak.

She'd known how important it was they give a convincing performance of being in love. It was shocking how easily she'd entered into her part of it, and she only had herself to blame if she was still trembling.

Cole's attorney Jim Darger, an attractive man in his fifties, who knew their secret and was totally loyal to Cole, had taken several pictures of them. She feared he might have caught that kiss which had lasted far too long for two people who hadn't been in each other's arms yet, let alone shared intimacy.

The moment she'd felt Cole's sensual mouth

coaxing hers apart, a quickening in her body had driven her to respond without conscious thought. The urge to meld with him wasn't something she'd had control over. It had simply happened.

She must have shocked him, because he'd clasped her tighter against his rock-hard physique—whether to hold himself up or her, she wasn't sure. All she knew was that the full contact of arms, legs and mouths had charged every atom, whipping up a storm of desire in her she'd never experienced in her life.

The sound of someone's cellphone ringing had insinuated itself into the very private party Catherine had been having with her new husband. The reminder that they weren't alone had caused her to pull away from him, her face instantly burning.

Three people had just witnessed something Catherine couldn't explain. You didn't kiss a man like you were starving for him unless—unless the physical attraction was explosive. Even then she should have been able to slow down her response.

Once goodnights were said, Cole's arm hugged her waist as they walked out to the limo with Jim. During the ride back to the hotel the two men talked ranch business while Catherine studied the new diamond ring circling her finger.

He'd given her a two carat solitaire, a stone whose facets caught the light. It was exquisite. The slim gold band next to it reminded her she had some shopping to do. Before tomorrow evening she

intended to present him with his own wedding ring.
Maybe one with a garnet.

From what she'd learned, the Ruby Mountains
were named for the red garnets found by some of the
early explorers. A ring would let all those women
know he was taken.

She groaned when she realized how possessive
she'd become already. The possibility that their
marriage could be annulled in the near future was
anathema to her.

Before long they arrived back at the hotel. Within
the hour they'd eaten a delicious Italian meal sent up
from one of the restaurants. After a waiter had
cleared everything away, Jim handed them the forms
to fill out. There were so many questions to answer.
The background questions took forever.

"What are our chances?" she asked him anxiously.

"You have a strong case, Catherine. Cole is well
known in this state, and can provide for all of you.
He's the biological father's brother. You have the
biological mother's notarized letter designating you
as the person she wants to raise Bonnie. Your time
spent in the ICU where you bonded with the baby
will stack the deck a little more in your favor.
Bonding is the crucial issue in adoption cases."

She took a shaky breath. "What might be the ob-
stacles?"

"There aren't any," Cole insisted, his expression
implacable.

"I'm afraid there is *one*," Jim asserted. The furrow

between Cole's brows deepened. "It's a little like insider trading on the stock market. You know something no one else knows and make a move, leaving everyone else in the dust."

Her mouth felt unpleasantly dry. "That's what I was afraid of."

Cole jumped to his feet. "It's not a good analogy. This isn't money we're bilking out of people."

"True, but you're depriving other couples of being given a chance to be considered."

Catherine lifted beseeching eyes to Jim. "Then we've got to pray the judge will overlook that aspect when he considers the positives. I didn't force Terrie to write that letter. In fact I didn't seriously consider the idea of adopting Bonnie until Terrie was dying."

"I'll put that in the deposition and file it with these papers. Have you answered all the questions?"

"Yes."

Cole nodded.

"Then all I need are your signatures at the bottom. I'll date them."

Once she'd affixed hers she glanced at him again. "How long do you think it will take before we can get a hearing?"

He gazed at her speculatively. "Judge Lander has a busy court docket, but I think I can safely say a week."

A week…

Sensing her disappointment, Cole's hand covered hers. "Jim will get it done sooner than that."

The other man pushed himself away from the

table and stood up. Smiling down at Catherine, he said, "The Farraday name will have more pull than anything I say, but I'll try my best."

"Thank you, Jim. We love Bonnie. You have no idea how much this means to us."

"I think I do." He regarded both of them fondly. "For what it's worth I applaud you for the unselfish step you're taking for that little baby. The minute I know something I'll be in touch."

"If the judge rules in our favor, the case will be sealed?"

"Absolutely. No one will have access to the record so your secret will be safe. I've known Buck for years. I attended his wedding to Lucy and understand why Cole wants his reputation protected. Now Lucy can never be hurt. It will be up to you if you ever decide to tell Bonnie her true parentage."

Catherine's gaze swerved to Cole's. He always seemed to know what she was thinking because he said, "If the time comes we feel it necessary, then we'll tell her." She gave him an assenting nod.

"Well, my work seems to be done here. I'll be going and leave you two newlyweds alone."

She got up from the table and gave Jim a hug, which he reciprocated.

While Cole walked him to the elevator, Catherine hurried into her bedroom to change. The word "newlyweds" had caused a strange flutter in her chest.

She unpinned her corsage.

After the mistake she'd made kissing Cole the

way you would as a prelude to making love, the worst thing she could do was waltz out there in a minute to talk to him wearing a nightgown.

The fear that her heated response might have surprised him in a negative way gnawed at her, but she honestly hadn't been able to hold back. Embarrassed just thinking about it, she quickly removed her wedding finery and slipped on jeans, which she coordinated with a short-sleeved cotton sweater in a lilac color.

"What have you got there?" he asked as she darted from the bedroom and hurried over to the fridge behind the bar.

"The flowers you gave me. They're so beautiful I want them to stay fresh." She moistened a paper napkin to lay over them, then put the corsage on one of the shelves. Once the door was shut she turned to him, hoping she appeared composed. What a fraud she was.

His suit jacket hung over one of the chairs. He'd loosened the collar of his shirt and pulled the tie away. She felt his shuttered gaze from across the expanse.

"I haven't taken time off to play in a long, long time," he began. "Have you?" The question caught her off guard.

"Not that I remember."

A faint smile tugged at his lips. "That's what I thought. How would you like to fly down to Laguna Beach tomorrow? We'll spend a few days sunning in the surf. Forget our worries. It will give us some time to relax and get to know each other without deadlines."

"I'd like that a lot, but—"

"You don't want to leave Bonnie." He could read her mind.

"That sounds pathetic, doesn't it?"

"No. You're making sounds like a mother."

She rubbed her palms against womanly hips. "It's just that Bonnie has needed so much love and attention. Now that she's in foster care, I go by to see her every day, either before or after work."

His indulgent eyes had been following her movements. "Then let me suggest something closer to home. After we visit her in the morning, we could drive over to Lake Tahoe for the day and have dinner somewhere before returning to the hotel. Each day we'll go someplace different, and the day after that, until we have news. What do you say?"

She felt her heart expand. "I think you already know. It's a wonderful idea. I—I haven't known you long, but I believe you're a wonderful man." The words had come out of her mouth before she could stop them, but in all honesty he deserved to hear the truth.

"If it turns out we can adopt Bonnie, she's going to be the luckiest little girl in the world to have you for a father." She dragged her eyes away from him. "Goodnight, Cole."

Four days later they got the call from Jim to meet him in the judge's chambers for the verdict. He stood inside waiting.

Catherine's heart was beating so hard she thought

she would faint. Cole put a supportive arm around her while they waited for the judge to enter.

"Be seated," he told them.

The judge took his place and put on his glasses. "Mr. and Mrs. Farraday? I've read over your adoption petition. It's an unusual case. Your recent marriage concerns me, in that the two of you haven't lived together, therefore no climate has been established to measure. On the other hand, for you to enter into this union tells me of your unqualified love for this child who has no mother or father living. I find it commendable that Mr. Farraday, an upstanding member of the community and this state, wants to father his deceased brother's child. I'm also impressed by Mrs. Farraday's impeccable record as a social worker.

"I'm further moved by Terrie Cloward's testimony that if Mrs. Farraday hadn't intervened on her behalf from the beginning of her stay at Girls' Haven she would have run away, putting herself and the baby in jeopardy. Her plea that Mrs. Farraday become the adoptive mother has been duly noted.

"I would like to say I was particularly touched by the part in Mrs. Farraday's deposition concerning her feelings for the baby while she was in the hospital those five weeks, fighting for her life. The depositions taken from the hospital staff and the temporary foster mother, Carol Wilson, not only verify her constant devotion, they assert that the baby has bonded with Mrs. Farraday. I'm of the opinion that if it's at all possible, that bond should not be broken."

He took off his glasses and leaned forward. "After weighing everything carefully, I hereby grant full custody of Bonnie Cloward to the Farradays. Let it be noted in the record that, as of today, she will bear the legal name Bonnie Farraday. Congratulations."

"Cole—"

His hand squeezed hers until she felt the new wedding band she'd bought him pressing into her skin. He had a strength he wasn't aware of, but she was so happy she didn't care.

"Thank you, Your Honor," they both said at the same time.

He smiled. "Mr. Darger? If you'll come forward, I'll give you the signed order allowing the Farradays to pick up their daughter at the Wilson home immediately."

Cole crushed her against his hard body. "We did it, Catherine," he murmured into her hair. "Little Bonnibelle is ours."

Catherine sobbed for joy. "If it weren't for you—"

"Bonnie needed both of us for this to happen."

A beaming Jim walked over to them, waving the order in his hand. Cole clapped him on the shoulder while still holding onto Catherine.

"That was a brilliant piece of work you did, getting those other depositions, Jim."

"I told you bonding was everything with this judge."

She kissed the other man's cheek. "We'll never be able to thank you enough."

CHAPTER EIGHT

COLE'S four-seater Cessna glided to a flawless halt at Elko Regional Airport. He flashed the pilot his thanks for a problem-free flight from Reno. With precious cargo in the seats behind them, he hadn't wanted anything to go wrong.

He'd called ahead to his brother, asking him to meet him and bring the suburban. "Come alone," he'd advised him. "I'll explain when we see each other."

From the co-pilot's window he watched John get out and walk toward the plane. Since Catherine had agreed to marry him, the excitement filling Cole's veins kept intensifying in quantum leaps. In about a minute his hatless brother was going to get the surprise of his life.

While Catherine was busy unbuckling Bonnie's carrycot, Cole climbed out on the hot tarmac behind the pilot.

John spoke first. "Hey—long time no see."

So much had happened in the time he'd been away that Cole didn't know himself anymore.

"What's up?" Though John sounded his same old self, lines of grief were still etched in the bronzed face that resembled their brother's. It was the face of Cole's little girl.

"Plenty."

John stared at him quizzically. "You look…good. Different…" He tucked his thumbs into the side pockets of his jeans. "Mind telling me what's been going on? The family's starting to worry."

Cole sucked in his breath. "Everyone can relax. You're looking at a married man."

While he left his brother standing there dumbfounded, he turned to Catherine, who handed him the carrycot. Their eyes met in a private glance before he helped her to the ground with his free hand.

Those pure blue orbs reflected anxiety. His sent her a message not to worry.

"John?" He drew his new family toward his brother. "Meet my wife, Catherine, and our little girl."

His brother did a double take. Beneath his tan, his face paled from shock.

With the advantage of surprise on his side, Cole drew the baby out of her infant seat and cradled her in his arm, being careful that the receiving blanket shielded her eyes from the rays of a blazing noonday sun.

"Bonnibelle?" He kissed her pert nose. She'd enjoyed the flight and was awake and alert. "Say hello to your Uncle John, who's going to love you like crazy."

His brother looked with wonder into her adorable face. Cole knew the second John recognized the Farraday brand, because a strange sound came out of his throat followed by a low whistle.

In the next instant his brownish-black head reared. Awestruck hazel eyes flew from Cole to the blond vision standing next to him. They filled with male admiration before switching back to Cole again, his gaze saying it all.

"Congratulations, you two." John continued to stare at them. "You're a dark horse, you know that, bro?" he growled, before breaking into a yelp of joy, erasing the grief lines noticeable a minute ago.

The noise made the baby cry, but she settled down quickly after Cole put her against his shoulder and rubbed her back. Since they'd picked her up at the Wilsons' a few days ago, he'd spent day and night with her.

Between him taking cat naps on Catherine's couch, and her in the bedroom, they'd alternated getting up with Bonnie for her feedings. Once installed at his house, however, their sleeping arrangements were going to change…

They'd already achieved a certain harmony that made him sensitive to the silent entreaty Catherine had just sent him.

He flashed his brother a glance. "Let's get Bonnie out of the heat. Then we'll answer all your questions."

In another minute John had helped them with the luggage while Cole assisted Catherine into the backseat. With a minor adjustment of the strap through the base, he put the carrycot holding Bonnie next to her. But he found it impossible to be this close to his wife without touching her.

Since the ceremony he'd been living for the next opportunity to satisfy his increasingly growing hunger for her. Cole wasn't above using his family to force her to play house with him. In time he would get her to respond to him when they were alone.

At the moment his brother provided a convenient audience for him to give her unsuspecting mouth a long, deep kiss. When he eventually tore his mouth from hers, John would have to have been blind not to see the blush that swept into her face before he started up the car.

Once out on the highway he gave Cole a furtive wink, obviously no longer wondering what his big brother had been doing away from the ranch all this time.

Cole grinned back. They'd always been close, and for the most part could read each other's thoughts without speaking.

"Okay." He relented at last, sensing his brother's impatience for an explanation. "What do you want to know first?"

John shook his head. He looked through the rearview mirror at Catherine. "You're the beautiful mystery woman Janine told us about—the one who came to the house the day of Buck's funeral."

Air locked in Cole's lungs while he waited for his wife's response.

"I was the unwitting intruder, yes. From the beginning Cole and I had a stormy relationship because— Well, it doesn't matter now why. But when he asked me to marry him, I turned him down flat."

"That had to be a first!" John chuckled before glancing at Cole for his reaction.

Cole nodded. "Remember last fall, when you told me I was a hard man to be around sometimes?"

"*Sometimes*— I've said that to you more times than I can count, but I do recall you were particularly difficult to reach back then. I thought it had to do with the ongoing range war over grazing rights."

"That's a problem that never goes away," Cole muttered. "But the truth is, I couldn't take it when Catherine turned me down."

"I—I couldn't take it either," came a tremulous voice from the backseat. "I loved Cole. Saying no to him turned out to be the biggest mistake of my life. When I discovered I was pregnant, I knew I needed to tell him. But I didn't want the pregnancy to complicate the issue between us, so I kept him in the dark as long as I could. He kept coming to Reno to see me, and I continued to say no to him, all because of my stupid pride. Ultimately he found out I was expecting. That's when it got really bad, because I knew I'd hurt him by not telling him. In the end I realized I'd been a total fool. Unfortunately it took until last week to get up enough courage to ask him to marry me because we had a daughter who needed her daddy as much as I did."

Even if the story had been manufactured, the throb in her voice couldn't be faked. It reached down inside the core of Cole's psyche, moving him in inexplicable ways.

"Incredible. So how did you two meet?"

"At a resort on the north end of Lake Tahoe," Catherine volunteered.

She had to be thinking of the one they'd gone to earlier in the week while they'd been waiting to hear from Jim. She was doing such a superb job, Cole was happy to sit back and let it all happen.

"One of the condos in my fourplex had a fire. I had to find a place to stay for a few days. When I went outside for a swim, your brother was doing laps in the pool. We more or less collided."

"It was fate," Cole proclaimed with a satisfied smile.

Another low whistle issued from John's lips. "This is going to knock the family up one side of the Rubies and down the other."

By now they'd entered the property, and would be coming up on the lake soon.

"It will get Penny and Rosemary off my back."

"No kidding."

"While Catherine and I settle in at my house, do us a favor and break the news to everyone? We'll be over for dinner later."

His brother's head jerked toward him. "Your place isn't exactly set up for a baby."

"All we need for tonight is a crib. Tomorrow we'll figure out everything else."

"I'll bring over the one we used for Susie. It's in the storage room somewhere."

Cole thumped his brother on the shoulder. "Thanks."

"We appreciate your coming to pick us up," Catherine chimed in. "Cole's told me so much about his family. I've been looking forward to meeting all of you."

"You don't know the half of it. To be frank, our family has feared this day would never come!"

Cole made a grunting sound. "Now that it has, better make room for more Farradays. Bonnie's going to need a little brother or sister before long."

Brother or sister—

What?

Catherine broke out in a cold sweat.

A "real" marriage she understood. Cole might have been giving her time to get used to the idea, but she realized he expected they'd be sleeping together soon. If only he knew that she could hardly breathe, waiting for it to happen.

However, another baby wasn't something they'd ever discussed. If he was looking forward to getting her pregnant, then they needed to talk as soon as possible.

After they'd circled the lake to the house, Cole climbed out of the suburban with Bonnie, visibly excited they were home. She could tell because that air of restlessness about him while they'd been in Reno had left him.

While John took their things inside, Catherine hung back on the porch, ostensibly to look at the view. When he reappeared he told her he'd be back with the crib.

She put a hand on his arm to detain him. "That's very kind of you, John, but I've been thinking about it, and I'd rather your family didn't know anything about us until we come over for dinner. We'll get the crib then."

Or *not*.

She trembled. It all depended on Cole's reaction once they'd talked.

His eyes danced. "You're asking me to hold back that kind of news?"

Catherine liked John a lot. No doubt she would have felt the same way about Buck.

Her eyes implored him. "Do you mind?"

"Nope. We *are* a pretty terrifying lot." Then he grinned. "Now that Cole's a married man, he might as well realize up-front he's no longer the big boss around here."

She kissed John's cheek. "Bless you."

After waving him off, she walked inside the house. There was Cole at the living room window, chatting with Bonnie while they stared out at the spectacular vista. She studied them for a minute.

He'd bonded so completely with the baby, and she to him. If there was going to be an annulment after all, the two of them would be fine.

Riddled with fresh pain, Catherine searched for the diaper bag among their suitcases. The sound brought Cole's dark head around.

"I'm pretty sure Bonnie needs changing," she explained, uncomfortably aware he could sense she was feeling guilty about something.

She spread the changing pad on the first piece of furniture she came to, which happened to be a brown leather couch. Cole crossed the expanse and laid the baby down without saying anything. Her nervousness increased so much she had trouble unfastening Bonnie's pink stretchy suit.

"H-how did I do?" she blurted.

"A propos to what?" came his deceptively mild query.

"Wh-what I told John."

"Since I wasn't out on the porch with the two of you, you must mean while we were in the car?"

She moaned. "Yes."

"I believed your account to the point I decided we'd lived your version in a parallel universe."

"If John is the litmus test, do you think we passed?" She slid a fresh diaper beneath the baby.

"What do your instincts tell you?" He answered with another question. Cole was angry. She didn't blame him. They'd had no secrets until now.

He stood by with the baby wipes and ointment, unaware of his physical impact on her senses. They were crying for the assuagement only he could give. But when he learned the truth, she might never know rapture with him.

She kissed Bonnie's tummy. "They don't. John's wonderful, just like you, but he's not my brother."

"He was snagged when you threw out the line about you asking me to marry you. John's aware it would take something that dramatic for me to get off my high horse and come crawling back to you. It was the part of your story that turned the corner for him."

Her pulse accelerated. "I'll remember that," she quipped, to cover her hectic emotions. "Won't we, sweetheart?"

When she'd finished snapping the material around the baby's tiny feet and legs, he picked her up. "Come on, Bonnibelle. It's time to give you and your mommy a tour of our home. This is where we're all going to live forever."

There was that word again.

She started to shake and couldn't stop. Cole was saying that now, but when he learned what she had to tell him...

The bachelor pad turned out to be a modern two-bedroom rambler, with two bathrooms, a den, and a great room with a wood-burning fireplace. Everything was done in a light tan color, with high ceilings and lots of bare windows giving their own close up views of the pine-tree-lined lake and the fabulous Ruby Mountains.

A sweep of open area from front room to kitchen made it seem larger. No curtains or frills. No knick-knacks. Just good, basic functional living, with the beauty of the architectural design of trusswork and cutouts providing the interest.

He'd made a concession to window coverings in

both bedrooms, but he'd left the blinds open. Cole was a man who worked out in the open and obviously wanted to create that same feeling indoors.

Catherine loved everything about it.

Though she could see some of her things, including her favorite McKnight painting of Corfu to add color, most of them would have to stay in storage. Of necessity having a baby in the house would guarantee a lot of clutter.

Cole had promised they'd drive to Elko to outfit the second bedroom into a nursery. For the moment it contained a twin bed and dresser, nothing more. For a niece or nephew to sleep over, perhaps?

At a glance it was clear he'd wanted no hint of past memories when he'd had this built. If he needed to touch base with his life before his wife died, all he had to do was sprint around the lake to the main ranch house.

Maybe it was wrong of Catherine, but she was fiercely glad no other woman had lived here with him.

While they finished walking around, Bonnie started making noises. "Sounds like she's hungry. You can set your watch by her."

She felt Cole's masculine chuckle resonate in every cell of her body. "Lie down in our bedroom with her. I'll bring the diaper bag." They still had several bottles of the prepared formula they'd brought on the plane. The rest was in an extra suitcase.

When they entered the room, Cole must have noticed her surreptitious glance at the king-size bed.

"I bought everything new when I moved in." Meaning his wife hadn't slept in it, in case Catherine was wondering.

It was scary how fast he connected the dots, no matter how obscure to anyone else. But then he wouldn't be the head of the Bonnibelle if he didn't have that remarkable capacity necessary to run a successful cattle empire.

Meeting Catherine had kept him away from his work a long time. Yet he hadn't touched on the subject.

That was because of Bonnie. She had him wrapped so tightly around her baby finger, Catherine hardly recognized him as the forbidding security guard. One who'd been prepared to drag her from the car if she didn't confess what she was doing there the day of Buck's funeral.

Driven by pain, she now understood, and she had no doubt that man would have carried out his threat—to hell with anyone who might be watching.

But the rugged black-haired male who'd just come back in the bedroom and laid down next to her and Bonnie bore little resemblance to the other man.

After handing her the bottle, he propped his head with his hand to watch them through veiled eyes. The baby drank thirstily, making loud noises.

His mouth widened in amusement. He was such a beautiful male. Catherine had to close her eyes against his overpowering charisma.

"You're a true Farraday, Bonnibelle. No one enjoys a good meal more than I do."

Catherine had thought he was going to say Buck, which only proved how total was the transformation from uncle to father.

CHAPTER NINE

AFTER Bonnie's feed, she was out like a light.

As Catherine's eyes slid away, they met the storm-cloud gray of Cole's.

"It's time to tell me what you were doing out on the porch with John." His low, penetrating voice wasn't quite a demand. "What did I say that put you off? You were different before we even got out of the car."

She swallowed uneasily.

Cole was so intuitive she could never hide anything from him. After her experience with him the first time they met, she didn't dare hold back. He'd only find a way to get it out of her. His methods guaranteed success.

She didn't want to fight with him. Especially with the innocent baby sleeping peacefully between them.

"If you must know, you and I never talked about— about having more children."

The quiet that fell after her comment could hardly be described as comfortable. She could almost hear the air crackle with tension.

His brows arched quizzically. "Isn't that part of what a real marriage implies?"

"Yes," came the lame concession.

"So what's the problem?" he infused in an unruffled tone.

She choked out, "The problem is *me.*"

"In what way?" he persisted.

"Not so loud. We're going to wake the baby."

Unable to handle the nature of their conversation being this close to him, she rolled off the bed, careful to leave Bonnie undisturbed. Cole followed her into the hall.

Before she reached the living room she felt a pair of strong male hands close over her shoulders, arresting her movements. His body heat permeated the silky material of her coffee-colored blouson. Combined with his natural scent, it all worked like an aphrodisiac on her senses.

He lifted the silvery gold strands away from her neck. "I'm the one who's been a fool," he whispered, letting his lips graze her heated skin. "I've been trying to give you time to get used to me. But it appears I've unwittingly sent the wrong signal."

"I-it's not that—" she tried to tell him, but the feel of his mouth created exquisite pleasure, robbing her of the ability to think clearly.

"Surely you know how much I want you?" His hands slid down her arms to her caress her hips. "I haven't been able to hide it. Bonnie might have been the catalyst to bring us together this fast, but believe me— I felt the desire to make love to you even as you were evading my questions in front of the ranch house."

"Cole—" she cried in absolute panic. Much as his admissions thrilled her, she couldn't let this go on.

His hands stilled against her trembling body. "What is it? I know you want me too. It isn't something you can hide."

"I—I'm not trying to. But first there's something I have to tell you that could change everything."

He twisted her around. She glimpsed silvery eyes molten with desire. "Don't be silly," he murmured against her lips, gripping her waist to bring her against him.

With undeniable mastery he explored her mouth, tasting and finding every part of it. The fire he'd lit was starting to engulf her. This was a husband's kiss, hot with desire.

Her husband. A man who might not want to claim that title once he'd heard what she had to tell him.

"Please, Cole—" She fought for air, really frightened now, because she could feel herself succumbing to the wanton needs he'd aroused.

"Don't you understand I *want* to please you?" he growled softly against her ear, sending little sparks of delight through her sensitized body.

He was too drugged by passion, too intent on making love to her, to listen. With Bonnie asleep for the next few hours, there was nothing to interfere with this ecstasy.

She shivered voluptuously, because she was

drowning in a sensual haze he'd created that was sapping her power to resist him. Somehow they wound up against the wall, their mouths and bodies insatiable.

"Hey, Uncle Cole—"

A young male voice called out with excitement. At first Catherine thought she must have dreamed it.

"Mom said you were back. Where've you been?"

The voice was coming closer.

Catherine struggled to surface, but she didn't make it in time.

"Oops—" the boy exclaimed.

Incredibly it was Cole who managed to ease himself away from her. Luckily she was still pressed up against the wall, which worked as a support until she could compose herself.

Cole turned to their young intruder. She could hear his ragged breathing. "Hey, Gavin—haven't you learned to knock yet before you barge in on people?"

The dark-haired boy wearing jeans and cowboy boots couldn't be more than ten. He hunched his shoulders, eyeing his uncle warily. "Sorry. I didn't know anyone else was here."

Of course the news that Cole was back had spread. But relief swept through Catherine that John had kept his promise.

"Exactly my point," Cole barked at his nephew.

Before another word was said, Catherine needed to talk to Cole in private.

"Hi, Gavin," she spoke up. "If you'll give me a

minute with your uncle, then he's all yours. Wh-why don't you go out in the living room?"

He stared at her like she was the great mystery of the ages. "Sure."

She reached for Cole's hand and drew him into the second bedroom, shutting the door behind them. When he turned to her, she hardly recognized him for his wintry expression.

His brows had formed a black bar above his eyes. "What's going on with you?" He grasped her upper arms.

Her throat tightened. "I was trying to tell you b-before you started kissing me. I didn't know having more children was included in our agreement."

She felt his fingers tighten around her flesh. "When I explained that I wanted a real marriage, you said you understood."

"I did, because I realized you meant we'd be sleeping together. But until you mentioned bringing more brothers and sisters into the world I had no idea you'd included that as part of it."

For a second she thought she saw a glint of pain in those cloudy depths.

"I guess I should have known, but all I had on my mind at the time was Bonnie." She tried to swallow but couldn't. "Naturally it's your dream to rear a family. So what I'm trying to tell you is that it's still not too late to annul our marriage. That's why I asked John not to say anything to the family yet."

Cole's hard mouth had taken on a whitish tinge. He was livid. She didn't blame him.

"I'm going to leave for Reno in the next few minutes. All you have to do is explain to Gavin I'm the woman who had your baby, but we couldn't work things out. After considering what was best for Bonnie, we decided to let you raise her."

His eyes had formed slits, which caused her to speak faster and faster. "In private you can tell John the whole truth and this will all be over."

Her eyes glistened, but she refused to cry in front of him. "You've won Bonnie legally. She's where she should be. I'm glad I was the one who could help you, but you're not in love with me. In time the right woman will come along. Love will happen naturally, the way it's supposed to. She'll fill that ache in your heart and give you the family you dreamed of having with Jenny."

"What's this about?" came a voice of ice. "Your idea of revenge for the man who destroyed your dreams?"

She backed away from him, shaking her head. "You couldn't really have asked me that question. I'm doing this to help you attain *yours*. To satisfy your curiosity, the man you think I was involved with was a pathetic teenager my own age. It was the first time for both of us, and from every aspect a miserable mistake. Telling him I was pregnant scared both of us to death. I never saw him again."

Maybe she imagined a momentary bleakness lurking in the recesses of his eyes.

Taking advantage of his bemused state, she rushed past him and opened the door. Before he could stop her she made it down the hall to the living room.

Gavin was sitting on one of the chairs, playing with a small, battery-operated video game. He flashed her a surprised glance. She smiled at him, reached for her purse and suitcase and flew out the front door. By the time she made it to the truck, Cole was almost at her heels.

If the gods were kind, it would be unlocked.

They were more than kind. His keys were in the ignition.

"Whoa, Uncle Cole. Was she ever mad!"

"She's scared."

Catherine reminded him of a graceful filly who needed special handling to get her to come to him willingly. It was his own fault for pushing every damn button guaranteed to make her skittish.

Gavin looked up at him. "Of you?"

"Not exactly. It's complicated."

He pulled out his cellphone and called Mack.

"Hey, boss—glad you're back."

"It's good to be home, but I'm without transportation at the moment. Do me a favor and catch up to the woman driving my power wagon. If you hurry you'll reach her before she hits the highway."

"What woman would that be?"

"My wife."

Mack chortled. "Hey, Cole—it's me you're talking to."

"Don't I know it. I'm counting on you to manage the impossible."

After a pause, "I'm on my way. Then what am I supposed to do?"

"Bring her back to my house."

"What if she doesn't want to come?"

"She will. Tell her Bonnie woke up feverish and is inconsolable."

"Who's Bonnie?"

"Our daughter."

"Maybe I'm in the middle of my own dream."

"It's no dream. I got married in Reno. Tell you about it later." He clicked off.

Gavin was all eyes. "You really got married?"

"I sure did. Want to come and take a peek at your new little cousin?"

Catherine had the turnoff from the Bonnibelle in her sights when a truck barreling down the road behind her whizzed past, kicking up dust. She couldn't believe it when the driver started to make a U-turn in front of her, forcing her to apply the brakes.

An authentic cowboy, maybe late forties, jumped down from the cab. He strode toward her in a well-worn Stetson.

Cole had sent him, of course. She was surprised she'd gotten this far before being apprehended. No one walked out on Cole. She dashed the moisture from her cheeks, but anyone with eyes could see she'd been sobbing.

He approached her, removing his hat. Squinting at her, he said, "Good afternoon, Mrs. Farraday."

That was all she needed to hear. The feathers were out of the pillow now. Air rushed from her lungs.

"I'm Mack Irvine, by the way."

Cole's ranch manager...

"How do you do, Mack?"

He held the hat in front of the brown plaid shirt covering his chest. "Cole says you need to get back to the house quick. Your daughter woke up and started to cry. He's pretty sure she's running a fever and needs you."

Catherine didn't believe it for a second, but she had no desire to argue with the man Cole not only revered but depended upon. What went on between her and her husband shouldn't have to upset the running of his ranch. Especially when the histrionics were a by-product of her own flawed nature.

She'd run away. Just like she'd done over and over during her teenage years. When she couldn't deal with reality, her answer was to take off. Apparently certain patterns couldn't be broken no matter how hard she'd fought to change them.

But for once in her life she had to go back and face the consequences. She owed it to Cole, who'd been nothing but wonderful to her and deserved to hear all the truth that was in her. What he decided to do with that knowledge wasn't her right to determine.

"Thank you for telling me," she said quietly. "I'll turn around."

Mack looked vastly relieved. He nodded, put on his hat and walked back to his truck.

CHAPTER TEN

COLE saw the power wagon coming from a long way off. While he waited for his wife to materialize, he made coffee, then propped his hip against the counter while he drank it.

At long last he was going to have the luxury of being in his own home with Catherine. No more interruptions, no deadlines.

Thanks to Rosemary, who'd come for Gavin and had gone crazy the second she'd laid eyes on the baby, she'd taken everyone home with her. No doubt at this moment the whole family was marveling over the latest addition to the Farraday clan.

Cole's eyes smarted. Maybe Buck was looking on too, from wherever he was.

He heard the truck pull up in front. In a moment footsteps sounded on the porch. She hadn't come charging back. He braced himself, not knowing if that was a good or bad sign. He'd married a complicated lady.

"Hi." The husky voice he'd loved from day one sounded deeper than usual.

"Hi yourself." He studied her where she was standing next to the kitchen table. She'd been crying her eyes out. He lifted a mug. "Coffee?"

"No, thank you." He could see her throat working. "Cole—"

"Bonnie's been kidnapped by the family. We'll be lucky if we see her again before sometime tomorrow. Gavin thinks she looks like his dad. Rosemary insists she's the image of Penny. You have to wonder how long it will be before someone says she resembles Buck."

A little sob escaped her throat. "I see you in her already."

"Spoken like a loyal wife."

She flinched. "I didn't give a very good impression of one earlier. Forgive me. I didn't mean to run away like that. I'm afraid it's an old habit when I don't want to face something unpleasant."

Sucking in his breath, Cole put the mug down. "Is the idea of getting pregnant again repugnant to you?"

She subsided into the nearest chair. "No."

His frustration grew. "Are you afraid of intimacy because of your former experience?"

"I-it's not that," she stammered.

He rubbed the back of his neck where the muscles were bunched. "Then it's me. You wanted Bonnie enough to marry me, but now the reality is too much for you to handle. Is that it?"

She flashed him a tortured look before she jumped

up from the chair. "I don't think I can have more children—that's why!"

Her answer flooded him with such great relief it took him a moment to respond. Unfortunately she read something else in that brief silence.

"You see?" she cried in undeniable turmoil, staring at him with wounded eyes. "I had sex with a boy, and my high-risk pregnancy probably ruined me for any more. My punishment for doing something I knew was wrong. But I didn't know how wrong until you talked about providing Bonnie with a brother or sister."

Tears gushed down her cheeks. "Do you have any idea how it killed me to hear you tell your brother you were looking forward to having a bigger family wh-when I was afraid we couldn't? And all because it was *my* fault?"

The rise of hysteria in her voice propelled Cole toward her. He crushed her in his arms. "Have you been checked recently by an OB who's of the same opinion?"

She burrowed her head against his shoulder. "No. I've been afraid to."

He rubbed her back in an attempt to console her. "Medical science has come a long way in the last decade to make conception possible for millions of couples. You know that."

"I don't think it's far enough for us, Cole." She sobbed against him, wetting his shirtfront. "That's why we need to get an annulment. My past mistake shouldn't prevent you from having the life you want."

She threw her head back to look at him.

What he wanted was to take away the pain from her drenched blue eyes. "I've got everything I want right here in front of me. The rest we can work out. Who knows? Maybe I'm infertile."

Her hands formed fists against his chest. "Don't be ridiculous! Haven't you heard anything I've been saying? You're too good a man to have married me. I'm like a tumbleweed out on the desert. I came from somewhere, but who knows where? I've rolled along here and there, with every gust of wind. I know nothing of my roots, whereas you can point back to your Farraday ancestors with pride."

Her trembling body bespoke her agony.

"Catherine—"

"Let me finish. I sensed how honorable you were the first time we met. You're a breed apart from any man I've ever known. Bonnie will never know how blessed she was that you claimed her. But when she grows older, what will be her opinion of a mother with no family, no clue to her background?"

He clasped her face between his hands. "Listen to me—what matters is what you've made of yourself! That's all that matters where any human being is concerned! Knowing your pedigree doesn't give you a pass in this life, Catherine. We all make mistakes. I've made a ton of my own. Some I'm not particularly proud of. Until you came into my life, I was a mess."

She shook her head. Her eyes were still swimming in tears. "I don't believe it."

"Gavin could tell you. So could the other children—*Uncle Cole's mean.*"

She sniffed. "If you're so awful, how come he came running into the house whooping it up because you're back?"

"Because children are forgiving. Haven't you noticed?"

"Yes," she confessed.

"Adults have a much harder time of it. I know one woman who needs to forgive herself so she can make this man happy." He kissed her luscious mouth. "I'm in love with you, darling. So much it hurts."

"But you can't be—"

"Let's get something straight, then we never have to talk about it again. If this weren't the real thing, I wouldn't have asked you to marry me under any circumstances. After meeting you, I discovered I wanted you, long before I saw Bonnie. The second I saw her, I wanted her too. Since then I've tried to show you in every way but one. Maybe going to bed will help."

Her eyes grew slumberous. "I think it will." She slid her arms around his neck. "Oh, Cole—" She pressed kisses all over his handsome face. "I've been wanting you to make love to me forever—I adore you." Her voice shook. "You have no idea how much."

For an answer, his mouth came down on hers, urgent and avid. Flames of desire licked her veins, turning her into a breathless supplicant. She didn't remember being carried to the bedroom. All she knew was that she was in his arms, trying to satisfy her craving for him.

Hours later, when the stars had faded over the Ruby Mountains and the sun was about to come up, she had to give herself a talk about leaving him alone. He was in a deep sleep at last.

She should have been sated by now, yet she realized the craving for him was worse than before and would never go away.

Out of the semidarkness she heard a velvet voice whisper, "Come here." Cole pulled her on top of him, trapping her legs.

Her breath caught. "I didn't mean to waken you."

"That's the first lie you've told me all night," he teased, kissing her in a certain spot.

Her face crimsoned. "Do you know how embarrassing it is to want your husband so much you have no shame?"

"There's no shame when two people love each other as much as we do. Only a hot-blooded woman like you could ever hold me. When my time comes—"

"Stop—" She put a hand over his mouth. "I don't ever want to think about that."

He pressed a moist kiss to her palm. "Naturally I'm hoping it won't be until after a lifetime of loving. But when it does happens—remind me to thank my little brother. Without him I would never have known this kind of happiness."

"Cole, darling—" she cried in an aching voice.

Once again her world spun away in a ritual of giving and taking and unspeakable pleasure. Catherine's entrancement was so total she didn't realize at once that someone was ringing the doorbell.

"Sweetheart—"

"Ignore it and they'll go away. I have other things to do," he whispered, plundering her mouth.

The bell pealed again.

"Cole?" She tried to breathe. "I think we'd better get it. Maybe something's wrong with Bonnie."

"Someone would have phoned."

"Maybe it's Mack."

A groan escaped. "All right. I'll get it." He pressed another hungry kiss to her mouth before rising from the bed.

She watched her gorgeous husband shrug into a toweling robe and leave the bedroom. In another minute she could hear Cole say, "Gavin—where's the fire?"

"The family wants you and Catherine to come over for breakfast, but they were afraid you wouldn't answer the phone."

"Then why didn't you just come in and tell us?"

"But yesterday you told me not to barge in!"

"That was yesterday."

"You don't sound mad anymore. I guess she's not afraid of you anymore either?"

"Nope."

"That's good, huh?"

"Yup."

Catherine had to cover her mouth to hold in her laughter. If this was how things were going to be on the Bonnibelle from now on, she could handle a hundred lifetimes of it.

CELEBRITY WEDDING OF THE YEAR

Melissa James

Melissa James is a mother of three, living in a beach suburb in New South Wales, Australia. A former nurse, waitress, shop assistant, and perfume and chocolate demonstrator, among other things, she believes in taking on new jobs for the fun experience. She'll try anything at least once to see what it feels like – a fact that scares her family on regular occasions. She fell into writing by accident, when her husband brought home an article stating how much a famous romance author earned, and she thought, 'I can do that!' She can be found most mornings walking and swimming at her local beach with her husband, or every afternoon running around to her kids' sporting hobbies, while dreaming of flying, scuba diving, belaying down a cave or over a cliff – anywhere her characters are at the time!

Dear Reader,

I am so happy to be taking part in Mills & Boon's centenary celebrations with this Marriage of Convenience anthology!

Mills & Boon have been crafting happy endings for one hundred years now – and I am so glad to be part of that tradition. In a world where that doesn't happen as often as it ought to, I love to read stories of hope, that have a positive outcome, that show the best of humankind. I also love to to create stories of love and commitment and tender romance. I am proud to be an author for Mills & Boon, and give people stories they can read over and over again, to come back to as an old friend when life can become overwhelming.

In *Celebrity Wedding of the Year*, I have taken the traditional marriage of convenience story and given it a fun twist. I hope it becomes a friend on your bookshelf, one you can turn to for a guaranteed smile.

Happy reading, and thank you for joining in our centenary celebrations!

Melissa

PROLOGUE

1977

It seems rock wild child Billy Browning is at it again—with the wife of the founder of Solutions for Poverty. Nice one, Billy...

1982

How brief "forever" can be in the music industry. End Game's guitarist Billy Browning has left his wife and two-year-old daughter Mia for a blond starlet fifteen years his junior...

1996

Billy Browning has checked himself into rehab for the seventh time—but he has had full custody of his daughter Mia since his ex-wife died last year. Child psychologists worry about the child's exposure to his wild lifestyle. Where is Mia while her father dries out again?

2000

The most successful lead singer of End Game has

called it quits. After four years C.J. Hunter has left the band for reasons unknown and gone into hiding. Guitarist Billy Browning has called for auditions for a new singer, but seems to be busier doing the rounds of international parties with his press secretary Michelle Glaser, who is half his age. His third marriage ended a month ago, which seems to be Browning's maximum mourning period.

2001

Since C.J. Hunter left End Game he's gone from strength to strength. The former rock god won a Grammy for "Shades of Gray", the number one song he wrote for End Game. He refused his invitation to the Grammys, concentrating on his studies at Sydney University. He's in his second year of medical school, and has ambitions to enter the research field.

The world of rock music is poorer for his leaving it.

2007

It seems Billy Browning never changes. Despite his vigorous denials, it seems he's in a relationship with Nicole Neilson, the estranged wife of his long-time friend crooner Martin Neilson. So much for loyalty, Billy!

A source close to Browning said today, "I don't know how much longer Mia can put up with her father's lack of morals. She's such a nice girl."

CHAPTER ONE

The Present Day

THE entire End Game family, including every lead singer since the band's inception in 1975, turned up in a "Who's Who" of rock to attend Billy Browning's wedding to Nicole Neilson. Browning married Nicole only four days after her return from Vegas, where she obtained a quickie divorce from crooner Martin Neilson. The private ceremony was surrounded by tight security. The couple are said to be very happy.

Browning and Neilson are said to be cruising in the Caribbean for their honeymoon. Browning's daughter Mia was unavailable for comment, but her publicist said to expect a special announcement from Mia soon.

The former lead singer of End Game, C.J. Hunter, approached for comment, said he'd never seen Billy so happy.

Martin Neilson apparently sent a telegram wishing them all the best.

A Month Later

"So that's it?" From the plush chair of the large, well-appointed office, Billy Browning frowned ferociously into his specialist's face. "I pay you an indecent amount of money to keep me healthy—"

"You're almost sixty, Billy," Dr. Bascombe said bluntly. "I haven't found the fountain of youth, and with your past..." He shrugged. "It was bound to catch up with you, even if you have been clean and healthy for the past five years."

"Hepatitis B," Billy whispered in horrified wonder. Shaking his head made his short silver hair shimmer in the glaring halogen lights of the private sanatorium. "There's no cure. It's not fair... I've tried so hard to change my life..."

His fourth wife, Nicole, squeezed his shoulder with sympathy. "You *have* changed your life, Billy."

A semi-conservatively dressed Billy glared at his doctor. "So why did this happen? Didn't I follow your every meticulous instruction to the letter?"

"Dad, it's awful, but it's not the doctor's fault." Mia Browning turned to the doctor. "What can we do to help?"

The doctor smiled at Mia with relief. Billy's temper tantrums were almost as famous as his revolving door love-life, and far more frightening. "We have drugs to stabilize the progress of the disease, and with a good diet and gentle exercise regime, it hopefully won't get worse for a few years."

"There's also a lot of herbal tonics that'll help, darling," Nicole said softly, and Billy smiled at her, albeit after a struggle.

"There *are* herbal tonics that *will* help." Her husband gently corrected her grammar with the pedantic nature which few of his fans knew. Nicole, who'd loved him for twenty-five years and knew he used his corrections to cover his fear, let it go with a smile.

"More than anything else you need absolute rest for three to six months, Billy," the doctor inserted.

All three of the Brownings stared at him; it was no wonder, given the paparazzi contingent camped outside. Since her father had married Nicole four weeks ago their life had become a circus again.

"Absolute rest, Billy," Dr. Bascombe repeated, looking stern. "You don't want to know what will happen if you push yourself, or allow life—and the press—to stress you."

Billy and Nicole sighed together. Even though yesterday's news was supposed to be old, Billy's past still haunted them all. Nicole had left Martin five months ago, and flown to Vegas for a divorce last month. The paparazzi still ran regular updates on *why* Billy would "steal" his friend's wife, and then marry her within days of her divorce being made legal. There'd even been a TV viewer poll with outrageous reasons for the "wife swap".

Mia sighed and bit her lip. From experience, she knew she had five minutes to come up with something before Nicole started crying and Dad began exploding. Entertaining was Dad's forte, not forward planning. The only plans he'd ever made that had worked had been flashes of spur-of-the-moment brilliance that always shocked Mia when they came.

She frowned. "Dad, you have to rest. You can't handle this situation about Uncle Martin. If I finish the book faster, he can come out earlier—"

"No." Billy said it firmly. "In this industry, timing, reputation and public perception are everything. Martin's been there for me through women and rehab, and he helped bring you up. He didn't blame me when Nicole came to me, blowing his cover. We have to wait until the book's release."

Uncle Martin had asked for six months before he went public with his love for his longtime secret partner, Dane Wilson, and openly announced that he was gay to his adoring female fan base. Mia, who was co-writing his autobiography, knew he was doing the right thing. In giving Uncle Martin these six months for people to wonder why Nicole had left him for Dad, the groundwork had been set.

"We have to come up with something else," Nicole said quietly. "I wouldn't hurt Martin for the world."

Mia smiled at her new stepmother. Nicole was small, plump and smiling, comfortable in her wrinkles and greying hair. At fifty-three, she was the oldest of Mia's stepmothers—and the nicest.

It had rocked her world to discover she hadn't really known her father until he'd got together with Nicole. It had been only then she'd discovered the reason for Dad's decades of stupid behavior and successively younger women—and for the clean-up of his life five years before. It had all been for the sake of the one woman he couldn't have, and couldn't live without.

He'd changed his world for Nicole.

Mia, though thrilled for her dad's happiness, felt rudderless. It wasn't just Dad and Nicole who needed a break, but until Dad was better she needed a plan.

Laughing green eyes flashed into her mind...a crooked, lazy smile and a voice like a rough angel.

Don't be stupid. That's not what counts here!

The crucial thing was that he was *the* C.J. Hunter. Every magazine in the country—and his very active fan base—still wanted to know about his life since he'd vanished from their world at the height of his fame. Since he'd won a second Grammy a few weeks ago, media interest had spiked.

Yes, yes—C.J. was perfect for this—if only he was up for it.

She bit her lip. They'd never truly been friends—but he was still close to Dad. Bribe, blackmail or call in the world's biggest favor. If she could only get him to do it, she could give her dad what he needed right now—and it would even help kick-start her own new career.

Billy smiled and whispered in Nicole's ear. "She

only gets that look when she thinks of him. I've been hoping since the wedding."

Nicole nodded, smiling at the girl she'd considered her daughter long before she'd gone to Billy. "I wonder if she even knows how she feels," she whispered back. "She wouldn't look at him at our wedding, but he couldn't stop looking at her…"

Billy nodded, a smile curving his mouth despite his health shock. "She's so much like Sarah." And she'd learned her mother's lessons too deeply.

For all his mistakes, he'd always known whom he loved. He didn't think he'd ever met a girl who knew her own desires and needs less than Mia did—and maybe that was his fault as well. He had to make it right. If Mia didn't take action on her happiness soon, for once he'd take over and stage-manage his daughter's life. He wasn't above using his illness to help if he had to. He knew C.J. wouldn't be hard to convince.

"We need a distraction," Mia announced. "Something has to happen that makes the paparazzi chase after someone else."

Billy lifted a brow. "Sorry, love. I don't think Paris or Angelina would announce something outrageous for an old rocker like me."

Mia rolled her eyes. "No, Dad, not the *usual* suspects. We want someone who'd cause a media flurry if they did something…out of the ordinary."

"Of whom were you thinking—and what would they do?" Nicole asked.

Slowly Mia looked up, seeing two hopeful faces

grinning at her—and she smiled back, feeling a rush of long-unfamiliar excitement. "I think it's best if the two of you know nothing. Plausible deniability and all that... But, suffice it to say, when everybody's good girl does the unexpected, hopefully the tabloid readers of the world will want to know about it."

He was completely wasted.

You wish, Hunter.

So he wasn't the kind of wasted he'd indulged in during his rocking days, but after thirty-six hours of Emergency Room roster, C.J. felt a little bit dizzy and totally inarticulate, as if he'd been drinking vodka straight for hours. He wouldn't risk driving his car home. It was in the hospital car park. He'd pick it up tomorrow or the next day, depending on when he woke up.

With a grin, he grabbed a cab outside the hospital and headed homeward. Ten whole days of freedom in a row before he began his surgery rotation: his last as a resident. Six more months and he'd be fully qualified, ready to start on the research track.

All the way home he thought of nothing but sleep, glorious sleep. Hitting the sack with a vengeance. A big, beautiful, empty bed—just him, splatted across the pillow-top mattress and catching lots of Zs.

The cab pulled up in front of his old house in a quiet Sydney street, and with a lazy smile he overpaid the guy who was smart enough to know when a guy wasn't up for a chat on the cricket or footy. He turned to the house. Sleep, glorious sleep...

Or not.

You've got to be kidding me!

Today of all days she showed up? Talk about turning a guy's hidden dreams into nightmares.

Though it had been more than seven years since he'd walked away from the world of rock music, her memory haunted him. Mia's silky pale skin and masses of glossy black hair, the dark brown eyes that looked on the world with an amused tranquility he ached to know, and her luscious, indescribable mouth jerked him awake in a sweat at night even now.

He'd loved her quaint sayings, her quick laughter, her reliable good sense, quiet irony and ruthless honesty: a refreshing reality check in the world of me-first rockers. He loved her curvaceous figure in a world of women who believed half-starved scrawniness meant beauty. Even the way her cute little John Lennon glasses perched on her nose had always turned him on...

But what *hadn't* done it for him was the way she'd always looked at him—like he was one species removed from a cockroach. Even four weeks ago, at Billy and Nicole's wedding, tearing his gaze from her had been an effort—but after the cool "hello to an old friend" hug, whenever she'd caught him staring her return glances had held amused disdain.

So why was she camped on his doorstep? And why *right now,* when his brain was so fuddled with exhaustion he couldn't find his defenses if they screamed in his ear?

And why was it still Mia that turned him upside-down and inside-out when he got a dozen offers a day even now, if a female patient or relative recognized C.J. Hunter of End Game as the exhausted doctor holding the patient notes? Other women made it clear they found him attractive, whether they knew his name or not.

And still it was Mia...

He slung his backpack over his shoulder and walked toward her. She was sitting on the top step of his half-renovated old house in Sydney's inner west: as good a hiding place as any, and light-years from his life of fame. "Well, this is a turn-up for the books. Mia Browning's actually sitting on my doorstep."

Mia uncrossed her legs from their odd, intricate weaving that always fascinated him, reminding him of a contortionist, and stood. Damn, how did that little half-smile of hers—like she had a delicious secret she wouldn't share—still make him think of all the things he shouldn't?

"Hi, C.J. Hope I'm not intruding?"

His mother would be horrified if he uttered one of the ungracious sentences that sprang to his lips. So he did the polite thing—or as polite as a man could be when firing on half a cylinder. "I was about to make coffee." *Before bed. Lots of bed.*

Bed and Mia. Not good in the same sentence.

He led the way into the house and straight to the

still-ugly-from-the-70s kitchen. But for once he didn't think of the renovation work to come. A massive caffeine hit was his only hope of sanity. Maybe when he had it he'd wake up and realize she was nothing but a mirage.

Mia put down the duffel bag she'd brought inside and said, "So, how've you been since the wedding, C.J.?"

Just hearing her voice, soft and pretty, with that tiny slur on her "s"s, gave his fingers that old itch— the one he'd never been able to scratch. Not to mention that she was so close to him her breath touched his skin—

Don't look at her.

He filled the kettle, set out mugs and cleaned the plunger from two- or three-day-old grounds, fervently hoping the milk hadn't gone off. He'd slept at the hospital the past two nights. "I'm fine, thanks. And you?"

"I'm fine—but Dad isn't."

At that C.J. swung around, spilling the coffee from the scoop. "Billy? What's the matter with him?"

Mia took the scoop from his hand, brushing his fingers as she did. "Sit. You've had a long shift, by the looks of you. Have you had breakfast?"

Grateful, cross-eyed, and too damned turned on for his level of exhaustion, he sat at the dining table. "Sort of."

"Don't tell me—a donut grabbed out of last night's box at five a.m.?"

"Pizza—and four a.m.," he corrected, rubbing his hand over his two-day growth of stubble. Wondering what she thought of him. Wondering why he cared after all this time.

But he knew why. Just like four weeks ago, he couldn't stop looking at her. Her thick fall of straight black hair, her curvy body, the way she tossed a quick smile over her shoulder, still did things to him he couldn't say out loud. Not to mention that she still had the sweetest butt he'd ever laid eyes on. Why couldn't she have put on twenty kilos and be all dimpled with cellulite?

"How old was the pizza?"

Her glasses slipped down her nose as she worked around the kitchen—the same glasses that always made him ache to kiss that slightly stubby little nose…and the rest of her… "Huh…what?" He rubbed his forehead. Right. Pizza. Age of pizza. "I'm not sure."

He reared back when she crouched in front of him, her face filling his line of vision with its little crinkle between her brows that sent a shaft of unwanted tenderness through him. So serious, so practical, and somehow so adorable—and he was the same sucker for her he'd been a decade ago.

"The doctor needs someone to look after him." She touched his hand, and the whole dizzy-and-inarticulate thing got worse—he was an incoherent wreck. "Coffee will be ready in twenty—along with a *decent* breakfast. Go shower, shave, and change into something ready for sleep. You know you want to," she added with a glimmering smile over her shoulder as she stood again and turned back to the kettle.

She really shouldn't smile like that at a guy with little to no control over his body's responses. "Thanks." The word was like a growl. Man, he hoped she thought it was tiredness. Because if she gave him that ol' cockroach look…

She took his hands and lifted him from the chair. "You're really exhausted. Go sleep, C.J. Shower and eat when you wake up. We'll talk later. I'll still be here."

"That's supposed to help me sleep?" he muttered. He lifted a hand when he saw her mouth fall open in obvious surprise. Mia's open lips acted on him like Mia and bed in one sentence, and he was *way* too tired for this. "Scratch that. I'm going."

At the door, memory—and curiosity—returned. "I won't sleep until I know. How's Billy—and why are you here? A call would have sent me to visit him."

She knew that. How many times had she called him in the past, only to see him running? And not only to see Billy, if only she knew it. Any chance to just look at her, to have her smile at him because he'd put himself out for Billy again, gave him a combination of soaring higher than on any medical substance he knew and weeks of frustration, because it never went further than a single smile. He'd lived on her last hug for weeks.

What a sucker.

She turned back from the coffeepot, and gave him the serious look he still adored after all this time. "Dad's got Hep B."

C.J. closed his eyes for a second. It didn't need deciphering—not with Billy's age and years of body abuse factored in. "He never took the vaccines I recommended?"

She shook her head. "He thought cleaning up his act was good enough. Dad and needles never got on." Her smile was rueful, accepting.

"What's he on?" He named the newest wonder-drug for treatment of the disease.

"He's on all the best cocktails. That's not the problem. He needs months of total rest—and since his wedding to Nicole…"

Again, he didn't need things spelled out. He knew all about groupies and media frenzies, which was why he'd left the life after four years.

Not that he regretted his time with the band. He still counted the guys among his closest friends, and his songs and royalties still gave him, his parents and his sister's family the luxuries in life whenever they wanted them. Not bad for a kid from the second-poorest suburb of Sydney. Auditioning for End Game had changed his life.

"Martin won't come out yet?" he asked, not really needing her head-shake. "So what can I do?" She wouldn't be here if she didn't need something from him. It couldn't be for his medical skills. Billy had the best.

"I was hoping you'd ask." The glow in her eyes was relief and hope—and a touch of admiration. She needed him at last…and it acted like a trip switch on him. *Yes, Mia, I'll do whatever you want if you keep looking at me like that!*

"Just spill," he said gruffly, hating the power she still held over him, when she couldn't care less. "I've worked thirty-six hours straight, I'm half-asleep, and this is a serious situation. What do you want?"

"I know it's serious," she snapped. "He's my father!"

His brows rose. Placid Mia hadn't given him that amused, sort of indulgent look, as if she was removed from the human race and all its over-the-top emotions. She'd snapped back. What was going on here? Despite there being no cure for Hep B, it wasn't as if Billy would die any time in the next decade, given the quality of treatment these days.

"So…?" he prodded deliberately. "Come on, Mia. We both know you're not here out of love for me. What do you want?"

To his surprise she blushed, and fiddled with the teaspoon in her hand. The way she worried her lower lip with her teeth made him want to find ways to stop her worrying so much all the time—but everything about Mia got to him. Always had, probably always would. He'd come to terms with it years ago, when she'd made it more than clear that she'd always be off-limits to him.

"Just say it, Mia," he repeated, more gently this time. "You know I'd do anything to help Billy."

She drew in a deep breath and smiled that hopeful smile at him again, like he'd become her personal savior.

Bad mistake to unleash *that* on a tired, aroused man—or maybe it was calculated? *Damn, damn, damn.* Now he almost wanted the cockroach look back. Anything to stop this crazy tangle of thoughts in his head.

Showers-bed-Mia. Wet and smiling at him…

Then her words soaked into his fogged skull and shock ran right through his body, like someone had used crash cart paddles on him. "*What* did you say?" He hung onto the door lintel for support.

He'd fallen asleep. That was what it was. He was dreaming of her again.

Then the words came back to him, like a tennis ball rebounding in his face over the net.

"I want you to elope with me."

CHAPTER TWO

ALL her life Mia had loved peace and silence, but when you were waiting for a man to answer a proposal of marriage it got downright unnerving. C.J. was staring at her as if she was an interesting disease he'd like to cure—if only he could work out what kind.

"Well?" she said—or squeaked—when she couldn't stand it any more.

He gave her a slow smile. "I'm waiting."

"For what?" Hadn't she said enough?

"The rest," he said patiently. "You never call me unless Billy needs something. You never could stand the sight of me. Even the other week at the wedding you wouldn't look at me or talk to me. There must be a reason why you picked me to elope with."

Couldn't stand the sight of him?

The sight of C.J. Hunter couldn't revolt any woman. Even in ancient black track pants, a crumpled polo shirt and runners that had seen better days, he was too easy to watch. Lithe and quietly athletic, with a runner's build instead of a weightlifter's, his once shaggy, reddish-brown rocker's hair was short and dark…and those eyes, deep and green, and his lazy, just crooked smile—

No. The *sight* of him wasn't anything she could complain about. She'd always appreciated his looks—what girl couldn't?—but that was as far as she'd allowed it to go, with her mother's grim example in front of her all her life.

Okay, so she'd been a bit disapproving of all rock stars. And she'd assumed he'd end up like her dad… but then, she hadn't known Dad well enough to see that his love for Nicole had governed his behavior for years. She hadn't known about C.J.'s ambitions for the rest of his life.

The universe was obviously teaching her the stupidity of assuming anything.

"It wasn't personal." Her gaze fell from the compelling honesty in his. "I was sixteen when we met. I judged you by the other party animals around me, and not for yourself. I'm sorry if I was rude."

"You were never openly rude, Mia. Bad manners were beneath you. You just didn't want to know me. You always kept me at a distance." He shrugged. "I always want to sing 'She's So High Above Me' when you're around."

Despite her best will, she felt the blush creeping up her cheek, but she gave him a straight look, demanding answers. "What's that got to do with— with—?" She tried to say "my proposal" and hated herself for chickening out. "With what I just said?"

He shrugged, and how he made it look sexy she'd never know. But with C.J., it was another of life's annoying mysteries. "Why me?"

Now her heart pounded so hard she could almost feel it hitting her throat. Her negotiation skills would never be more needed than now. "It's to help Dad. I need someone really famous who's walked from that life. If you'd been a fame-chaser it might have created a stir, but you with your second Grammy the other week, and me with my—" She skidded to a halt. No one apart from Dad, Nicole, Uncle Martin and Uncle Dane knew her secret yet. Though the first book was done, and due for release in a few months, she knew they'd fall all over it if she added a final chapter as Mia Hunter—if she could get C.J. to go along with this caper. "Um, and both of us being on the reclusive side—"

"Instant sensation. Got it—and good thinking," he said dryly. "It seems my past comes in handy for something. Is that the only reason?"

"You care about Dad. I know you wouldn't betray his confidence."

"Thanks," he said dryly. "High praise, coming from you."

Oh, darn it. She was blushing again! She rushed into speech. "And you're the only famous man around my age I know who isn't a slimeball. You're a decent guy."

After a startled moment he burst out laughing. "I didn't know you'd even thought that much about me.

But that's a reason for a nice girl to ask a guy on a date, not to offer marriage."

She felt her blush grow deeper. "Well, um…" She made a strangled sound, and then said it. "All I'm offering is a fake marriage to make the media chase us around and take the heat from Dad."

Another moment—two, thirty seconds… It stretched out and out, until the air around her felt like it would snap. "I see," he said, his voice strange. "I guess I should've seen that coming."

Could any more blood pool in her cheeks? It was spilling down her throat. What had seemed so easy, so straightforward in the doctor's office now seemed like a road pitted with unseen potholes.

"So what's the rest?" he asked, no longer sounding exhausted; cynicism had bolted straight past exhaustion and taken first place. "And don't tell me you don't have it all mapped out, Mia. You always have a plan."

"You—you mean you'll do it?"

Oh, *curse* her breathlessness! She was supposed to be cool and in control here.

His brow lifted, giving him a look of superiority she didn't like. "I'm not agreeing to anything until I know what I'm letting myself in for. Have you been to the lawyer's office yet, to draw up a contract?"

Her reaction must have been obvious, because he shrugged: the picture of a cool, uncaring male leaning against the doorpost. "You'd never put yourself in a situation you couldn't control. You'd want it all in writing, and for me to sign something that sets boundaries and enforces your 'hands off' policy."

Mia gaped at his perception.

He laughed outright. "Four years as part of End Game, and you thought I wouldn't know that about you?" He shook his head. "You kept your disdain for lowly musos up on a handy shelf for you to grab and toss at us any time you needed it."

Her hands curled into fists; she swallowed down the lump of pure anger. Cool and in control. That was the key to winning. "So you'll sign the contract?"

"No."

The shock shivered straight from her brain down her spine. Where was the straightforward course she'd set for this plan? She'd thought C.J.—always easygoing, and looking to Dad like a second father—would be happy to follow her lead. Dad would get his rest, C.J.—well, he'd enjoy it…and *she* could kick-start her new life. This was the perfect way to catapult interest levels in her book.

Well, two out of three wasn't bad for her—but when it came to C.J., obviously another assumption had bit the dust.

"Why not?" she demanded.

C.J. looked into her eyes. "I've never given you reason to doubt my word. If you want me in on this you either trust me or find another sucker."

The words were uncompromising, but as she looked in those eyes, deep and darkest green, his own personal Amazon, all she could think was that if she wasn't careful she could get lost in them and never find her way out.

No man will ever control me! Even a man with eyes that cold-burn into my soul.

She squared her shoulders. "I guess I'll find the other sucker." Her hand flicked a wave. "Go and sleep, C.J. I'll leave breakfast for you and get out of your hair."

"I thought I was the only *really* famous reclusive guy you knew that was decent?"

She shrugged. "So I pay a B-grader from somewhere and enforce the contract."

C.J. shook his head. "You honestly think that'll work? Give him everything Billy has to match what the paparazzi will offer for a scoop on why 'squeaky clean Mia Browning' eloped with him? He'll still take your money and theirs, and run with both. And if you sue him he gets another fifteen minutes of fame and hopefully a contract. The clock keeps ticking, the media surround Billy and Nicole, and he gets sicker."

Feeling sucker-punched, she glared at him. "Are you digging holes in my plan for the fun of it?"

He put a hand over his mouth to stifle a yawn. "Your first plan was pretty good, leaving out your control freak nature and the contract."

She frowned. "So…you are thinking about it?"

"What's there to think about? You still haven't told me what the plan is—apart from a fake marriage to fool the squizzes."

"Squizzes" had been C.J.'s derogatory term for the paparazzi when he'd been part of End Game, after all the endless intrusions into their lives. Nobody knew where he'd gotten the term from, but in the end they'd all ended up using it. The memory made her smile. But as she was about to comment on it she looked at him—*really* looked— and closed her mouth. By the way he was rubbing his jaw, with whitened fingertips, exhaustion was taking over again.

No wonder he sounded cranky.

She drew in a breath, recalling every word of her perfectly rehearsed plan. "We head to Bali or Fiji for an overnight wedding on the beach—probably Fiji; it's closer—and allow 'a source close to the couple' to leak the news about an impulsive marriage they don't expect to last beyond a few weeks."

His answering grin was wry. "I can't count the amount of 'close sources' who know more about my life than I do."

She laughed. "I know. I wish I knew what jerk gave me that 'ice cream' tag—sweet, but freezing cold."

"You mean it's not true?"

"About as true as you sleeping with a fourteen-year-old, or Dad's last three stints in rehab," she shot back, hurt, even though his tone had been teasing.

After a moment the grin faded, and he nodded. "Fair enough. It seems you're not the only one who's made stupid assumptions. Sorry, Mia. Go on."

So he really thought it of her—sweet and cold?

Was that how everyone saw her? Granted, she'd given due respect to her mother's warnings, but—

What had he said she did? Put the human race at a distance…?

She shook off the self-doubt. There was no time for it. "We stay on some exclusive island until some bright squiz gets a shot of us getting hot and heavy or romantic—"

"So that much touching is allowed?" he murmured, with another grin.

"—and then we take Dad's jet to another island, or North Queensland. When they find us there, we head somewhere unexpected…your pick," she went on, as if she hadn't heard him. If he made another "ice cream" comment, she'd—

"The Northern Territory," he said promptly. "I haven't hiked around Kakadu or Litchfield Park for a couple of years." He nodded. "I'd love to show you around—and May's perfect. The wet season's just ended, and the weather's gorgeous."

"H-hiking in the Outback?" Mia blinked. *That* didn't fit her plans at all…

His brow lifted again. She was starting to dislike that brow. "What? Did you think I'd go for five-star resorts and demand limos and Bollinger on Billy's credit card?"

"Actually, I was thinking I'd need to buy hiking gear," she shot back.

He shook his head. "You had the cockroach look on your face. I surprised you. Your plans revolved around my indulging in playing the star again. You thought I'd want to use this as a way to get back into the business."

Despite her anger, she had to take the hit. Contrary to all appearances, she'd thought maybe he *would* want an opportunity to be famous again. Her primary focus was and always would be her father's health, and C.J.'s choosing the fame track once more, wanting ritzy locales for their honeymoon, would make it easier for the paparazzi to find them... To her shame, a tiny part of her admitted the glitz and glam of a celebrity honeymoon wouldn't hurt sales of her book, either.

She bit her lip. Was this the moment to tell him about the book she was writing and her plans for the final chapter? But how could she write a convincing chapter about her marriage if he knew from the start? Also, he might refuse—as was his right—or throw her out. She wouldn't blame him if he did. His privacy had become almost the stuff of legend...and she'd hate such exposure if their positions were reversed.

She knew that even if he agreed to this, and she wrote the chapter, she would have to run it by him before it was added to the book. It was only right.

But for now she couldn't make herself say the words, so she decided to placate him. "If I offended you—"

He cut in. "You must have gone into psychosis when you found out I finished university by correspondence while I was in End Game and made medical school."

She'd been shocked all right. She'd never even *seen* him studying—but she'd spent most of her time hiding out herself, studying or writing in her journal. Being a sixteen-year-old finding somewhere to belong in one ritzy hotel after the other hadn't been easy; finding friends had been harder. They'd envied her too much to see the loneliness in her life. Not one young person she'd met had wanted to know *her*— they'd wanted to meet C.J. through her, which had made her despise him more.

She frowned, looking around the homey kitchen. She should have realized she'd need to change her plan the moment she saw this house. What had happened to the opulent apartment overlooking the harbor he'd lived in during his End Game days?

"I sold the apartment," he said, with uncanny accuracy. "This is close to the university campus and the hospital. My neighbors are mostly elderly, and don't know what End Game is." He gave her that deep look again. And when she stared back her pulse pounded and she was all flushed and—and lost in those forest eyes… "I said when I left that I wasn't looking back."

And she hadn't believed him for a moment. When he'd won the first Grammy she'd expected him to ditch university and take up a solo career or song writing, but he'd done neither. He'd penned two more songs—"Issues" and more recently "Defiance" the song that had won his second Grammy—but he hadn't collected either of his Grammys personally, only sent a pre-recorded message.

Goaded as much by her self-admission as by his words, she snapped, "All right, I apologize *again*. I was wrong. I'm *sorry*. Now, can we get on with why I came?"

Instead of backing down, he grinned. "That was cute, Mia. I've never seen a woman give an apology with such disdain." He mock-bowed, with the crooked smile she'd *used* to think was pretty sexy. "Good job."

With that, she lost it. "Oh, shove it. Forget everything I said—especially about you being decent. You're too busy punishing me for the past to take me seriously. I'm not a child anymore, in case you haven't noticed. Thanks for your time. I'm sure Dad and Nicole will appreciate the cleverness of your sarcasm and your patronizing attitude in their time of need."

She stalked out of the kitchen, heading for the front door.

As she fumbled to open the lock she felt a touch on her arm. "Mia."

"What?" she yelled, biting back tears. "This is *my father's life,* and all you want is to have fun at my expense."

"I'm sorry. You're right. It's about Billy, not you and me. I'll do it."

She didn't hear him. "I've barely seen you in years. I was a *kid* when you joined End Game and just out of my teens when you left. So if I offended you by the way I looked at you sometimes, get over it!"

The grip on her arm grew tighter, just enough to stop her jerking the door open. "Mia, I said I'll do it."

"I spent *years* dodging slimy passes from half the men in Dad's world from the time I was fifteen, and you think a no-sex contract is an *insult?*" she panted, trying to get the door to work one-handed.

"What?" Suddenly she'd been swung around and was facing him. His eyes were blazing in front of her face. "What did you just say?"

CHAPTER THREE

C.J. SAW Mia's hackles fall as fast as they'd risen. She shrugged one shoulder, her gaze on her thumbs, which were flicking in and out of half-curled fists. "You heard me."

But her words didn't have the tight edge that grated against his tired nerves—and suddenly she wasn't a girl looking down at him from a lofty intellectual and emotional height, but small, vulnerable, defenseless...and he was the world's biggest jerk.

"Not—not the guys in the band?" he demanded, with a protective fury roaring through him. If he'd seen it, just once—

She shrugged again. "Of course not them. They're like my uncles. You know the ones I mean—the hangers-on."

He wanted to punch something—preferably someone. How the *hell* could they? She'd been barely fifteen when Billy had swooped on her at her mother's funeral! She'd been *grieving,* for God's sake. And from that time she'd wandered the world with the band, learning by correspondence, watching Billy's diet and stopping his drinking and drugs—

Looking back now, he could see how hard the life must have been for a teenager. She'd rarely met friends her own age, or had normal teenage fun. Always curled up in a strange room watching TV, reading, looking after everyone, or scribbling in those journals she loved.

Having joined End Game six months after she'd joined the entourage, C.J. had always taken care to act around her as if she was his sister, no matter that her bouts of teenage sarcasm, her superior taunts and occasional practise sessions of budding womanhood on him had driven him half-crazy at times. Poor kid had had to learn to grow up on someone, and she'd chosen him as either the safest bet or, at twenty, the closest in age.

It seemed other guys in the industry hadn't shared his scruples. All they'd seen was another pretty girl hanging around. They'd probably treated her as fair game when Billy was off pleasure-seeking, or away the three times he went to rehab after she came to live with him.

It had to have been one hell of a childhood, between a bitter, abandoned mother and a loving but basically self-absorbed and addicted father, dragging her from one place to another, from one new "mother" to another.

His mind was too sunk in exhaustion to deal with *that* revelation as she deserved. But he'd stop baiting her, patronizing and punishing her for demolishing his twenty-something self's over-inflated ego.

"How about we start today's conversation again?" He smiled at her. "I've just come off a thirty-six-hour shift in the Emergency Room, and my bedside manner's gone down the plughole—even for an old friend. Can I ask you for coffee and breakfast while I shower and shave?"

Mia blinked, still flicking her thumbs, nibbling the inside of her lip. Slowly, so serious she made it an illustration of cuteness, she nodded. "All right."

He grinned, taking care not to touch her. "Thanks, Mia. I'd appreciate it. Normally I shower, fall into bed and wake up a few hours later starving. When the rhythm breaks like that, it's hard to get some serious REM time."

She smiled back, her eyes warm and shy behind her glasses. "I'm sorry I lumbered you with this when you're so tired. A decent breakfast is the least I can do. There's a good deli on the main road, right?"

"Yeah, it's my favorite place for brunch—at least on a weekday. Too many celebs hang out there on weekends." A thought grabbed hold. "And the squizzes."

Her brows lifted a little. "It's Sunday."

"Exactly. So why not start as we need to go on? I'll grab a quick shower and be right with you. Some espresso, eggs, tomatoes and mushrooms on toast…"

She sucked her lips in and still managed an

adorable half-smile. "Looking into each other's eyes...holding hands..."

And our first kiss. He knew it was going to happen; he could feel it. She'd latched onto his excitement and run with it.

Time to test the waters. "It'll have to be convincing, Mia." He did as she'd just said and looked into her eyes, taking her hands in his. "If we're not compatible, we need to know before this idea becomes public."

Mia took a step back, right into the door, her body stiff and the look in her eyes saying she suspected the worst of him.

"For Billy's sake," he said patiently—at least he hoped he sounded patient, and not half as eager as he felt. "If we don't do it right they'll suspect a cover-up, and Billy's worse off than ever. If we're not compatible we're forewarned, and we can fake it."

After a long, hanging moment, Mia frowned and nodded. "All right." Her words were barely above a whisper. She looked down at their linked hands; her fingers uncurled, and laced through his. They brushed his palms as they moved.

Heat flashed through him.

It seemed compatibility wouldn't be a problem for one of them. He hadn't reacted this strongly to a woman since his girlfriend in first-year university—before he'd joined End Game. After that time he'd never known if a woman wanted *him,* or the fifteen minutes of fame being with him would bring.

Mia's eyes drifted closed as she stood passive, waiting for the kiss with a look on her face that sat somewhere between anticipation, distaste and martyrdom. She was probably thinking about the sacrifices she made for Billy, or ways she could get him to sign her stupid contract, while *he* was already going nuts just feeling her hands in his.

Caught somewhere between lust and anger, he bent closer to Saint Mia the Martyr, and brushed his mouth over hers.

Whoa, *brother.* If this was what kissing a saint felt like, no wonder people had been going on crusades for centuries…

Mia's gasp was faint, a sweet indrawn breath, but her luscious mouth opened and she swayed towards him. C.J. groaned and pulled her closer. No way could he ignore that honeyed temptation. After years of forbidden fantasies Mia was a woman—and she wanted him.

If he could get her to marry him without that stupid contract the moment was now—and he had about a minute to convince her.

He lifted her chin and kissed her, deep and hot, reveling in the feel of skin to skin. Their mouths spoke far more sense without words. Reveling in her fingers winding through his hair, her body soft and pliable, her tongue twining with his.

"C.J.," she whispered, just when he was upgrading from thrilled to ecstatic.

Mia wanted him at last.

He nipped at the full, silky lower lip, and kissed her again. "Mmm?"

Though she kissed him back, she winced a little. "You need to shave."

Feeling dazed, he looked down at her. She was smiling, but her satin-soft skin had become tender from his two-day bristle. Weird, the shot of satisfaction that filled him, seeing the marks he'd put on her. Like he'd branded her.

You wish, Hunter. She might have enjoyed the kiss, but as far as she's concerned she's here for Billy.

He smiled, but it felt rueful. "I knew I should have shaved last night."

"Go and do it now. We need to start putting the plan to work." She turned him around, pushing him toward the bathroom.

Obviously she needed space. He'd made his point; he could give her time. He turned and winked at her with a grin. "At least we don't have to pretend we like kissing each other."

He wanted to pump a fist in the air when she blushed. Score one for male ego, zero for feminine resistance and prejudice.

What was that?

Mia had only one answer—and she didn't like it. Her mother's warnings from childhood came back to haunt her. *My entire life changed with Billy's kiss. I didn't even know who he was, but it was as if he showed me heaven.*

And that was how she'd felt when C.J. kissed her—like she was floating…

And then your father left me, Mia—and my life fell apart. Promise me you'll never marry a man like that!

Wasn't that what she'd just proposed?

No! The real message was *don't fall in love with a man like your father.* No way would she fall for C.J.—even if his kiss sent hot shivers down to her toes and made her feel like she was melting. She always chose serious, stable guys to date—

And not one of them has made you feel as if you're floating in the stratosphere—that you finally belong somewhere.

She wouldn't let it happen! Control, keeping calm and collected—and making him sign the contract—was the key to surviving this. A sham wedding, a runaround "honeymoon" and then splitting for the media, releasing her book while she was still inside her own fifteen minutes of fame. How hard could it be?

"Mia?"

She started. How long had she been lost in thought? C.J. was already showered, shaved and dressed in dark jeans and a deep green V-neck sweater the shade of his eyes. His hair, freshly washed, was mussed in the half-curls he was famed for.

Oh, man, she was in trouble…*deep* trouble…if just the sight of him could make her feel as if she was halfway through a marathon—breathless, flushed, *thirsty*…

In too deep, and she'd never known it until now.

She'd known the man more than ten years, and managed to ignore him most of the time. She'd always found him attractive—okay, *gorgeous*—but why was it she suddenly couldn't keep her eyes off him? Couldn't stop thinking things she had no right to think, her body alive with feelings she couldn't stop?

"You keep looking at me like that and I'll rip the contract up right before I take you to bed," he said softly. That semi-crooked lazy grin wasn't so indolent now; it had taken a wolfish edge that made her pulse rocket and her sensible head do a weird, slow spin…

No!

She spun around to the door, realizing only now that she hadn't even moved since he'd left the room. "Dad needs us to be focussed. We should make a start on our public face, so the wedding doesn't come out of the blue."

His chuckle was low and soft—a man who knew he had a woman right where he wanted her—and it terrified her. "Whatever you say."

He put his hand to her back as they walked down the path to the road. She moved away, slow and deliberate. To move fast implied fear.

"You're going the wrong way," he called as she strode ahead of him.

"Oh." Feeling that dratted blush, she turned back to him, but when he took her hand in his she pulled away, trying for a light but deliberate feeling.

He didn't let go. "No one will believe we're crazy about each other if you keep avoiding me." He held tight to her hand as they crossed the road, C.J. keeping his long, loping pace slower for her. "You have to *be* with me to make this plan work."

"No one's looking now." Cool and calm, pointing out the flaws in his argument, as he was to her. Ignoring the sweet, tingling warmth creeping up her arm from his touch.

"This street's filled with elderly folk. When the media gets hold of this, the first people they'll come to will be the neighbors—and at least two of them are peeking through their curtains now."

She sucked her lips in and nodded. "You have all the bases covered."

He grinned at her. "Quick thinking for a guy who fell over his jaw when you proposed marriage to me, huh?"

"You don't have to keep reminding me," she muttered, feeling like Oscar the Grouch without his trash can.

"Fair enough. No more reminders of how you proposed to me, but I reserve the right to tease you on our twenty-fifth anniversary." He grinned at her.

She choked on laughter, relieved at the sudden harmony of a joke. "Yes, darling." She mimicked Nicole beautifully. "And I'll tell you it was worth the humiliation."

He laughed and squeezed her hand as if they were old friends—or long-time lovers.

The shot of wistfulness in her heart was surely just the loneliness of a woman who didn't have a special someone in her life. C.J. *wasn't* that special someone—just a blind for the media.

"Getting back to the topic, I've lived with the paparazzi for eleven years, and been dodging 'em for seven. I've learned how they work."

She nodded. "We can make good use of our combined knowledge."

"Relax, Mia." He sounded serious suddenly. "You don't need to worry that I hold all the aces."

She turned her head, gaping at him. "What…?"

He led her across the road, not looking at her. "Since the kiss. Yes, I know you liked it—but so did I. It's a fallacy that guys get turned on by any woman—at least it is with me. And the whole groupies-and-one-night-stands thing got old for me really fast."

Feeling acutely uncomfortable, she snapped, "What are you trying to say?"

He shrugged again. "If you're scared that I'm on top since the kiss, or that I've got a hundred women to compare it to, it's not true." He still didn't look at her as he said, "You do it for me, too, Mia. You always have."

What did she say to that? Should she admit that he "did it" for her, far more than she'd ever dreamed? That her whole body was still *alive,* on alert from just being near him, that she was waiting for the next kiss like a dog waiting for a signal to bolt to her dinner bowl?

She pulled her hand from his, fumbling in her bag for her sunglasses as a good excuse. "I'm not comfortable with this," she said, almost scared to look at him.

"Okay." He sounded just as quiet, maybe even uncomfortable too. As if he—

As if she'd just said something that made him feel stupid, because she wouldn't give him the same honesty. Well, wouldn't *she* feel stupid? She already did—because she was chickening out *again* after C.J. had been strong enough to be truthful with her.

As they reached a corner, she made herself face him. "I think we should both sign the contract. I think we'd both be better off with…boundaries."

"Safe, you mean?" he said, not backing down, not allowing her to.

She squared off, looking him right in the eyes. "I won't make apologies for that, given the troubles I've had in the past."

"Not from me, Mia."

Unaccountably she blushed again. She knew *that*. He'd never once tried anything on her. "I'll sign the contract if you will."

C.J. shrugged, and pressed for the pedestrian crossing light leading over the main road. "We'll have to fly out quickly. I've only got ten days off before my surgical rotation begins. I won't apply for extra time. Even if I could, it's my last rotation before I'm qualified to apply for research consultancies."

He hadn't answered her about the contract, but the tightness of his jaw and the clipped tone warned her not to push the issue. "How long is each rotation?" she asked, curious about his life.

He took her hand back in his as they crossed onto the crowded thoroughfare. "Four to six months. I've been rotating, as intern and now registrar, for over two years."

Her hand felt so *snug* lying in his. So comfortable, yet—oh, she didn't know what. But it had never happened to her before. "What kind of research do you want to get into?"

"Whatever I can get for the first few years. It's very competitive. I'll probably be dogsbody at first, drawing blood and playing with the centrifuge." He shrugged. "You have to pay your dues."

It seemed the dues were endless with medicine. He'd already given up fame and the adulation of that world for study and long hours.

He must be very dedicated to stick to it, with so much to go back to.

"What's your ultimate goal?" she asked, wondering if he'd answer.

She felt his gaze touch her before he spoke. "I'd like to research brain diseases. The mind is an amazing thing, and the brain the most intricate organ. Things happen for no reason we can find sometimes—a fully-functioning person can become someone totally different without warning. I want to find the warning signals, the reasons."

The moment of unexpected insight almost blinded her. "You've always wanted to do this, haven't you?" She didn't need to ask, really, but she wanted to see if he'd answer. "That's why you joined End Game.

To earn the money to get you through university and into research."

"Yes."

That was it. No embellishments, no explanations. She supposed she didn't deserve it. He'd opened himself to her, and she'd given only shocks and rules in return.

She'd offered a sham marriage, a "hands-off" contract, and undeserved judgment.

They reached the main road, tense and silent. "I'm usually recognized by the time I reach the grocery store. There's usually someone trawling for shots around here on weekends. We need to make it look real."

The warm tingling filled her again; her palm felt connected, her hand—safe. "I never thanked you for doing this," she said softly.

"I don't need you to. I owe Billy, for what he did with Michelle when I left End Game."

Her head turned so fast she hurt her neck. "What—?"

"Not here." He threaded their way through the crowd coming the other way, moving faster when someone gasped and asked if he was…was he…?

"It's C.J. Hunter," a guy muttered, in the kind of awe-envy ordinary guys often used when in the presence of rock royalty.

Without even cracking a smile C.J. kept walking, dragging Mia by the hand, acting as if he hadn't heard the awestruck twentysomethings.

Her dad would have stopped, smiled, signed autographs, but C.J. obviously had meant what he'd said. He was never going back…

But he'd agreed to her plan, and she hadn't even had to blackmail him. He'd agreed for her dad's sake, even though it obviously meant turning his quiet life upside-down.

Another gasp. "And isn't that…with him….um… isn't she…?"

Mia grinned. It was the inevitable reaction when anyone saw her. They knew she was *someone*…and she'd finally gotten past the resentment and was using it to her advantage. "Just call me the 'um' girl," she murmured as she stumbled in C.J.'s wake.

A low chuckle told her his hearing was as sharp as ever. "Probably better than an 'it' girl."

"And probably better than skinned knees," she retorted as she almost fell. "Can you remember I'm only five-foot-four when you're claiming the street?"

He slowed his steps, but didn't smile as she'd expected. "Look tense, Mia. It's started."

She bit her lip and frowned, hoping it was good enough. "Shouldn't we look like we're in love?"

"Not now. The squiz knows I saw him."

A moment later the call of "C.J.!" proved him right.

"He took a few shots. If the guy's got a BlackBerry, he'll e-mail the pic to his editor and know who you are in about three minutes. Our work here is done. We'd better get my car and make arrangements for that flight."

"Don't you need to eat?" she asked, concerned. No sleep, no food...

"I'll get drive-though."

"Dad's made his jet available anytime. He and Nicole will go into hiding as soon as our news comes out."

"Good."

She almost stumbled again as he changed direction with shocking suddenness. "Would you mind slowing down, six-foot-three man?" she panted as she ran after him.

He grinned back at her and increased the pace. "I could haul you over my shoulder."

"I'd—break—it." She sucked in a breath as pain stabbed her ribs. "I have a stitch."

"Run through it," he panted mercilessly as he pulled out his phone. "It'll fade. Hey, Dave?" he spoke into the phone. "I need help. Get to the corner of Park and George, will you? ASAP? Thanks." He snapped the phone shut. "We have three minutes to dodge the squiz. He must have got the call. He's gaining on us."

"C.J.! Mia! Have you any comment on...?"

Curious pedestrians parted for them as they ran, but they parted for the reporter as well. C.J. pulled her along, and Mia ran harder, gasping for air and holding her side with her free hand. The reporter bolted after them, yelling questions.

A couple of people in the crowd tried to stop them, asking about C.J. and her dad. "Sorry," she called as she passed. "We're—in—a hurry..."

A nondescript sedan pulled up in front of them as they reached an intersection.

"Get in." C.J. shoved her into the backseat.

The driver screeched off, just as the journalist caught up with them.

"Mia, this is Dave, a friend from work who lives down the road from me," C.J. said briefly, still catching his breath.

Mia, unable to do anything but clutch her sides, smiled and nodded at the man, who was busy turning into side streets and laneways.

"Want to tell me what's going on, C.J.?" Dave asked as he roared through the backstreets. "Why are the press chasing you? Is it the Grammy? Or can't I know?"

After a pause, in which Mia sent him a frantic look, C.J. said, "Dave, this is Mia Browning—Billy's daughter."

"Holy—" Dave choked off the rest and started chuckling. "No fame or women for years. Now the Grammy and Billy Browning's daughter. C.J., when you fall off the wagon, you really do it, don't you, man?"

C.J. threw a casual arm around Mia. Though his voice was warm and indulgent, she could feel his tension. "When you meet the one, you can't let that stuff matter."

"Correct me if I'm wrong, but didn't you and Mia meet, like, years ago?"

"Why do you think I *haven't* dated in years, Dave?"

Mia blinked. Oh, he was *very* good! Even she

almost believed that line, said with all the stiff embarrassment of an Aussie male admitting to the dreaded emotion *love*. The only emotion an Australian male was allowed to show in public was over sports.

She whispered in his ear. "Brilliant."

He turned his face and kissed her before she'd finished the word. And she couldn't remember anything else—not the plan, the contract, the car, Dave, or the media chase. There was only C.J.'s touch, his kiss, and what he made her feel...

A loud sound of throat-clearing startled her. "Can we keep it PG, kids? And remember I don't know where we're going!"

Mia came back to reality. She was lying across the backseat, her sunglasses tossed somewhere, with C.J. lying on her, totally aroused, kissing her throat, nibbling along her collarbone... She almost forgot where she was again.

Just like her mother.

It took all her will to push at his chest. "We need to sign the contract as soon as possible—and Dave wants to know where we're going," she whispered.

He looked down at her, soft, unfocused, his face filled with passion, then his eyes grew cool, distant. "To the hospital, thanks, Dave. I'll pick up my car." He turned to her. "My family deserves to meet you and know what's happening before they read about my marriage in the tabloids."

Mia's stomach lurched.

CHAPTER FOUR

C.J. SAW her expression—shocked because he had a family to consider—and didn't know whether to be amused or exasperated. He'd always thought of himself as a reasonably normal and decent guy until he'd met Mia.

"You want me to meet your parents?" She sounded strange.

He frowned. "Of course. Your family knows. Why shouldn't mine? My parents and sister would be hurt any other way."

"You're…close to them?"

He wondered if she'd even noticed he was still lying on her, still fully aroused. "Yes, of course. They're my family."

Did she know her fingers were playing with his hair? And that it was driving him crazy? "Tell me about them."

"My sister's married with four boys—she's still trying for the girl she wants. Jess was always a girly girl, and she wants a baby to put ribbons on and frilly dresses. Right now she spends her afternoons going from one sport to another." A thought occurred to him. He checked his watch. "Arlen and Patrick start soccer in about half an hour. Mum and Dad usually go to watch. We can meet them there."

She sucked her lips inward. "Um…C.J.…."

"Here we are," Dave announced cheerfully. "You probably have two minutes before they show up here with cameras, guys, so I recommend a quick exit, stage left."

The words acted on him like a stinging cold shower, reminding him what was going on and why Mia had come to him. He pulled her arms from around him and sat up.

"Thanks a million, Dave," Mia said, as she handed C.J.'s friend a piece of paper. "Here's the phone number for Dad's plane—just in case."

"Let's go, Mia," C.J. said, pulling her towards the car park.

"Give me the keys. You're still too tired to drive," she said as he pulled her along to his car. He nodded and handed them to her. Control freak she might be, but in this case she was right.

Once they were on the road, he said, "It's obvious you have a problem with meeting my family. Want to tell me why?"

"It's not that. It's the timing and…and the plan…and the contract." Her uncertainty was so palpable he could almost take its pulse. "Can I meet them later? After we do this thing? Can we call them from Fiji, and tell them the truth?"

Do this thing. Like marrying him was taking nasty medicine. She was harping on that stupid contract as if it could kill her reaction to him. "What's the matter? You've only got the guts to tell my family from a distance? Or are you afraid to face the people who love me and act as though you give a damn? Worried you'll actually like something about them— or me—and live with the fallout when they know you were only using me?"

She kept her eyes trained on the road. "Yes." In her voice was a mixture of defiance and fear, anger and acute embarrassment.

"You don't pull your punches, do you? I'm doing you the favor, if you remember." He heard the anger and cynicism in his voice and almost winced—but, hell, she deserved it.

"No," she retorted, flat. "You're doing this for Dad, because you owe him. This isn't about you and me. We may not like each other very much, but we both love Dad."

The adrenalin that had kept him going since seeing her on his doorstep began to fade, and the ex-hausted shaking re-emerged. It took all his will to control it—he'd shown enough weakness around her. "All right, let's skip the traditional 'meet the parents' and head straight to the airport. You don't have a problem if I tell them before we sign the papers? Or if I sleep all the way to Fiji?"

"Of course not." Her voice was like frost. "You can sleep now, if you like."

He shrugged. "Once I crash out, I'll be asleep for hours. We'd better head to my place. I need to pack some gear. I gather that bag you left in my place has your clothes?"

"Yes."

"Let's head back and get it, and get the show on the road. The sooner we start, the sooner Billy gets better and we can end this." Was that *his* voice? He sounded so cold, so uncaring. She knew how to bring out the worst in him just by not giving a damn, when he wanted her so bad he was in pain with it.

He had to get her out of his life before he became as obsessed as a stupid schoolboy with his first crush. Just as he'd been when he'd joined End Game and had first seen her.

He wasn't that person any more. He wouldn't allow Mia's bad opinion of him to direct his life and choices.

"Whatever you want." She shrugged in turn, pushed her glasses up her nose, and concentrated on the road. "What do you want for breakfast?"

"I don't care." Anything would turn his stomach now—but he wasn't about to tell her that. From now on he'd show no weakness, give no mercy.

She'd really blown it. Why had she said it? One word spoken because she didn't know what to say or what the truth really was, and she'd lost him.

While the jet streaked across the sky toward Fiji,

Mia was jotting down notes on the autobiography—
the gentle outing of Uncle Martin he'd asked her to
co-write with him—but she couldn't concentrate.
C.J. hadn't spoken since they reached the hangar.
He'd gone to the bathroom, emerged in shorts and a
tightly stretched singlet top, showing his lithe,
muscled form to perfection, and fallen to the bed
without looking at her.

"That's good," she muttered fiercely. "It's what I
want. He—he knows his place…"

He knows his place—but do you?

That was the problem. This was *her* plan, *her* way
to save her dad and help launch her book, but while
C.J. was *doing* everything right, he wasn't *thinking*
the way she'd expected, didn't want the things she'd
planned for.

And whose fault is that? She'd thought of him as
an accessory to her plan: a faded rock star who'd be
grateful for another fifteen days of fame. She hadn't
thought about how it would change his life, or
whether it would hurt him.

But he'd become real to her now, and she couldn't
make that go away. When she'd seen him so exhausted, yet still worried about her father; when he'd
talked about his family, his surgical rotation, his ambitions for the future—

When she'd seen the look in his eyes when he'd
thought she wasn't paying attention. All that deep,
hot yearning…

He wanted her, and he wasn't ashamed of it. And

she'd thrown his passion and his courage back in his face.

Bruck-bruck-bruck. Chicken-chicken-chicken...

The lessons of a lifetime had been drilled in with the sharp point of her mother's abandonment and bitterness. Mum had done all she could to make Dad stay—and to discover he'd only stayed as long as he had because of Mia had been a humiliation her mother had never recovered from.

I should have known a man like that would never stay.

And so, while every cell and pore of her body— a body that felt as if it had awoken from a Rip Van Winkle sleep—yearned to touch him, to go to him now and *show* him he wasn't alone in this crazy fascination, her mind and heart kept her butt glued to her seat, kept her reading the same page over and over.

Bruck-bruck-bruck...

And she hated him for knowing it. Hated herself more for doing nothing about it.

Hated him for being asleep, yet was relieved too.

She'd never been through such a wringer of emotional change before today, and she couldn't even blame C.J. She'd come to him.

She had to talk to someone or she'd go crazy.

Without thought, she picked up the sky phone and called Nicole. "Hey. How's Dad?"

"He's sleeping right now. How's everything going?"

Mia read into the simple question, *when can we have some peace?* "I'm with C.J. We're on our way to Fiji for a quickie wedding. The press has already got some pictures of us together."

"I knew C.J. would agree after what Billy did for him."

Nicole didn't even seem surprised. She briefly wondered if she and Dad had always known C.J. *did it for her.* "What did Dad do?" she half-whispered. If C.J. woke up and heard, she didn't know how he'd react. "He mentioned something about Michelle."

"C.J. needed space when he left the band. He was exhausted after the bout of glandular fever he had. Remember when they had to cancel the British leg of the tour?"

Yes—and she'd thought C.J. had been burned out with too much partying.

"He'd passed his final-year uni by correspondence, but half killed himself doing exams throughout the last tour of Europe. They worked around his schedule, but often he had to finish a concert and bolt off to find the next exam room…"

Mia sat still, filled with horror. "*That* was where he kept disappearing to?" She'd assumed he'd disappeared with some groupie or other. She'd thought he'd been playing the rock star when he'd been in his room, studying, or facing another exam.

She was appalled. So shallow, so ready to judge C.J. by her dad's life…the stupid, impulsive decisions he'd made not because he was self-absorbed, but because he couldn't have the one woman he loved. Yet while she'd given her father second, third, fourth and fifth chances, she hadn't even given C.J. one chance.

"...so, while C.J. went into hiding Billy took off with Michelle. He paid her double to act like they were together. She never even liked Billy, but it was good for her career." She laughed. "I was so jealous until Billy told me what was going on."

After a long silence, Mia mumbled, "I see."

And she did. She saw far too much about herself she didn't like.

That's not the point, is it? It's keeping Dad healthy. C.J. will get over it. It's not like he cares about me. Half the time he almost hates me.

The jet began its descent. "I have to go, Nicole." She added, painfully, "Thanks."

"For what, sweetie?"

"For being so good to me," she said quietly. "For making Dad happy."

Nicole said warmly, "You're welcome, Mia. Think beyond this week, sweetie. C.J.'s a good man."

Yes, he is... And not least because he was still here, after all the provocation she'd given him to walk.

She hung up the phone and crossed to the bed. He was lying on his stomach, taking up most of the bed. He'd barely moved since he fell there.

Looking down at him, she felt something strange fill her. He looked so peaceful: a man who was doing what he wanted to do with his life, who knew his direction and was following it.

She envied that direction, that certainty. She'd

taken too many years to find her direction, and it had only come through a chance remark of her father's that maybe her journals would make a great story about a kid in the public eye.

C.J. sighed and flipped over, mumbled something, and slept on. Mia wished she could let him stay there—but he could sleep the night through at the nearest hotel in Nadi. They'd hop to an island tomorrow, once they were married.

She was marrying C.J. Hunter.

Strange, but never once had she thought of it that way: she was marrying a man half the young, unmarried female population would die to be with, and she'd taken it for granted. She'd taken his assent for granted, even his kiss.

You haven't been with a woman in years…

He hadn't even denied it.

Bloop, bloop…

The sound came from the sky phone. Wanting to save him from waking, she grabbed the phone. "Hello?" She said it just as she realized it could be the press. What would she—?

"Mia? It's Dave. Is C.J. there?"

"He's asleep," she said softly, carrying the phone back to her seat. "Can I help?"

"It's already hit the fan. The journo must've run my license plates. Half the Sydney press are outside my door."

Her stomach dropped. "Oh, Dave, I'm so sorry."

"Well, they're here, so no use in being sorry," he

answered impatiently. "I sneaked out the back way to get to work, but the other half of the press is at the hospital. They're asking the staff about you and C.J. There's not enough security to get rid of them all. Some are pretending to be patients' relatives and we can't sift them all."

"Oh, no." So many consequences she hadn't thought of, so many complications to C.J.'s life and career—just because she'd put her dad's needs before his…and her own.

"Mia? What is it?"

She looked over at the bed. C.J. was awake. He rolled over and sat up in a moment, rubbing his eyes. "What is it? Who's on the phone?"

"It's Dave. There've been—consequences," she whispered, feeling helpless.

He took the phone. "Dave—hi, mate. What's up?" He listened, nodding, his tired face growing hard. "Okay, let's make use of this. Tell 'em all that you're auctioning off the rights to what you know via the net. Use my C.J. Hunter webpage. Password is doctorclown. Whoever pays the most by to-morrow gets an exclusive. My sister will do the same… Nah, mate, best if you don't know any more—but give them all you've got. Make a splash of this. Yeah, truly, Dave, it's fine." He listened, nodding and smiling. "Yeah, that's fantastic, Dave. Go for it—and enjoy the zeros, okay? I'll call soon. Yeah, okay, mate. Bye." He disconnected and looked at her. "Right, Thunderbirds are Go on the plan. I'll call my parents and Jess and get the rest of it in motion."

"What rest?" she demanded, bewildered.

He sighed and rubbed his jaw. "Your dad and Nicole should know as little as possible or the squizzes will hound them, mission failed. If they give an angry, confused denial of knowing we're together or married then my family, who are healthy and hate taking my money, can take over. Let them invent as many lurid details as they want. Jess is a drama queen—she'll love this. There's only two bits of info she needs. One: we're getting married on a Fijian island tomorrow. The press will send their Fijian counterparts here by morning. Two: after some appropriate kissing for the Fijian press to send back, we'll be at Mum and Dad's in a day or two. And she's not to be there so it doesn't look contrived. Then we disappear to the Outback and lead them on a chase— and then we break up a few weeks later, in spectacular style." He looked at her with a slight twist to his mouth. "It'll look best if we both date other people pretty quickly while we're at it."

She stared at him in awe. He'd taken her plan and run with it, filling all the holes with cement the press wouldn't be able to see through—Dad and Nicole would be left in peace after one bewildered interview. "It's—perfect," she agreed, feeling left out and alone. Out of control with this plan *again*. Wondering if she was alone with the distaste the thought of dating someone else sent through her.

He nodded as if he'd expected her approval. "I'll call Jess now, then my parents. I won't give them all the details in case they crack under pressure. Just that Billy's sick and the press can't know it. We can trust Jess to do whatever we want."

Again, all she could do was nod and agree. "I think we're about to land in Fiji."

"Better call Jess now." He called his sister, dealing with it as quickly as possible.

Mia, hearing his sister's laughter and squeals of delight as he told her everything, realized C.J. was right: she'd revel in her task. She'd tell the press what they wanted to know, and keep the truth to herself.

"I'll call Mum and Dad from the hotel, Jess. Remember they can't know any of this, except that Mia and I fell in love a few weeks ago and decided to elope. From there, have all the fun you want."

Mia heard Jess laugh again, and felt like grumbling. Did C.J. have to be right about *everything*?

"We'll have to sleep in one room," he said as he strapped himself into his seat. "Or they'll never believe us. But I'll sign the stupid contract if you want."

She hesitated, listening to her deepest instincts for the first time. "No. It's not necessary, C.J." She smiled at him, aiming for—she didn't know what. "I know I can trust you," she said softly. "And— and—" But she couldn't finish it. *I want you, too.* No "hands-off" contract could keep her safe from herself.

But, if anything, he grew colder. "There's no way you'd trust me unless you'd talked to someone

and checked up on everything I told you." It wasn't
a question.

Shamed, she nodded. "Nicole told me about Dad's
plan with Michelle, and why you left. I didn't know
you were sick." She turned to him, her eyes pleading.

"You didn't want to know." The words were flat.

"No." She looked out the window to the warm
blanket of darkness over Nadi. "I don't know what
to say to make this right. I don't know how to make
it up to you."

After a few moments, he murmured, "Yes, you do."
You do it for me, Mia. You always have.

How she must have hurt him back then. What a
blind fool she'd been, pushing him away, never
seeing how similar they were. She need not have
spent all these years alone in a world where she'd
never belonged.

"Do you want to hear it?" she mumbled.

She felt the warmth of his hand over hers. "After
years of waiting for you to admit you were wrong
about me? You bet I do."

The smile curved her mouth. He was giving her
another chance to start over.

Turning her hand over so her fingers twined
through his, she used her free hand to cup his jaw in
her palm, and kissed him with a mixture of joy and
urgency. Heated pleasure ripped through her with
every touch, even the tiny movement of his fingers
against her cheek. Oh, what he *did* to her…

She moaned and moved as close as the seats

would allow, and kissed him deeper, lips, tongue. Her hands were winding through his hair, caressing his neck and shoulders. She was gulping him down like a pre-menstrual woman finding a cache of chocolate.

The bouncing of the jet's wheels on gravel parted them—and instead of chickening out she smiled right into his eyes. "How am I doing with that groveling?"

"Not bad." His grin was the lazy one she loved. "I'm sure you'll find other ways to improve with time."

She laughed and swatted him.

"I'm still waiting," he murmured, as the jet taxied around to a hangar.

She mock-sighed. "You want the words?" Her hands fluttered up. "I didn't know, C.J. I really didn't."

"Know what?" he whispered in her ear, warm laughter in his voice.

Acutely uncomfortable, she shrugged. "I knew you unsettled me, but not why. Until you kissed me. I didn't know it could be like that—like you clobbered me over the head."

After a stunned moment, he burst out laughing. "Clobbered you over the head? You really don't have much experience at this. Didn't you ever whisper sweet nothings with one of your library lovers?"

She was still wanting to kiss his smiling mouth, but the words sank in and she blinked. "My what?"

"The international literary boys. The study sharks. The algebraic-mafia characters you hung out with in libraries around the world." He was still chuckling.

"It was fun listening to you trying to understand them, and they you."

"How do you—?" Then it came to her. "You needed quiet places to study." He nodded. "You watched me?" she demanded, with a sneaking sense of pleasure that C.J., who could have got any girl he liked, had wanted to watch her.

"Sometimes." He grinned. "I was intrigued by the looks you gave them—I'd never seen you give such respect and admiration to anyone before."

Mia opened her mouth to refute it, but an innate sense of honesty stopped her. Apart from the original band members, whom she still saw as her family, she *had* despised him and everyone in their world back then.

It had kept her safe. Stopped her mother's history repeating.

He knew she wanted him, but to admit she liked him, that she'd never felt so *alive* as when C.J. touched her, made her throat swell and close up. Her heart pounded and she felt like the worst kind of traitor...or was it fool?

C.J. was too much of everything: too intelligent, too insightful, too—too gorgeous. Too strong. Too sure of himself and what he wanted.

He wasn't *safe*. He'd never stay long. Not with someone like her.

"I'm sorry if I hurt your feelings," she said, feeling the uncertainty of quicksand beneath her feet.

"I haven't forgiven you just yet." He grinned at her. "But you've got ten days to make it up to me."

Her breath lodged in her throat. She knew what he hadn't said. And the worst part was that her body went into hyper-drive, flying on warp speed, just *thinking* about it. If holding hands and kissing had changed her irrevocably, what would—?

Would—?

Say it. Making love. Making love to C.J....

Oh, where was the nearest funny farm? Half of her was dying to throw herself into his arms and whisper, *Yes, please,* and the other half wanted to bolt back to her old life, despising every man who came into her orbit unless they were safe. Safe from her own body's needs finally coming to life after twenty-seven years' dormancy.

"We have time, Mia," he said softly, touching her chin with his fingers. "We don't have to work it all out now. We're here to help Billy, and we like each other. Let's go with the flow."

Go with the flow? Panic welled up in her. That was what her father had done all his life, and he'd left a string of broken hearts on the way. It was what her mother had done...

She didn't even remember meeting her dad until she was six or seven. He'd been her hero, the cocky, confident rock star with a jet-setting lifestyle. He'd give her a day to remember, showering her with gifts, and then disappear again for months, leaving her to a bitter mother and the grief of missing him. She'd heard from him every so often, but he'd always been recording, or on tour—or with a new woman.

Watching him on TV had been like visiting him through prison bars. It was her dad, but she couldn't touch him, or show him off to the kids at school at parent-teacher interviews. He was exciting and glamorous, but he wasn't *real.*

She couldn't go through that waiting torture again. Too many years waiting for affection, for the *attention* that never came...

"Control doesn't make you safe, Mia," C.J. said, breaking into her thoughts with the same accuracy as earlier—mirroring her deepest fear. "Everybody gets hurt sometimes. But if you stop reaching out, stop taking risks, you don't live at all."

"We've arrived at Nadi International Airport," the pilot announced cheerfully just as she was about to snap back with some flip answer to cover the fact that he scared the living daylights out of her. She unbuckled her belt and reached for her duffel.

"I'll get it."

"I'm not helpless," she snapped, unable to stop the words tumbling from her mouth. "I've done everything for myself since I was fifteen. I don't need you to look after me!"

He handed her the duffel. "I don't think you've got a clue what you need, Mia—but at the rate you're going, pushing everyone away, you'll end up a lonely woman. And long before you're old."

After a moment she said, in a shaking voice, "Be glad I'm not into clichés, or I'd slap your face."

His laughter had an edge—anger or bitterness, she didn't know. "Wake up and smell the coffee, Mia—this plan of yours *is* a cliché. You're as human as the rest of us. Hiding behind your books, behind your superior attitude, looking after Billy all these years, hasn't kept you safe. Everyone gets hurt sometimes."

She wheeled back around on him, her eyes flashing with all the turbulent anger inside her. "I hide? And you don't? I'm afraid of hurt—but are *you* any different? You were attracted to me, or so you say. How would I know that? You never once told me you liked me, what you wanted from life, or where you went when you studied. Did you ever come to me in all those libraries and once say, *Hi, Mia, look how much we have in common?* In four years you never showed me you thought of me as anything but a kid to pat on the head! What was that but hiding—hiding who you were, hiding yourself and your feelings from me? Was I supposed to come to you, a four-years-younger fish out of water, when you had girls screaming your name every night? So where are *your* friends and lovers to prove you're not lonely too? Don't preach to me about taking risks, because you hid behind your C.J. Hunter image then and you hide behind your wondrous nobility now, *Dr. Hunter!*"

She ran down the stairs and out into Customs before he could say a word.

CHAPTER FIVE

C.J. FOLLOWED her through the airport, into the limo, and from there to a quiet, classy hotel near the ferry terminal. He didn't speak a word except to the Customs guys.

What could he say?

He'd been pushing and prodding her, forcing her out of hiding, in denial the entire time that he himself had anything to hide—then she'd ripped the blinders from his face and showed him up for the hypocrite he was.

What a jerk. He'd been obsessed with Mia all those years, but he'd never once shown her. He'd done exactly what she said—patted her on the head, treated her like a kid. Thinking, because he couldn't stop fantasizing about her, that she had to know how he felt—and he'd believed she'd rejected him without a word.

But Mia had been a teenager who'd lost her mother and her quiet life, who had been dragged into a glittering world by the father she adored but barely knew. Billy had dragged his daughter into his jet-setting life, but he'd never let her in to his most private world.

She hadn't even known he loved Nicole until a few months ago.

She'd been far more lost in the End Game world than he'd realized.

Even if she *had* wanted him, to approach the lead singer of her father's band and say she liked him would have felt ridiculous to her. How would she have been any different from the groupies that had surrounded the band?

No wonder she'd always seemed so little-girl-lost beneath those superior looks. Mia had lost everything, and he'd been angry with *her,* punishing her for crimes that were never hers. Because she'd been an uptown girl and he'd been a downtown boy, he'd expected her rejection…and his sense of inferiority had made it a self-fulfilling prophecy.

If she thought of him as a jerk, he deserved it.

So why had she come to him with this plan, believing she could trust him?

She'd showered and changed into a pair of shortie pajamas that sent his pulse racing, but she climbed into bed without looking at him. "I assume we can share the bed without a debate over who gets more of it," she said stiffly.

He looked at her, covered by a sheet to the neck, and felt a shaft of tenderness streak through him. He'd seen her in action—dealing with Billy, with the band members and all the self-obsessed jerks in their world. Tact was Mia's middle name—except with him. With him, she'd always been off-balance. Why had he never noticed that before?

"Mia, I've been a real jerk today. Can we start over?" he asked softly.

She glanced at him through her floppy fringe, and if it was a defense mechanism it was so *cute* he ached to kiss her. "Again?"

He held up a hand. "I'll be better after twelve hours' decent sleep. Scout's honor."

She bit her lip. "I know I shouldn't have sprung all this on you when you've had so little sleep. Let's forget today—well, the worst bits." She smiled at him with an enchanting shyness.

"Keeping the good bits?" He slid into bed beside her.

He was in bed with Mia, wearing almost nothing, her lovely hair spreading across from her pillow to his.

Tomorrow she'd be his wife.

Judging by her blush and the darkness of her eyes, she was thinking the same thoughts and wondering the same things. *Wanting* the same things.

"Depends on what you think the 'good bits' are." Her words were almost a whisper.

His heart was pounding so hard against his chest he couldn't breathe properly. "I definitely rate kissing and touching you as the 'good bits'."

Her eyes turned dark, languid. Breathing faster, she moved closer—but her words broke the mood. "What's your real name?"

Lost in the wonder of having her still want him after all he'd said to make her hate him, he blinked. "What?"

She lifted one shoulder in a shy shrug. "What do the letters C.J. stand for?"

He groaned, caught between desire and desperate embarrassment. "Can't we stick with C.J.?"

Her lashes fluttered down; she sucked in her lips in a way he'd begun to recognize as *I don't know what to say* mode for Mia. "But…everyone calls you C.J."

"Yeah," he murmured, hoping for an encouraging tone. She obviously had a point, and would get to it if he let her.

"Including the press, your fans, and…the girls you've been with." Her cheeks were crimson.

Thinking he understood, he gathered her close, running his fingers through her hair, exultant that she might be jealous, trying to hide it in case he was wrong and scared her off. "There haven't been as many as you think."

"That's not it." With a small, frustrated sound, she splayed her hands across his chest. "That's C.J. Hunter." She looked up, her eyes soft, unfocussed without her glasses, her body pliant against him, driving him nuts with need. "I always felt kind of intimidated by the whole C.J. Hunter thing…but—" she smiled shyly "—I think I like you."

Slam. Just like that it happened. He'd always known that if Mia ever came to want him it would be in spite of his being C.J. Hunter, never because of it…and with her words he fell headfirst in love.

Or maybe he'd loved her all along and had been hiding from it. Because he'd always known she was too sweet, too high, too pure for the likes of him.

She didn't like the rock star or the doctor. She liked *him*.

"Christian," he murmured, trusting her with the embarrassing truth—the name he'd always hated and been taunted about right through school. "Christian James Hunter." He prayed fervently that the James in the middle would break the connection. How his parents could have saddled him with Christian when his surname was Hunter, he'd never understood. The kids at school had been merciless. *Ha-ha-ha—you hunt Christians! Don't kill me coz I went to church yesterday!*

But Mia's eyes lit. "Christian," she said softly, that secret, feminine smile curving her luscious mouth. "Oh, that's so…sexy. Kiss me, Christian," she murmured, drawing his name out with sensuous emphasis as she pulled him down onto her.

The slow, tender kiss took him by surprise. The heated passion they'd known until now, as addictive as it was, couldn't compare to this sweet poignancy…and he knew, much as he was dying here, they wouldn't make love tonight.

Some things were worth waiting for—and, while he'd been waiting more than ten years, to Mia this was all new. One step at a time, one connection, one kiss. She *liked* him, and for now it was enough.

"Ah, *Christian,*" she purred as he kissed her

throat—and for the first time in his life he loved his name. Loved it on her lips, spoken as if he were the only man on earth.

"Mia," he groaned, when her hands explored beneath his shirt. "I've only got so much self-control, sweetheart."

"So?" she whispered in his ear, and he shuddered. She kissed his ear and trailed down his neck, and he forgot his scruples… For a minute—or was it ten?

But when they were half naked, and she was arching up to him, moaning softly at the feel of his skin on hers—oh, *man,* she was even more beautiful when she was radiant with passion—a final moment of sanity came.

It hasn't even been a day. She'll hate you for this tomorrow. And it'll be two to three years before you can maintain a relationship. Six months' surgical rotation followed by long hours in research or a hospital ward.

No woman should have to put up with that—especially Mia, who'd lived all those years with a father who worked long, erratic hours and put his career before her needs…

"You'd better be sure, Mia, before we go too far. I want you like crazy, but this can't last," he growled. "Not with the life and career I have."

The cloudy desire in her eyes was doused in an instant. She pushed him off her and scrambled back into her pajama top—and he cursed his stupidity in opening his big mouth. "You're right," she said tersely. "This can't go anywhere."

"You want me," he growled, with all the frustration inside him. Knowing she was right, and mirroring his thoughts, only made it worse.

"That's obvious. I'm not going to lie for the sake of stupid pride." She sighed, sitting on the opposite side of the bed, looking out at the water lapping against the beach outside. She turned to him, her eyes remote, cool—that damned cockroach look. But now he knew more about her he could see the vulnerability hiding beneath. "Thank you for playing Devil's advocate, Christian. It can't have been easy."

Easy? Nothing about his feelings for Mia was easy. In fact everything was *hard*—physically as well as emotionally. He wanted her like crazy, but he'd almost ruined this for them both. Somewhere in the past twelve hours he'd forgotten, almost begun to believe he could play this game for keeps.

He wasn't heel enough to ask her to share a life that only differed from her current life with Billy in geography—and in sleeping arrangements. He'd get all the benefits, Mia all the waiting, left behind and lonely.

"It's okay." He still sounded gruff with desire. "Just remember this is your show, Mia. I'm just asking you to be sure it's what you want." He grinned and winked, and she'd never know what an effort it took to sound playful. "Whatever you want, I'm up for it." *In the worst kind of way...*

Her smile turned shy at his words. "Thank you, Christian," she whispered, and he loved the sound of his name on her lips. "I'll remember that."

"So we're okay?" he asked huskily, unable to stop staring at her. Lovely Mia, shy Mia, cranky Mia, passionate Mia—every mood enchanted him. *She* enchanted him.

He was such a goner.

"We're good." She leaned over and kissed his mouth, soft and sweet—and the next thing he knew they were tangled in the sheets, kissing and tumbling over and over in the oldest dance known to man and woman.

"Christian...*oh*..." She arched up against him as he kissed down the line of her breastbone. "What you do to me," she whispered. "It's never felt like this..."

The hardest thing he'd ever done in his life was pull away again.

"Christian?" she faltered, her cheeks flushed and her eyes starry—he'd done that to her.

He smiled down at her, aching, wishing. "We have a big day tomorrow—and four hours' sleep out of forty-five..." Not knowing how to finish that, he let it trail off.

"I'm sorry," she cried, sounding stricken. "I've been...taking advantage of you when you're tired." Her cheeks were crimson.

He took her face in his hands. "You have no idea how much I want you to take advantage of me." Grinning down at her, he moved slowly, letting her feel his aroused state again. "But for Billy's sake we have to stick to the plan." He rolled off her, pulled on his shirt, socks and running shoes, and headed for the door. "My mind's buzzing. I'm going for a run before bed."

Bed and Mia: a delicious, irresistible combination…and she wanted him. She was all his for the taking. A fantasy come to life—

If only he could live up to the forever promises they would be making tomorrow.

With a curse he kept inside his head, he left his adorable bride-to-be and pounded the coral sand until his vision blurred, his head pounded with exhaustion, and he couldn't physically contemplate the magnificent temptation awaiting him in his bed.

"I now pronounce you husband and wife." The celebrant smiled at the barefoot couple who wore traditional Fijian wedding clothes, flowers in their hair. "You may kiss your bride," he prompted Christian gently.

Her new husband lifted her hands to his, kissing one palm, then the other, and Mia quivered. He drew her against him and kissed her, slow and gentle.

And though she loved every moment of it she felt like a liar, giving those vows to love him in sickness and in health for a lifetime. If he'd lied too, she wouldn't feel so bad—but she couldn't ask. If he had feelings for her, she'd made a fool of him; if he didn't, she'd made a complete idiot of herself.

Bruck-bruck-bruck…

How ridiculous is this? I'm kissing the man of a million girls' dreams, and wondering about my faults.

That was the problem. The thought that C.J. Hunter could want her terrified her…but *Christian* was beginning to terrify her just as much. Because he was becoming the man of *her* dreams, and she only had nine more days with him.

Christian pulled away. "We should sign the papers and get on with alerting the media."

Her heart lurched. While he'd kissed her she'd wondered how to make him stay; his mind had been on the plan.

"I'll call Jess and Dave. If they both make the leak the same day it'll make a bigger splash." He led her to the little pavilion where a table stood with their marriage papers.

"Okay," she replied, sounding lame.

He frowned down at her. "What's wrong, Mia? Isn't this what you wanted?"

She pulled a self-deprecating face, wishing she didn't feel so sad at his ability to keep his mind on the job. After all, she deserved nothing better. "Yes, of course it is."

"Jess is pretty excited by all this. She loves being in on the secret and being able to dole out the goss one delicious slice at a time. She hasn't had her fifteen minutes of fame since I left End Game, and as my sister she'll not only be believed, but be paid well for her 'exclusives'." He grinned, and signed the papers with a flourish, handing her the pen. "Simon, her husband, doesn't like accepting anything from me but presents for the kids."

"Okay," she murmured, hating the melting power his grin had over her even when he was all business. She couldn't help an insecure glance up at him, nibbling the inside of her lip. "She doesn't hate me for this, does she?" Though she'd never met Jess, it suddenly seemed important that his family like her.

Christian's face softened. "She wasn't even angry. She'd have done it for our dad, and she knows how much Billy means to me."

The celebrant congratulated them. The paid witnesses—resort staff—hugged them exuberantly, wishing them happiness.

Christian drew her close. "For the witnesses—or the cameras," he whispered as he kissed her again. But it wasn't so gentle. Passion simmered and grew a life of its own. She kissed him back with aching hunger, holding nothing back.

Each kiss could be the last, depending on media coverage.

CHAPTER SIX

C.J. HUNTER'S Secret Wedding?

Rumors of a secret wedding between C.J. Hunter and Mia Browning have been confirmed by two sources close to the couple. Billy Browning and his wife Nicole are still in hiding, but Mia's publicist, Gavin McClintock, has confirmed the romance between the two. He added that there will be an official announcement soon.

Did she have the slightest clue that he was completely crazy about her?

Christian—she even had him thinking of himself by his hated name!—watched Mia, still in her traditional wedding dress, her hair falling over her shoulders and breasts, nibbling her nails instead of the tiramisu she'd chosen for dessert. She wouldn't meet his gaze, and hadn't since he'd cuddled her for a photo requested by the resort photographer. He'd kissed her palm with lingering desire before he'd let her scuttle back to her side of the table…and scuttle she had, with the whole frightened rabbit thing going on.

When he'd tried to call her on it, she'd whispered fiercely, "You said there wouldn't be any hype tonight. I'll—I can start the show tomorrow, right?"

"Someone could have arrived early," he murmured low. "Or if anyone recognizes us they could take a few candid shots and make some cash."

Her startled glance around the room was endearing, because behind her defiance lay something deeper. She was so palpably nervous. Was she frightened he'd make demands on her? Strangely, the thought inspired tenderness instead of frustration, because every instinct told him Mia hadn't had anyone in her life for a long time.

Just like him.

She wouldn't be so frightened if she didn't want me. She'd be in control.

She was so *adorable*. She was his bride—and he'd promised it would be her choice. No seduction, not even persuasion. He had nothing to give her beyond this honeymoon.

Time for reassurance. "I think the tiramisu would taste better than that," he suggested, pulling her finger from her mouth.

She glanced up, startled, and her glasses slipped down her stubby little nose. "Oh." She fiddled with the fingers he held, trying to make him let go. "I—I was thinking."

"I can see that." He took pity on her. "Mia, don't

think so hard. I told you—whatever happens between us is your call."

If anything, the warmth streaking her face grew deeper, hotter. "I know that." She snatched her hand from his.

"Not in public—darling." He reclaimed her hand, and took the other as well. "We never know who's watching…even in the bedroom."

"So we keep the curtains closed!"

He softened again at the panic in her voice. "We're in the electronic age, Mia. Any housemaid could be bribed to put a tiny camera in the bedroom."

She gaped at him in that endearing way she had. "Eeew," she gasped. "Then—then we can't possibly…"

And, he noted in half-shamed satisfaction, she looked more cheated than relieved.

He grinned. "I've had some experience with how some of the more unscrupulous operators work. I've had these kinds of intrusions." "Patients" coming to him in the hospital, or a so-called patient's relative, and a dark-haired, sweetly shy waitress at his favorite restaurant he'd actually liked and asked out three years ago. "I bought a sweeper. I packed it. They can't get us in private. We only need to show affection out here, where you're safe. Whatever happens in our room will be for you and me alone." He kissed the hands he held and felt her quiver. "Remember, we *want* them to follow us. Once Dave and Jess go into action, and Billy denies all knowledge, they'll flock around us and leave Billy and Nicole alone."

She frowned, looking down at her dessert, then pushing it away before looking up with a brilliant smile. "You seem to have the plan well in hand."

He was about to tease her when he saw her nibbling the inside of her lip. *Insecure. Lost,* he translated. How he'd come to know her so well in just over a day, after barely seeing her in years, he had no idea—but he was sure he was right.

"Let's get out of here," he murmured low. "For a walk along the beach," he added when the fear flared in her expressive eyes. "We'll have to cuddle, of course, and kiss once or twice, in case anyone's watching."

With a defeated nod and a sigh, she got to her feet, leaving her dessert untouched.

Christian smiled to himself as, leaving the restaurant, she gazed up at him in her best imitation of an adoring bride—she looked almost cross-eyed with fear.

Man, she was so damn adorable, and he loved her so much—but, though he ached to make love to her, he wouldn't. That he knew he *could* seduce her was useless knowledge, because loving her would become his most painful memory. It would be over soon after the honeymoon, and he had nothing to give her after this week. Not even time.

It didn't stop the battle inside him—body and heart against good sense. Loving her, wanting her, forcing himself to do what was best for her. In all these years nothing had ever stopped that fight.

But right now he'd take what pleasure he could get. He wrapped his arm around her waist as they walked, loving the feel of her against him, so curvy and feminine.

"It's warm here for May," she said with a quiver in her voice, as her arm snaked around his waist in return. She looked up at the clear sky, dotted with stars. "It's hard to believe it's so cold at home."

He bent toward her ear. "It's almost always balmy here. A perfect place for a honeymoon, don't you think?"

He felt a shiver ran through her. "Um…I suppose so."

His body won the fight against reason for a moment. "It *is* our honeymoon, Mia. No matter how it started," he whispered, letting his lips brush her ear.

A faint gasp came to him; she quivered at the touch, then turned in his arms, going up on her toes as she lay flush against him. "Ah, Christian…" Her voice was all husky as she said his name. Her mouth was seeking his, *wanting*.

His lightest touch could make her want him; hers made him forget his scruples. So when her lips touched his every thought flew out the window as he lifted her against him and kissed her back.

Every time they kissed it felt like the first time… but it could be the last. Despite all his plans he wanted to just wing it, to go with the flow—

More like get totally lost in her touch.

He'd always known Mia was dangerous—she'd turned him into a stammering wreck the first time he'd seen her, and that was *before* they kissed. But now…

Now you have to stop it.

He pulled away, the man in him exulting that it was always *him* ending their kisses, loving that she got lost in his touch and forgot the stupid *plan*. "I think that's enough for public display. Good work, Mia."

The flushed passion in her face faded the moment he pulled away. "Of course. I'm—that was what I—"

She shook her head and lapsed into silence—and that look she'd been trying to hide all day replaced the sweet, dawning desire. With a bland smile to fool any hidden cameras she led the way to their room, as if leading him to bed, but she didn't look at him once. She grabbed her PJs and disappeared into the bathroom as soon as the door closed behind them.

He sighed, sat on the bed, and made the calls to Jess and Dave.

It took half an hour to crawl right through the bathroom, checking for any electronic devices, before she'd risk the shower, but she couldn't ask Christian for help. He'd taken over everything in the past day—including her thoughts and her body's needs.

In the end she did an awkward undress and redress, putting on her bikini to shower.

She knew Christian was disturbed by the change in her. She was too restrained, too quiet, not playing the bride as she ought. But it was either distance herself or—

No. No!

She almost broke the taps twisting them off. Even the hard rubbing down of her wet skin with a towel didn't help. *She wanted him.* Her body was crying out for him, every time he touched her she melted, and *he* was always the one bringing it to an end.

He obviously had self-control enough to stop. While she—

So humiliating. How could she be in control when every minute that passed with him made her feel more infatuated? She felt like an obsessed groupie, while he was completely focussed, utterly in control of the situation.

In control of *her*. And there wasn't a thing she could do about it.

"Mia? You okay? You've been in there a long time."

"I'm fine." She winced at the clipped tone of her voice. "Is it all in motion?"

A short hesitation, then he said, "Are you decent?"

She hastily shoved on the robe the island resort supplied. "Come in."

Bad mistake.

He opened the door, and the flash of desire tearing through her was nearly pain. *No* man should look so good and yet so sinful. He'd obviously gone running again while she'd showered. In his running shorts and a singlet top, he was all hot and sweaty, vibrant and utterly male.

She turned and picked up the scraps of material that had been her wedding outfit, glad for the shot of wistfulness at the death of her long-held dream of a traditional wedding—a wedding with a man who loved her, who'd asked *her* to marry him.

Glad, because at least one part of her wasn't running sky-high on hormones.

If she just didn't look at him, maybe she could…

"Are you stuck in that position, or do you just not want to look at me?" His voice was soft, husky.

Knowing.

It had to stop. She wasn't a teenage girl with a groupie crush. They were *married*—even if it was only for a few weeks. "Don't make me say it." She straightened and turned around, not quite looking at him. "You know what you do to me. Surely your revenge has been thorough enough? You seem to have no trouble stopping when you're kissing me, and you remember the plan when I forget everything but you."

"Mia…"

Feeling a dreaded lump rising in her throat at the tenderness in his rough angel's voice, she shook her head and pushed past him into the bedroom. "I'm tired. I can't deal with any more of my faults and weaknesses today. You shower. I'll sleep." *Please, God, let me sleep…don't give me a repeat of last night.* Trying to lie still while her hands ached to reach out and touch him…

"That's not fair." He spoke right behind her: everything she yearned for was mere inches from her needy body, and her entire frame shuddered with longing.

"Okay, it wasn't fair. You've been very nice today.

Don't make me say any more," she whispered. Her head drooped. "Please, Christian…"

"I don't want revenge anymore, Mia. I love how much you want me—and it's our wedding night," he whispered back, his breath stirring her hair.

Her throat convulsed. *Want, hunger, aching, craving…*

If he didn't stop she'd make a fool of herself *again*.

"It's our wedding night only because I asked you to marry me. We're only on this island because I came to you. Because my father's sick and you care about him," she managed to choke out. Fighting him. Fighting herself.

"Tonight has nothing to do with Billy," he murmured, still so close to her it was sweet addiction and beautiful pain. "Tonight it's just you and me, and just being near you is killing me. I've done my best to stop, remembered all the reasons this is a bad idea, but I can't fight it anymore, Mia. If you don't want to make love, you're going to have to tell me no. You'll have to stop me from touching you. Because just one touch and I'll be gone. Tell me no, Mia," he whispered, brushing his body against her.

The hot current of wanting from his body filled her senses to overflowing, every pore and cell crying his name. *Christian…*

Could there be a worse moment to discover she was crazy in love with him?

Two days ago she'd have scoffed at the thought that level-headed Mia Browning could fall in love with C.J. Hunter in two days—but now she knew better. Now she knew why no other man had ever come close to touching her heart.

It had been Christian's the whole time. She'd been in love with him for years—not with C.J. Hunter, but with the man beneath that the fans only caught in glimpses. Why else would she have avoided the only person near her own age, someone who could have been her friend, a brother figure? But she'd resented his big-brother attitude from the start, the patting on the head. She'd never understood why, when she'd craved a brother or sister's uncomplicated affection for so long, but she'd always been revolted at the thought of asking Christian to be her brother.

She'd been in love with him since her teens—and the discovery was bittersweet. Christian might not be exactly like her father, but *she* was her mother's daughter, as her father had always said…and after a lifetime running she'd made her mother's mistakes. She'd fallen in love with an extraordinary man, one dedicated to his profession.

"We shouldn't." It took every ounce of strength she had not to thread her hands through his hair, draw his body down to her and lead him to that big, lovely bed. "Please, let's get through this with every-thing intact and say goodbye with a smile. I don't want to hate you." *The same kind of hate my mother had for my father: the kind that stems from a once-in-a-lifetime love gone wrong.*

After a few moments in which she could feel her

heart beating, he said, "As a passion-killer, that's a winner…or it would be if I believed you." He lifted her chin, making her meet his gaze. "I think you've been trying to hate me for years, Mia—trying and failing, or we wouldn't be here now. You want me as much as I want you," he whispered, brushing his lips over hers.

With his lightest touch craving crashed into fear and knocked it out; longing turned into a lifetime of feeling alone, screaming that Christian could—*could*—

Her arms were tight around his neck before she knew it; her lips were on his at that same moment of memory and realization.

Don't subject yourself to a lifetime of loneliness, Mia. Don't be like me!

But I've always been alone until yesterday. Until Christian touched me.

Still kissing him, she pulled him by the shirt and drew him backward, to the bed.

Women like Mia ought to come with warning labels: *Highly addictive substance within.*

Christian held her close in the aftermath of the loving of his life, blowing away the strands of silky black hair that drifted across his mouth. Her head rested on his chest, and her fingers played over the skin of his stomach, arousing him over again—but he hung onto thin threads of control, not by will-power but by sheer tenderness.

Surely she wouldn't be able to make love again for another day?

He didn't indulge in the kind of clichés she claimed to hate, or else he'd ask, *Why me?*

But as he was coming to know the real Mia he could guess why he was her first lover—and why she'd chosen him now, tonight. Practical, straight-talking Mia was a romantic at heart…gentle, shy Mia, covering her deepest emotion with bravado and passion, *felt* something for him.

Dear God, how he adored her—but he couldn't speak it aloud or let her say it. He couldn't let it happen now, of all worst possible times, when Billy's health was at stake and he himself had months and years of an insane schedule if he was to reach his ultimate goal.

He couldn't ask her to wait, much as he wanted to. It wasn't fair. She'd already waited twenty-seven years for her life to begin.

Marrying a doctor was a dream for many women—but he'd seen the burnout and divorce rate among his colleagues. Heaps of guys not yet forty were on wife number two or three or even four. In that way they were little different to rock stars—the round-the-clock lifestyle slowly strangled the life from love. Partners and children left alone far too long couldn't stand the stress.

He wouldn't be free to be the kind of man Mia deserved for another five years, and by then she'd be married, with a baby—

The picture grabbed hold of him: pretty, exotic Mia, rounded, with a baby at her breast, looking up with an ecstatic smile as he walked through the door…

Christian, she'd say, all breathy—

"Christian?"

He started a little, and looked down at her with a smile. "Hey. Just thinking."

She didn't ask—but that was Mia. "It's late."

"Yeah." But he wouldn't sleep. Not with her lying beside him, knowing she was his for the taking—at least for now.

But though they both knew it had to end he couldn't shatter her illusions, or bring himself to hurt her with blunt reality, even for her sake. Not now, the night she'd made him her lover. A few days of honeymoon—who could it hurt? He'd make her happy for the brief time they had together, give her confidence to find her life, maybe even find—

He couldn't make the thought form. Not even if she deserved that kind of happiness. If eight days was all he had with the woman he loved...

Oh, *man,* her hands were so soft, threading through his chest hair, wandering over his stomach, trailing over his thigh. "Mia." With his final threads of control, his last shard of nobility, he took her hands in his. "We can't do any more now—it will hurt you."

"Hmm?" She dropped a lingering kiss on his chest. "It didn't hurt the first time, Christian—well, not for long." She smiled up at him in that short-sighted blurry way he couldn't resist. "I don't think this time will hurt at all." She nibbled at his ear and he was *such* a goner. "I think this time will be even more wonderful. Don't you?"

Yup, he was a goner—scruples and nobility heaped on a smoldering pile of desire and burning to ash. He cupped her breast in his hand and at the same time nuzzled her throat. "You lifting the bar, Mrs. Hunter?" Loving the sound of it. Mia Hunter. *His* wife, *his* bride. His lover.

Just *his*.

"Ah, *Christian*," she whispered, filled with instant passion, and without a moment's hesitation, without fear or nervousness, she drew him around and down on her.

CHAPTER SEVEN

REAL life intruded soon enough.

It was barely eight a.m. when the knocking began. Christian groaned and nudged Mia awake. "Only the press would be rude enough to wake us this early."

Mia moaned and snuggled into his shoulder, her lush body snug against the length of him. "Not yet," she whispered.

More knocking, and she sighed. "Haven't they heard the word 'honeymoon'?"

"They've heard it, all right. That's why they're here." Was the tenderness in his voice obvious? "They must have come over with the early tour group."

The third knock could almost wake the dead. "Mia, we'd better clean up…"

She sucked her lips in. Their clothes were everywhere, the sheets strewn across the floor. "Hurry!"

He shoved into his running shorts and singlet top while she scrambled into her bikini and sarong—

The knocks were getting louder, more insistent.

"Go away," he called, with the rough, gravelly

voice he was famed for, as they ran around clearing
away the evidence that was way too private for the
press—even for Billy's sake.

"C.J.! Is it true you've married Mia Browning?"

"Is she with you?" another voice, obviously
American, called.

"Some of the overseas press have flown out here
already." He met Mia's eyes and saw the same regret.
Their brief idyll was over.

"I'll call Brian to get the jet fueled," she whispered
as she picked up the sheets and bedcover, and laid
them on the bed. "You handle them. I'll act like I'm
trying to hide."

He nodded, wishing for another hour, another day
with her, uninterrupted, a chance to be a normal
couple. She deserved so much more than this...

He should never have made love to her in the first
place. What a jerk. He'd seduced her into wanting
it, even knowing it was always going to end like this
in the morning. Yet Mia's face was placid, in-
scrutable, as she picked up the phone and called the
pilot.

With a muttered curse, he went into action.

Flashes filled the room from twenty cameras the
moment he opened the door. "I'm on my holidays—
do you mind?" he yelled, with an exasperation he
didn't need to feign.

"Don't you mean your honeymoon, C.J.?"
someone yelled, and the reporters laughed. "Is it true
you married Mia Browning?"

"How does Billy feel about your eloping with his only child?" another yelled.

"Have you written a song for her yet?"

"You could name it 'Loving The Ice-cream-Girl'," someone called, and everyone laughed again.

"Say that to my face, you coward. You're talking about my wife!" he growled, his mind flashing back to Mia, flushed with passion, taking him heart and soul with her touch. Wanting him over and over through the night.

"So it's true?"

"Hey, there's Mia!" someone yelled. The reporters lifted their cameras high, aiming at Mia, whom he felt dash by, making a beeline for the bathroom.

"You've had your fun," Christian said flatly. "You've got your shots. Take them back to your tabloids and get paid. This is our honeymoon—can you take a hike?"

No chance. They'd follow them everywhere, no matter where they went, just as Mia had planned. Mission accomplished—and their very private honeymoon was over.

He slammed the door closed after another four dozen flashes, and pulled the chain across. "Right," he said as Mia emerged, her brows lifted, looking unruffled. "Complain to the manager. We can get them turfed out, but it won't last."

She disconnected her mobile phone. "Brian says he can land here. There's a strip at the back of the resort."

"Great. We have to make enough fuss to get the

squizzes off the island entirely. When they see us taking off, and in what direction, the chase begins." He hesitated. "If we fly back to Sydney I can introduce you to my parents and we can let the squizzes find us there. It should take the heat from Billy."

She smiled, nodded, and indicated the phone. "You might want to call your parents."

He picked it up. "Can you pack up our stuff? We'll need to make a quick getaway."

She grinned, folding their clothes and putting yesterday's stuff into the resort laundry bag. "Just call us Bonnie and Clyde."

How could she laugh? Surely she should be— emotional—after last night? She seemed to be taking everything in stride, while all *he* felt was the need to hit someone.

"I always knew Christian was carrying a torch for someone," his mother said happily to Mia late that afternoon, while Christian was arranging for another getaway on his old motorbike, installed in his parents' garage. "He's been so standoffish with the girls we introduced him to these past few years." The tall, dark-haired, curvaceous woman hugged Mia, who felt a mixture of sweetness and guilt. "But we know you won't have married him for his fame."

Mia blushed and hid it by hugging Mrs. Hunter— Patricia—back. "Thank you."

"I'm so glad you've got him answering to his

name." Patricia patted her shoulder. "He always hated the teasing he got on it, but it's a lovely name."

Mia, remembering her reaction to his name, felt her blush grow deeper. *That* wasn't a proper response to make to her new mother-in-law.

"So, what have you been doing with yourself since Christian left the band?"

Her blush grew. How did she tell her new mother-in-law she'd written a book that included her son? "I've been, um, looking after Dad…"

"There's nothing wrong with putting family first, Mia." Patricia patted her shoulder. "What are your plans?" she said briskly. "Come over for dinner once the honeymoon's over. Maybe it would help to have some feedback on what you want to do?"

A lump thickened her throat. Guilt and pain intertwined… When the honeymoon was over she and Christian would be over. Patricia would know exactly what Mia was doing with her life. And she might hate her.

She had to tell Christian about the book—and soon.

"I'd like that," she said huskily.

Patricia hugged her again. "You're family now, Mia. I don't have a fancy education or anything, but if there's one thing I do well it's mothering—and grandmothering," she added with a wink. "Remember that when you and Christian have children. I love having the kids over, and I'd love a granddaughter."

"Stop nagging, Mum, we've only been married just over a day!" Coming into the room with his father, who was an older version of him, Christian strolled over and took Mia from his mother's arms. He smiled down at her, warm and intimate—and even if it was an act for his parents she felt her whole body go into meltdown. "Speaking of honeymoons…"

"Let Mia finish her cup of tea. She looks like she could use it. She looks so tired. Did you keep her up all—?"

"Pat!"

Christian's dad, tall and lithe and dark, like his son, growled at the same moment Christian snapped, "Mum!"

Patricia gasped, seeing the heat flooding Mia's face. "Mia, I'm sorry. That's another thing I do well—putting my foot in my mouth." She bit her lip, but a little laugh escaped her. "Go and enjoy yourselves, kids, and we'll see you when you're back home."

At that moment someone knocked at the door. Michael Hunter peeked out the curtains. "There are about twenty people out there with cameras!"

"They've found us," Christian said, sounding creditably tense. "We have to go. Mia, are you up for a garage escape?"

Half glad to be leaving these people who'd made her so welcome in their family, despite their unorthodox wedding, she grinned at him. "Try me."

This had to be the worst possible time for him to get aroused thinking of the implications of those words! Lucky for Christian his T-shirt was hanging outside his jeans and his parents couldn't see…" Sorry to leave you with this, guys. Just tell them what you know—and hang out for as much as you can get from them. They don't deserve it for free."

"But, son—"

"Billy's sick, remember," he said, with the same tension. "He doesn't know about us. We don't want the press to find out he's sick, or they'll hound him. Can you handle this for our sake—and for Billy's?"

"Just watch us," his mother said stoutly. "We'll do what we can to hold them off." She kissed him. "Welcome to the family, Mia." His mum kissed Mia, whose smile quivered with emotion.

Trying so hard to hold it together for Billy's sake...

They roared out of the automatic garage door two minutes later, while his parents were fending off the press at the front door. As he swerved around the members of the press stupid enough to try and chase them on foot Mia snuggled into him, her helmeted head lying on his back.

In total trust.

Well, why wouldn't she? Now Billy has Nicole, I'm all she has.

Oh, God help him. Why hadn't he thought of that before he'd touched her? If this marriage had to end before it truly began, he should never have made love to her.

She knew that when you took her to bed, you jerk. She isn't counting on forever. She's not some silly weakling, or she'd never have survived life with End Game.

But, as he'd discovered in the past few days, what the mind knew the heart could discount, if it wanted something enough. As he wanted Mia.

As Mia wanted him. If she hadn't, he would never have become her first lover.

He couldn't make her repeat her childhood over again—and marriage to him would barely be any different to her life with End Game. Always at someone else's convenience, waiting... He should let her go, find someone else.

Mia jerked back, squealed, and clung to him as his body roared its protest, twisting the accelerator so hard the bike's speed shot to warp.

No matter how much he hated it he had to let her go—sooner rather than later. His future was all long hours and hard work. She'd spent enough time in the shadows of someone else's life. She deserved much better than he could give her.

C.J.'s Secret Wedding A Fact!

C.J. Hunter married Mia Browning yesterday in a Fijian beach ceremony after a relationship spanning only weeks, according to C.J.'s sister Jess Abrahams. "He always liked her, but the timing wasn't right," Ms Abrahams said. "They met again at Billy and Nicole's wedding. It all went from there."

Billy Browning is furious at the marriage. He claims to have no knowledge of a romance between the two famous recluses. "I can't

*believe she didn't invite us," was his only
comment by phone. He and wife Nicole, Martin
Neilson's ex, have gone into hiding.*

*Neilson, when contacted for comment,
wished C.J. and Mia all happiness.*

*However, a source close to the couple gives
the marriage a matter of weeks. "Mia doesn't
know what she's in for. C.J.'s a dedicated
doctor, and the divorce rate for specialists is
about the same as for rockers."*

"Oh…"

Mia felt Christian's gaze on her face, rather than
the vista all around them, but for once he couldn't
hold her attention. She couldn't stop turning, taking
it all in. For the first time in her life she couldn't see
a building, a car or a bus.

Kakadu.

Mile upon mile of untouched nature, a waving
sea of gum trees and rivers and rocks—and they
stood upon the biggest. A sunlit shimmer many
miles to the north might be the ocean—but it could
just be the glimmering silver of the gums and the
rivers melding. Hundreds of meters beneath their
feet crocodiles nested in the rivers, spiders spun
webs across trees, brolgas called for their mates.
Above them cockatoos squawked, kookaburras
chuckled and eagles spread magnificent wings,
sailing across a sky so bright she wanted to jump
into its diamond clearness. Here life went on without

politics or religion or greed or suffering…or the media. It made everything she'd ever thought of or wanted seem insignificant.

A wild paradise that touched a part of her soul she'd never known existed until this day, this hour.

"Oh, Christian, I've never…it's like…" She shook her head a little, turning west and south.

"Recognize it?" he asked, sounding odd—emotional somehow.

She turned to him, frowning. Speech seemed almost beyond her.

"It's Ubirr," he said quietly, his hand taking hers. "Remember the *Crocodile Dundee* movie? This is where his house was supposed to be."

"I watched a lot of movies on tour." She made a rueful face. "You watched that with me, didn't you?"

He nodded. "Remember what I said then…that I'd come here when I had time? This is my fifth trip."

"I can see why," she whispered. It was one of those places where you had to whisper: it inspired reverence. It was like the hand of God was so strong here no one dared interfere with it.

"I find a peace here I've never known anywhere else."

She squeezed the hand she held. "Thank you for bringing me here. For trusting me with your special place."

"I've never come here without wondering how you'd react to it."

"I—" She shook her head. "I can't explain…"

"I know." He drew her against his body; she wrapped her arms around his waist and his fingers twined through the ends of her hair. They stood there holding each other in silence as tourists came and went all around them. Some made hushed comments about the rock art left there centuries ago, now part of the landscape, giving it a sacred feel. Some stood beside them in the same rapt silence.

One person lifted their camera phone and took a shot of them instead of the land; lost in the world around them, and each other, they didn't notice.

C.J.'s Crazy Honeymoon!

C.J. Hunter has odd tastes in honeymoon locations. Instead of taking his bride Mia Browning to Ibiza, Lizard Island or the Caribbean, they're in Crocodile Dundee territory. This shot of them standing awestruck on Ubirr Rock in Kakadu was sent to us by a happy fan. The shot below, by another fan, shows them at the Kakadu Resort, joining in the barbecue sing-along beneath the stars last night. Neither showed off their musical prowess, preferring to sit in the background, allowing the song leader to remain in happy ignorance of the stars in his group.

A source close to the couple says the outback is C.J.'s preferred holiday destination…and by the look on her face in these shots Mia isn't arguing.

* * *

Christian emerged from the bathroom, a towel slung low around his hips. Mia had been writing in her journal when he'd deliberately walked by her naked, hoping she'd get the message and join him.

Fifteen minutes later she was still writing, so absorbed she didn't even look up.

"What is that?" he asked with a frown, still feeling let down, overlooked. "You're always scribbling in that notebook. You still keep a diary?"

"What? Oh…Christian." She looked up, sucking her lips in again. "This is…um…"

Oh…Christian. She'd forgotten all about him. They'd been married—what? Three days? And whatever she was doing, it was obvious she didn't want to tell him. "Don't worry, Mia. You keep scribbling. I'll make the arrangements for our next appearance."

With a little knowing smile, she said, "Somebody's feeling neglected." She reached out and twitched the towel from him as he passed. "You want to know what I'm doing in that notebook?" She pulled him down to her. "I've been meaning to tell you…in fact, I want to talk to you about it. You need to know before…"

But by then he'd forgotten all about his shower disappointment, and didn't give a hang about her scribblings. "Later…much later," he muttered roughly, stripping her with slow fascination, kissing everywhere he exposed.

Her eyes dark with arousal, Mia smiled and lay back on the bed, holding her arms out to him.

* * *

"It's so warm!" Mia slid into the hot springs with a happy little shiver.

Christian watched her lie on her back, floating, her lovely hair spreading across the water, and ached with a cocktail of pride and wanting. She hadn't complained once—not when the media had found them in Kakadu, and in the tiny hotel in Gove, in Arnhem Land. She'd just made plans to come back later— when—

They didn't talk about it. Another few days and she'd move into his house; another week or two and she'd disappear, claiming media pressure or his job as the catalyst for their breakup.

And then one or both of them had to start dating within weeks, becoming media darlings for another few months, until the doctor proclaimed Billy well enough to withstand the public eye.

He'd taken her to his favorite places, from the magnificence of Ubirr to the shared laughter of the "cockie show" at the Backpackers Hostel in Litchfield Park, which the proprietor insisted every patron watched in return for a stack of pancakes for breakfast. The squawking, dancing, well-loved birds waddling along "tightropes" and riding tiny unicycles had made them both crack up. They'd swum beneath waterfalls and ridden on aluminum boats in croc-infested waters. They'd climbed and walked, discovered new beauty in the world around them and in each other, and smiled for besotted fans when they were found. And they'd made love at night with a fever that grew every time.

She no longer wrote in her notebook until *after* they'd made love. She'd tried several times to tell him about it—some secret she had—but he didn't want to know, didn't want to get closer. He couldn't let himself know her beyond this. The more he knew her, the deeper he fell.

Why talk about the future? Why destroy what little happiness they could find?

Now he slid into the springs beside her, conscious of tourists with their cameras. The media hadn't found them here yet, on the Stuart Highway heading for Darwin, but it wouldn't be long.

Time for more honeymoon play.

He splashed her lightly on the face, grinning as she lost her ecstatic peaceful contemplation of sky and trees, sputtering. Laughing, she floated to her feet and splashed back, and they got into a water fight—

"Ooh!" With an odd squeal, she jumped at him. "Something's biting my toe!"

He chuckled, cuddling her. "Guppies, that's all. They don't hurt or poison you. They like to clean up your sores. Told you those hiking boots were the wrong ones; your toes are covered in blisters. Soft leather feels better at the start, but it rubs against your skin, whereas—"

"'Hard leather remains the same and doesn't create blisters,'" she mimicked him in a self-righteous tone, rolling her eyes with a grin. "Yes, dear, I got that point at the time—but *your* boots are ugly."

"Practicality over fashion," he retorted self-righteously. "No guppies are biting *me*."

"It tickles," she admitted, laughing.

"I can tickle your toes tonight, if you like," he whispered in her ear.

"Mmm." She turned her face and kissed him. "You're *good* at tickling."

Love-play had never been such fun before. With other women he'd always felt the pressure of expectation, the drive for fame or commitment. So few women he'd met had wanted only the fun of being lovers. It was ironic that the one woman who seemed to want just that was his wife…the wife he adored but couldn't keep.

Don't think about it.

He took the kiss deeper, forgetting for a moment how many camera phones might be aimed at them. He *wanted* to forget, to just be lost in Mia while he still could.

"C.J.! Mia! Look this way!"

He muttered a curse and grabbed her hand. "Time to cut and run again."

She laughed softly. "Let's find a hotel room and hide out for the day." She added in his ear, "My own personal guppy…"

She made him feel *good*—even when he was ready to deck someone. He chuckled. "You got it."

They bolted for the four-wheel-drive they'd hired,

ready to drive it to the car hire place and ditch it for another model to fool the squizzes for another day. They pushed past the clever journalists who'd found them this time, looking tense, ignoring their questions.

Mia yelled, "Why can't you leave us alone?" Only Christian heard the underlying laughter in her voice—and the sadness.

The plan remained in action. For Billy's sake.

CHAPTER EIGHT

"How's it going, mate?" Billy asked Christian two weeks later.

Cradling the phone between his shoulder and ear, hopping awkwardly into underwear and then his jeans, Christian left the bedroom and closed the door before he answered. "Mia's asleep. I start work in a couple of hours. How are you feeling, Billy?"

"I'm fine. Nicole and I are in a safe place. They won't find us. So you two do what you want to do—don't think about me. I'm getting plenty of rest, thanks to you."

"And Mia," he reminded Billy, with emphasis.

"Of course Mia. I meant both of you. Are things going well, C.J.?" Billy asked, after an obvious hesitation. "You sound tense. Is Mia okay?"

"When's the last time you asked that, Billy?" Christian asked bluntly, angry without warning. "When's the last time you wondered if she's okay or if she's happy?"

"I ask it all the time, C.J. Ask her if you don't

believe me." Billy's voice remained mild. "I've been waiting for *you* to take some action in her life for a long time, however."

"Why don't *you* take action in her life?" he snapped, losing his temper completely. "You're her father!"

"Do you realize how patronizing that sounds? I don't need to do anything for her. She's a grown woman, C.J., and she's doing just fine. Are you telling me you still don't understand her? She'd never *allow* me to interfere in her life. She's Sarah's girl to the core. By the way she reacted to you—the way Sarah did to me—I always thought you'd be good for her if you came to love her. Is she happy?"

"*Love her?* In case you missed it, Billy, this isn't *real*. We did this for *you!*"

"Right." Billy sighed. "For a realist, when it came to your feelings for Mia you were always in denial."

Like a balloon pricked, the fight and the anger collapsed, and he sighed too. "It's got to end any day, Billy. It's been four weeks already. What's the point in talking about it?"

"Why need it end so soon? Need it end at all? Don't say it's for my sake, C.J. I just told you it's unnecessary. Nicole and I are fine."

"Did you call just to make me feel bad?" he demanded wearily.

"Not at all. I hoped Mia's plan would be the perfect solution. You'd both been doing the dance too long. It was time for a turn in the right direction."

"What do you know about timing—or about Mia's needs?"

"I know more than I'd say you do—or you wouldn't be so defensive about her."

Oh, hell. He sighed again. He'd forgotten Billy's deep core of wisdom beneath the rocker image. "What do you suggest I do? Ask her to wait for me over the next six months of insane hours until I finish my residency? Then ask her to wait another five years while I work my way into research? I won't do that to her. She's waited all her life for her own life to start. She has to know what *she* wants from life, apart from taking care of people."

"You mean to tell me she hasn't told you yet?" Billy sounded strange. "I felt sure she'd have told you. You should ask her what her plans are, what she wants from her life, before you shove her out the door, C.J. You really should."

"How will that change anything? It won't give me more hours in the day to be with her, will it?"

"You cut ties too thoroughly, C.J. You're cutting Mia out of your life the way you cut music. You never learned how to reconcile all the pieces of your life." Billy's voice was colder than at any time since they'd met. "You'll let her go, the woman you've loved for years, for the sake of your blind goals. I hope giving your name to some new disease keeps you warm at night when you remember what it feels like to have Mia beside you."

With that, Christian's temper flashed up and

boiled right over. "With all due respect, Billy, fix your own mess for once. She needs to grow up on her own—without either of us directing her. I'm not asking Mia to stay so you can relieve your guilt because she doesn't know who the hell she is!"

"I don't *have* a mess with Mia. I never did. She knows who I am—and she's always known who she is. Right now, I doubt you know anything about her." Billy's tone was harsh, frozen. "Oh, and if I were you, I'd look around. Mia always was a light sleeper."

Was that the cause of the sudden dread pooling in his gut? Christian disconnected the phone.

And, when he turned, of course Mia stood in the doorway, her hair mussed with sleep, her eyes dark…and her face pale with betrayal.

He cursed his idiot mouth. Why had he let Billy provoke him to the point where he'd yelled? "Mia—"

"It's all right. Just don't speak," she whispered. She turned back to the bedroom and quietly closed the door behind her.

He didn't follow her. She was right. What was there to say?

When he came home after a two-day shift that had driven him to exhaustion, he stumbled into the house and into the bedroom. He was too *tired* even to eat after a fifteen-hour operation on a kid who'd landed under his quad bike and crushed half his bones. He'd had three four-hour shifts assisting his surgeon mentor with the op, and one hour off after each shift. All he wanted now was sleep—

And to see Mia.

He'd tried to call her four times in the past two days, but she hadn't answered. He'd given up after the last call. If she didn't want to answer he couldn't make her, but now...

The bedroom was empty. Her deodorant, perfume and brushes were gone, as was the group photo of them all at Billy and Nicole's wedding.

And their own wedding picture.

The room was as it had always been before she came to him. But it felt deserted, the bed ridiculously big.

Feeling like a total idiot, he yelled, "Mia! *Mia!*"

He left the bedroom and she came out of the spare bedroom, her face holding an almost ancestral calm. "Did you want something?"

He frowned at her, hating that his brain was soaked in exhaustion again. Wishing like hell that Billy had never called—that he'd never said what he had. "Why are you in that room?"

Her brows lifted. "I'm living my life, C.J. Preparing for our 'inevitable split'."

He swore beneath his breath. He'd blown it sky-high if she was calling him C.J. again—and the cockroach look was back. Worse still, he *felt* like a cockroach. She'd given him her trust and he'd abused it. Saying things he didn't mean was bad enough, but saying it to her father must have felt like betrayal. "Look, Mia—"

With studied patience, she sighed. "I'm not into autopsies. I have to stay for a few more days while we do the whole tense-at-dinner thing, and Jess goes into action on our breakup, but anything else is unnecessary. Your dinner's in the fridge. Eat, shower and sleep. I have things to do."

"What things?" he asked, peering past her. A laptop, strewn A4 papers across the spare bed and the small desk.

She gave him that look of amused contempt he'd always hated. "My scribbling."

He flinched again, remembering the derogatory term he'd used for whatever it was she was doing—and just as she was about to confide in him.

"That was childish and unnecessary." Her face softening, she frowned and waved her hand at the mess in the spare room. "I've been trying to tell you what this is for weeks. I'm…" She hesitated, shrugged, and plunged in. "I'm writing a book about the life and times of End Game—you're a part of it."

He frowned. Whatever he'd expected to hear, it wasn't that. "You're writing a book." It wasn't a question, but it was filled with incredulity—too much of it.

She flushed a little. "You really do think of me as a child, don't you? As if I've spent my life just hanging off my parents, not doing anything on my own."

He flinched again. Hell—could he make this any worse? Too late he remembered the years with End Game, Mia's nurturing of them all—even him—and that quaint advice she'd doled out now and then. How she'd cooked for them all rather than let them eat out every night. How she'd invented movie nights or asked for help with homework—160 IQ Mia— when one of them was about to do something stupid. Keeping them home and safe from the media circus at all the right times.

Mia was anything but a fool, yet he'd treated her like one…

And you're a part of this book.

It sank in just as he was about to grovel, apologize for his stupidity. "Is this thing going to be published anytime soon?"

She nodded. "Everyone else signed a clause giving permission for me to write about the band. I was going to contact you—" she flushed deeper "—and then Dad's health deteriorated…"

Fury like he'd never known—utter betrayal— filled him and overflowed. He felt literally sick with anger. "You mean you knew I'd say no, so you chickened out until an opportunity came along to sneak permission out of me in bed!"

She closed her eyes, but refused to soften it. "Not in bed. I just wanted to bring it up at a good time. But, yes, I did chicken out. I've chickened out of a lot of things." Her eyes opened, and she met his gaze with calm honesty. "I wasn't exactly in a position to know I could seduce you when I came to you—but it's interesting to know your real opinion of me."

"You married me for the sake of your father—why

not the rest?" he shouted, losing it completely. "You didn't even *like* me."

"So I'm not only a child who needs sending back to my father, but I was willing to trade my virginity for the sake of a book?" she asked quietly.

Hearing it put so bluntly shocked him into silence—and killed his anger. Oh, hell. Even he knew he'd done it now. "You should know me better than that," he growled, because he couldn't think of any way to refute it—and that left him open to derision.

And it came. One brow lifted. Slowly she shook her head, with a disbelieving laugh. "You accuse me of sleeping with you for profit, and *I* should know *you* better? Right," she sighed. "I don't think you ever knew me at all."

"Obviously I don't, if I couldn't conceive of you writing a kiss-and-tell on me!"

"And you've made that assumption about my book based on what? You've read it when I wasn't here?"

"What the hell else can it be?"

After a long moment of silence—a minute had never felt so long—she sighed again. "I see. Just so you know. I don't want to publish anything without the signed permission of everyone named in the book, but that doesn't really matter. Excuse me. I'll start packing. We'll go somewhere public tonight and end this."

She was right. It was time to end it. He turned away and let her do it. And the emptiness hollowing out his gut was only because this ending wasn't of his own scripting.

The Honeymoon's Over for C.J. and Mia

It seems the honeymoon's over for C.J. Hunter and Mia Browning. The tension between the two was obvious at Marchand's in Watson's Bay last night. After what looked like a short argument, Mia threw a glass of wine in C.J.'s face before leaving alone. A furious C.J. refused to make any comment.

A source close to the couple says Mia's already packed her bags.

"Well, that's it." Mia deposited her duffel and three shopping bags filled with stuff—all she'd brought here—in front of the door, ready to face whoever from the press was out there, waiting to pick over the carcass of their hasty marriage. She turned back to where he stood silent, bleak, just watching her.

"Thank you for putting yourself out for Dad's sake," she finally said, almost too soft to hear.

The bleakness in his eyes softened. "Mia, I'm so sorry…my lousy temper, and my privacy…"

"Don't, C.J. No need. I invaded your privacy. I didn't tell you about the book." Swallowing the lump in her throat, she lifted a hand. "I have to go."

He touched her face, some black emotion in his eyes hurting her. "Mia…we can be friends, right? One day?"

It was an olive branch—it was forgiveness, of a

form—but too much and still not enough. "I left you something on the kitchen table. I hope you like it." She turned away. "The taxi's here. Don't come out. It'll make a bigger splash if you don't. For—for Dad's sake. Goodbye," she whispered, and turned blindly for the door.

He opened it and she dashed through, the tears spilling down her face one hundred percent real. And for once the press wasn't there to see it. A politician's mistress had spilled his dirty secrets—money, abuse and sexual proclivities—in a letter to the editor, and now everyone wanted an exclusive.

They were yesterday's news…in more ways than one.

Christian stared at the door for a long time after she'd gone.

She was gone.

It was what she needed. Mia had never had the chance to just be free, to know herself. He couldn't ask her to stay, much as he ached to—man, he'd almost begged her, but looking in her eyes he'd seen the shattered heart beneath the calm she'd projected.

He'd ruined her trust. It was over.

He still had a life—the one he'd planned to have since he was a kid, the life plan he'd always thought was so brilliant…until she'd shown him how *empty* it was without her smile, her touch, her presence lighting up his life.

Damn it. He needed water to gulp down the choking ball in his throat.

And in the kitchen he saw it. A neatly bound bundle of papers, typeset, with a few stapled pages above. It looked like a contract...*Permission for Content.*

So she'd told the truth, he thought bleakly as he read the terms of the contract. She'd bound herself legally to terms that stated she couldn't print one single word about him without his signed permission—and its stamped date was April 15th.

Before she'd come to him.

His stomach churning now, he set aside the contract, unsigned, and turned his attention to the stack of papers below, held together with an elastic band. He knew what it was before he saw the words. *Um Girl: My Life With End Game by Mia Hunter.*

He was turning the pages before he knew it, one after another, and by the time he finished the book, six hours later, he knew he'd made the worst mistake of his life.

CHAPTER NINE

Five Months Later

> C.J. Hunter's soon to be ex-wife, Mia Browning,
> has hit the fame and talk show rounds in her
> own right, with her new book Um Girl: My Life
> With End Game. The intimate look at life with
> a superband from an insider's perspective,
> moreover from a woman who has been less than
> famous, whose life and interests have remained
> unknown throughout the years, is a compelling
> read. Mia has written not a shocking tell-all,
> with sex and drugs and groupies, but a warm-
> hearted portrait of the wild rockers who
> watched movies with her, took her to theme
> parks and helped her with homework. Cleverly
> avoiding shock-schlock, she's written a journal
> story with real entries from her teenage years
> until now, showing the good and touching as
> well as the loneliness in her unusual upbring-
> ing and jet-setting life.

Starting with her mother's heartbreak, and the world's belief that the fault rested with her father, Billy Browning, Mia shows both sides of the story, including her father's lifelong love for his current wife Nicole, and presents Browning's story with compassion instead of judgment. She doesn't attempt to hide the bad and ugly times, such as when hangers-on tried to use her to meet their idols, or when those surrounding the band treated her like a groupie, but instead of naming names she moves on to her next memory. By writing with truth and simplicity she proves the woman she's become—and she gives much of the credit for that to the father the press has spent decades lambasting, and to the rest of the band.

She has included a final chapter—not, as one expects, a tell-all against her ex, but about C.J. Hunter's kindness, his dedication to medicine and their good times together. She obviously harbors no bitterness against him. She says they've both moved on. Mia's current squeeze is her publicist, Gavin McClintock, and Hunter is said to be dating model Erica Chang.

While the book contains few shocks, it shows both sides of the divorce fence from a daughter's perspective, the reality of a teenage dream life and poster idols as human beings, with all the same faults, failings and endearing traits as any other person.

There is a frontispiece with the autographs of every member of End Game from the time she joined the band's travels, including C.J. Hunter. They all wish her success in her new life as an author. Browning and Hunter's wishes to Mia border on the touching.

Mia says she hopes children of divorce will read Um Girl and find healing and forgiveness, and the rest of her readership will understand the difference between tabloid sensation and the truth about those living in the public eye.

Her next book, due for release at the beginning of next year, is co-written with crooner Martin Neilson, but beyond that she refused to comment. Neilson said, "There is no one I trust more than Mia to get my story right." His ex-wife, Nicole Browning, said, "Mia's always been like a daughter to me. If anyone could tell our story with knowledge and compassion, it's Mia."

C.J. Hunter gave his blessing to his ex's new venture. He said he'd read and loved the book, and sent "all his love" to her.

The book, released three days ago, is already on bestseller lists around the world.

Two Months Later

Mia let herself into her new apartment with a relieved sigh, dumped her bags and looked around. Sydney.

Home. It felt so good to be back—even if this place, nice and homey as it was, didn't *feel* like home.

No place did that anymore, but she supposed that was natural. She'd been living out of suitcases and in hotel rooms for over six weeks, flying from America to Britain and New Zealand, and around Australia for talk-show appearances as her book crept up the bestseller charts. She'd had to hire an assistant to answer her fan mail.

So this was personal success…but it didn't feel as she'd thought it would. All she felt was tired. Lonely.

She tossed her bags on her bed and wandered out to the kitchen to make coffee. Nicole had stocked the kitchen, as promised. She felt a grateful little rush when she saw the homemade chocolate cake in the fridge, and the little note from her stepmother welcoming her home, signed with a heart and tons of kisses.

She'd go see her dad and Nicole today. They were back from their hideout shack in the Watagan Mountains near Newcastle. With a healthy diet and months of rest, Dad's health was improved, and, while he couldn't yet go on tour, he'd spent time in the mountains writing songs. The band's next recording session was due to begin next week.

She checked her watch. It was time. Dad had called the other day, telling her about his first public appearance since—

Her throat thickened, but she forced it down. *Don't think about him.* If Gavin had agreed to play her lover, to help foster the illusion she was over Christian and to keep her in the public eye until Dad was well, she had no idea *what* was between Christian and Erica, who was reputed to be as nice as she was beautiful.

It was only during the past months that she'd recognized her teenage resentment against Christian for the hidden jealousy it was. She'd resented him because he hadn't wanted her…or hadn't appeared to…and he'd not only *had* all the adulation that was every teen's fantasy, including hers, but he'd walked away from it without looking back.

She'd never understood how he could do that until she'd discovered the price of her own fame and longed for a few weeks of peace.

At least Dad was feeling better now, and the current End Game lineup was on her favorite morning show and she'd promised to watch. She flicked the TV on.

"Next up is the superband End Game, on life, biographies and their latest album—including two songs by, and with, Grammy-winning former lead singer C.J. Hunter." The woman beamed into the camera as Mia froze.

"So, C.J., how do you *really* feel about your ex-wife's success with *Um Girl*?"

How many times had he been asked that in the past few months? Christian made himself smile at the famous interviewer, leaning back in a relaxed stance beside Billy. "It's a brilliant book. I'm proud of Mia. Having read it, we're all proud of her."

The other band members nodded and murmured assent.

"*Um Girl* was a real homage to her life with the band—and to you. Her affection for you shines through every word. Do you regret the marriage ending?"

If the words had been scripted, they couldn't have been a better introduction to what he wanted to say. Her answers to his e-mails and messages asking to speak to her had never varied. *When I'm back in Sydney, we'll talk. Maybe we can be friends.*

He couldn't. It was as if something vital inside him had withered when she left. His research ambitions seemed to have crumbled to dust and ashes. He worked in the ER now, enduring each shift like a sleepwalker, a doctor on autopilot. His house was empty, the bed cold, and getting colder daily. He'd taken to sleeping in the lounge.

He taped every chat show that interviewed her, and watched them over and over. Billy wouldn't give him her address or new home phone number. She'd only come home this morning, he said. If she wanted him, she knew where he was.

Being apart from her was torture. He had to be near her, touch her one more time…

He'd given up trying to deny it. Without her, there was a blank wall in front of him he couldn't see around or scale. She lit up his life, his heart. Her gentle teasing, her sharing of his favorite things, her over-the-shoulder smile, the unashamed need in her sweet touch—they took away the darkness.

"I regret losing Mia every day," he confessed, his heart thundering. Was she watching? Billy had promised she would…

The interviewer's brows lifted in eagerness. The reclusive C.J. Hunter had actually answered a personal question for the first time! "So, the rumors of Mia and Gavin, and you and Erica—"

"I can't answer for Mia, but the rumors about Erica and me are just that," he confirmed. "I love my wife. Erica's dating one of my friends." Dave's reward for all he'd done had been an introduction, and he and Erica had hit it off immediately.

Erica was better off with Dave. With her long black hair and dark eyes, she had too much of a resemblance to Mia for him to look at her with anything but pain.

"I believe the two songs you've written for the new album are tributes to Mia?"

He nodded, unable to smile. He couldn't think of those months of sleepless nights, scribbling words and music, finding closeness to Mia in song. Billy, in daily contact with her, had promised she'd be watching. What was she thinking now she knew the truth—that he was nothing without her?

As if on cue, Billy got to his feet. "It's why we came today—why C.J.'s here with the band. We all want to be part of this tribute. During the time she traveled with us Mia helped us all to grow up, because she was there, because she trusted us to be the family she needed. Apart from Nicole, Mia is the best thing that ever happened to my life." He looked into the camera. "This is for you, Mia. Thank you for making me a better man." He motioned to the other members of the band.

Years ago Christian had sworn he'd never do this again, but as he took his place in front of the band he felt a sense of coming home. He wouldn't sing full-time ever again, but he'd spent too many years denying this part of him, trying to separate the singer from the doctor.

Billy had been right. The singer and the doctor were both parts of what made him who he was. No need for shame. He was C.J. Hunter, and that was okay.

"This is *'Denial'*. For the love of my life—my wife, Mia," he said into the mike. He played the first chord of the power ballad, praying she was listening, that she'd understand.

> *Only a fool finds out too late*
> *What he most wants, and denies*
> *The love he walks away from*
> *And lives his life in lies*
> *I was that fool, spent years in denial*
> *Of the light you brought to my emptiness*
> *With your touch, a simple smile*
> *Now you're gone, I am not more, but less*
> *Far less than I thought I could be.*

The chorus came straight from his heart.

Your faith set me free, but you were chained
To the needs of someone lost
If you could only know I was wrong
Thinking I could take the cost.
Losing you is the price I can't stand to pay
You deserve more than these clumsy words
can say.

As the song faded out, he spoke one final time. "I love you, Mia. Please—just one call, one message. Talk to me. Please."

He walked off stage without another word, leaving Billy and the boys to finish what he couldn't. His heart was too full, too aching, for anything more.

He left the studios and threw himself into his car, his pulse thundering. The Mia he knew, the Mia he loved, would have already called him, or left a message.

The silence deafened him. Oh, God, *please* let her car be outside his place... But the road in front of his place was bare, the driveway space in front of the garage was empty.

It was over.

CHAPTER TEN

CHRISTIAN let himself in the house and checked his phone for messages as he headed for the kitchen. Nothing. All his last hopes came crashing around his feet.

These past weeks—writing and rehearsing with the guys, working and barely sleeping—he'd allowed dreams to comfort him. Remembering the way she'd looked at him as they made love, the way she'd touched and kissed him, he'd planned for a reunion that obviously wasn't going to happen. He'd destroyed her faith in him.

At least he'd reconciled his past to his present, thanks to her. At least he had memories. The happiest few weeks of his life…

"I let myself in. I hope you don't mind. I made coffee, if you want some."

He blinked. The pretty voice, slurred with tiredness, didn't sound like a sleep-deprived hallucination. He turned to the sofa with the dented pillow and mussed sheets…and there she was, sitting upright, obviously tense. Her fingers were white around the mug. Her eyes didn't quite meet his.

Thank you, God. She was here…and, like an idiot, all he could say was, "Mia."

"You walked right past me." She sipped at the creamy sugar-laden mess she called coffee, her gaze on the curls of steam rising from the mug. "I thought if you found the coffee in the kitchen you might think you had a stalker."

He didn't know what to say—what to do. All his plans, all the heartfelt words he'd worked out in his head were gone. "You watched the show?" he said, feeling more stupid than ever. Would she be here otherwise, only hours off a morning flight from Auckland?

She nodded. "It's a lovely song—but I'm here for closure, Christian."

"That's a bad word," he managed to croak, through a throat so tight he couldn't breathe properly.

She lifted her brows. "In what way?"

He couldn't think. He could only say what was in his heart and hope it was enough for her. "Closure's only good if we want this to be over— and I don't. I love you."

She licked her top lip, then sucked it in. Mia thinking. "You said that on the show."

He nodded, watching her, moving closer. "I meant it. I miss you like crazy. Everything's gone blank without you."

She frowned, but didn't speak.

Obviously he hadn't said enough. "I meant what

I said to Billy," he said, hearing desperation creeping into his voice. But he couldn't sound as desperate as he felt.

She sat back, her eyes cold. Wrong thing to say. He rushed into speech again. "But that was because I was in denial, Mia. I was so focussed on my goals I'd forgotten how to live, to breathe, to enjoy life. I've always taken everything too seriously—including what I thought was you rejecting me. Then you came to me back in May, and I was *alive* for the first time in years. Within days you were my lover, and the best friend I'd ever known. I knew I loved you that first night, but I was still locked into my goal. I thought I'd be nothing without it—and that you couldn't handle my life. I thought I could live like you'd never been here, or that maybe we could get together again in a couple of years."

Her brows lifted. "First I was a child selling my body—now you think I'm a plaything to discard and pick up when you're ready?"

"I should have written down everything I was thinking while I was writing that song for you," he groaned, wanting to whack his forehead. He crouched in front of her, knowing this was it—now or never. "You're right. I didn't think of you as a woman. I thought of you as you were when I first knew you—with no life apart from the band. But you were a child then, and even after we made love, when you acted with greater maturity than me during the media chase, I treated you as a child. I discounted you."

She asked quietly, "Does a career make a person worthy of respect to you?"

"I was a jerk," he admitted. "If I'd respected you as you deserved, I'd have had to reevaluate my life goals to keep you in my life. So I thought of you as the child you'd been—as if I could give you back to Billy and find you later." His head dropped. "When I saw the contract and read your book I knew I'd made the biggest mistake of my life."

He lost his balance on his haunches, swaying back, and she grabbed his hands to steady him. Their first touch in months. He groaned again, and twined his fingers through hers, needing that contact, needing her more than air, more than life.

"So it took discovering that I had a career to make you see me as real? To write songs for me and go on national TV? What sort of love is that?"

The pain in her voice wasn't a testament to her loving him now, more to how much he'd hurt her with his stupid, wilful blindness. "Not the sort of love you deserve. I was blind, Mia, a selfish jerk not to see you for the extraordinary woman you've always been," he admitted, falling to his knees before her. A lump filled his throat as he asked the dreaded question. "Is—is Gavin good to you?"

"He's a good man."

At the odd note in her voice, like a hiccup, he looked at her. She was staring at their linked hands, her face pale, eyes dark—whether with pain or longing, he didn't know.

"Mia?" The lump in his throat turned sharp, hurting him. Was it anguish or hope?

"I wasn't going to—I can't do this," she whispered back, her breath coming shallow and fast. "I came here to—"

After a minute's wait, he asked softly, "To what, Mia?"

She gulped and turned away a little. "To say goodbye." The words were threadbare.

He couldn't answer. Their linked hands and the pain in her face was all the hope he had now. He couldn't sever it.

She frowned and waved at the sheets and pillow. "You've been sleeping here?"

"Mia." He lifted her hands to his mouth, his lips burning to touch her somehow. "Are you saying goodbye?"

"Why are you sleeping here?" Soft and insistent the question. Why so much hinged on it, he didn't know. Knew only that it did. Her gaze on him held a world of waiting.

"I can't stand it in there," he rasped. "I see you everywhere, but it's worst in there. I see you smiling at me when we made love. I go in that room and all I see is you. You own that room now. It's yours." His head fell again. "You own me, too. I'm yours, Mia. Whether you want me or not doesn't change it. I know that now. I've always loved you."

"Why did you leave End Game without telling me?" she asked softly.

"I'd planned to stay with the band another year, to take time off study and just enjoy myself, but I couldn't stand being near you and not touching you anymore." He shook his head in self-disgust. "But even leaving the band didn't change it. I called Billy every week, pretending to myself I was watching out for him, but I always asked about you, if you were seeing anyone. Ask Billy—he always knew." He sighed, and shook his head again.

"I never hated you." Her fingers squeezed his gently. "I tried to, because I never thought you could want me. If you were in denial this year, I was all the time *until* this year. You made me want to run to you, and run away at the same time, Christian. I wanted so much with you. It scared me…"

Her voice was soaked in emotion—and every pore and cell of him filled with pained hope, making his heart knock against his ribs. "We were both scared." He released her hands to touch her shoulders. Slowly, inch by inch, he drew her to him. "Love this intense shouldn't come so young, and if it does it rarely lasts a lifetime."

He held his breath. Would she accept the words, or pull away?

She wet her mouth, staring into his eyes, dropping her gaze to his mouth and back. "No," she whispered, leaning toward him. "It shouldn't. But it did. All these years…"

"Tell me, Mia," he murmured against her mouth, aching, needing the words.

"I can't say goodbye, Christian." The words seemed to burst from her. "It almost killed me last time. I can't do it again. I love you too much."

"Thank you, Mia. *Thank you.*" Happiness burst from the inside of him out, until his whole body felt like the Cheshire Cat: one big grin. "I swear you won't regret this."

"You better make sure I don't." Laughing, she leaned into him.

As she was about to kiss him, he held her off. There was a final barrier that had to fall. "Life won't be easy with me, Mia. I work long hours, and while I haven't tried to get into research yet, I still might. You'll always be waiting for me…"

"How little *you* know, buster. I'm a writer. My life and hours can be insane at times." She fell into him, dropping him to the floor and pinning him down. Her glasses fell to the ground, but she didn't notice. "Half the time you'll be waiting for *me* as I think up a new idea, get excited by a new book, or go on tour again. I'm planning to write a novel after I've done the edits on Uncle Martin's biography. It's about time travel and I can't wait to get into it." She whispered against his mouth. "But I'd rather be alone two days and get to sleep beside you than spend all day, every day, with any man *but* you. In fact, too much time with you would eat into my writing time. So I'll love you and let you go—as you'll have to do with me." She winked. "*Now* will you kiss me?"

Her eyes were shining. The crushing load lifted from

him. She was right. Mia knew herself—knew what she wanted—and he should have learned long ago to trust her. "You're an amazing woman, Mia Hunter."

"I love you, Christian Hunter. I've missed you so much—and my body's missed you like crazy," she whispered intensely, moving against him. "I need you *now*."

Her mouth claimed his with a heat and hunger and need to match his, and joy seared him to his core. He prayed to God she'd always be like this—loving him, needing him with an intensity to meet his own, taking him body and soul with a touch.

"Want to reclaim that bed?" She nibbled his mouth, her hands beneath his shirt, claiming his skin, his body, as hers. "Mine," she whispered, her eyes glowing as she smiled down at him. "My bed. My man."

His heart too full to speak, he kissed her again and stood, leading her to the bedroom, leaving layers of clothes on the way, hers and his falling together.

As he was lying her on the bed, she suddenly chuckled.

"What?" he growled, barely able to think beyond his need for her.

"Christian Hunter!" She grinned up at him. "You must have copped heaps as a kid!"

The bubbling joy in her eyes, the love in her face as she looked at him, took away the old sting. He grinned back. "Cut it out, woman. I told you I hate my name."

Her eyes lit with sensual playfulness. "Oh,

yeah…? Bet I can make you love it in seconds. Come here," she whispered, drawing him down to her.

Moments later she was moaning, "Ah, *Christian*," arching up to him as he kissed and touched her. And he had to admit she was right.

Again.

Queens of Romance

The Wedding Ultimatum

Rich and ruthless Rafe Valdez was way out of Danielle's
league. She'd turned to him as a last resort to help her family
but his solution was outrageous! The devastating, sexy
man gave her twenty-four hours to decide if she would
marry him, share his bed and give him an heir.

The Pregnancy Proposal

Tasha is overjoyed to discover that she's pregnant with
sensual tycoon Jared North's baby, but telling him is the
hardest thing she's ever done. For three years they've shared
an intensely passionate relationship – but marriage has
never been on the agenda.

Available 1st February 2008

Collect all 10 superb books in the collection!

 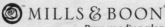
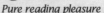